The Underdogs

Sara Hammel

Farrar Straus Giroux
New York

Farrar Straus Giroux Books for Young Readers
175 Fifth Avenue, New York 10010

Text copyright © 2016 by Sara Hammel
All rights reserved
Printed in the United States of America by
R. R. Donnelley & Sons Company, Harrisonburg, Virginia
Designed by Andrew Arnold
First edition, 2016
1 3 5 7 9 10 8 6 4 2

mackids.com

Library of Congress Cataloging-in-Publication Data

Hammel, Sara.
    The underdogs / Sara Hammel. — First edition.
        pages cm
    Summary: "A shy, overweight 12-year-old & her best friend take on the case of a
popular 16-year-old who died mysteriously leading to a breathtaking surprise twist"—
Provided by publisher.
    ISBN 978-0-374-30161-3 (hardback)
    ISBN 978-0-374-30163-7 (e-book)
    [1. Mystery and detective stories.   2. Murder—Fiction.   3. Country clubs—
Fiction.   4. Dogs—Fiction.   5. Overweight persons—Fiction.]   I. Title.

PZ7.1.H363Und 2016
[Fic]—dc23

                                                            2015018069

Our books may be purchased in bulk for promotional, educational,
or business use. Please contact your local bookseller or the Macmillan
Corporate and Premium Sales Department at (800) 221-7945 ext. 5442
or by e-mail at MacmillanSpecialMarkets@macmillan.com.

For Ollie and the rescues, who inspired this book;
Chris, who gave me the space to write it;
and Mom, who nurtured my dreams

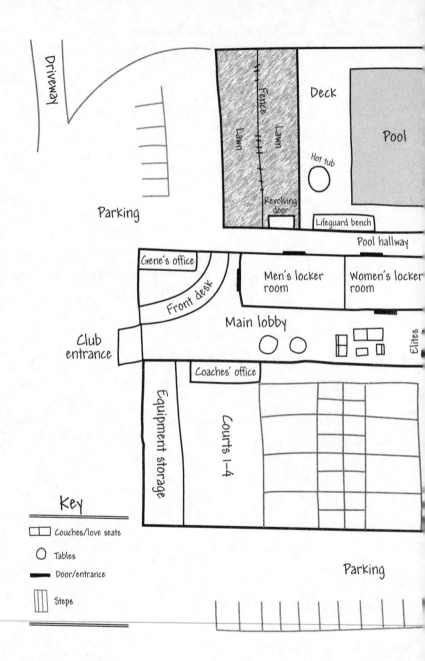

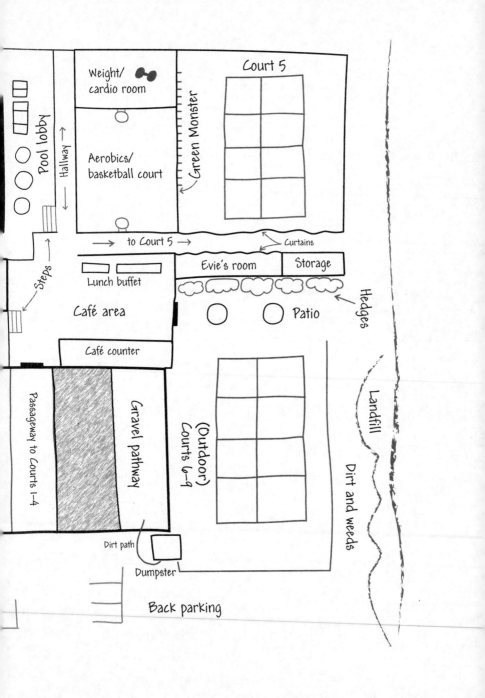

The Underdogs

August 4

The day they carried sixteen-year-old Annabel Harper out of the club they had to close the pool area because someone had vomited everywhere. They found the vomit before they found Annabel.

She did not have a hair out of place. Her champagne-blond bob framed her face in two perfect angles, even in death. She would have liked that. Her skin, from her shoulders to her tummy to her long legs, was still flawless and bronzed and a little slippery from the water, not blue or red or pale like you might expect.

They carried her away from the pool, through the women's locker room, into the lobby, and people stood alongside like a receiving line and gawked, but they would not have seen the perfection about her. They would have seen a big lump of dark blue plastic go by. I know because I watched them zip up the body bag.

Seeing Annabel like that was not the worst part of that day. It was Nicholas who got to everyone. He arrived later, as the sun arced higher in the sky and announced it was going to be a scorcher, and he ran to the revolving doors and pushed as hard as he could, shooting out like a bullet onto the pool deck. A detective rushed and grabbed his shoulders, pushed him back, but Nicholas wouldn't go. He was taller than the detective. Younger, fitter.

"What happened? What happened? What happened?" Nicholas screamed, the question growing louder each time. He was crying and he didn't care who saw. I watched from behind the glass in the hallway that led from the main building to the pool. Nicholas was Annabel's brother, almost like a twin but not. He was older by less than two years, protective and so fond of his baby sister. An equally blond creature who tanned in the summer like he was made for the sun, like it was summer that brought him to life. Nicholas, who was tall and muscular but not bulky—he had the build of a catalog model crossed with a soccer player—always said, *It's okay. We're forever young.* It was so wrong that Annabel would now stay young forever.

I remember Nicholas's face that day, twisted with pain. His voice, feral and telling us he would not be the same person from this moment on. He was this local hero, and so old for his years. Nice to everyone, so composed and mature. Only seventeen. He had saved a little girl's life earlier in the summer. That was quite a story.

I had to turn away when he started wailing. When the detective dragged him from the scene. That's when I saw Lisa

Denessen standing alone in the pool's viewing lobby, staring out the big picture windows, a strange look on her face. Half-smile, half-indifference. Or something more sinister; there was no way to be sure exactly what she was thinking.

So much goes on at the club, especially in the summer. There's always something juicy happening among the members, the staff, the aerobics addicts, the tennis people . . . Oh Lordy, the tennis people. They alone could star in their own soap opera: *As the Yellow Ball Turns.*

I remember everything, and I listen. People generally like me around this place. Apparently I'm a pretty nonthreatening figure, and unlike certain others I won't mention, I don't seem to alarm or offend anyone. People have gotten so used to me that sometimes I think I'm like wallpaper in this joint. So I hear and see more than I probably should.

You never would have thought that summer would turn out the way it did, but in retrospect, everything that went on—the betrayal and the tears and the raging hormones—was leading up to something dramatic.

After

With the drama unfolding around here faster than Rafael Nadal's serve, I had to find my best friend—*stat*. I knew where Evie would be. I cruised through the main lobby toward Court 5, my head down, hoping no one would stop me for a chat.

I knew pretty much everyone around the club because of who my mom is. She pretty much runs the reception area (some say the whole club), and she speaks her mind. I love her, of course. She takes care of me, and every summer she clears it with the owner so I can hang out here while she works.

I ran down past our little café area, where a bunch of policemen were milling around looking serious and drinking the club's free coffee out of Styrofoam cups. The club is arranged thusly: after you go through the entrance and pass through the main lobby, there are four stairs that lead down to the café—and when I say café, I mean glorified kitchen counter, refrigerator, and creaky, outdated frozen yogurt machine. Our lunch place served snacks, sandwiches, and one flavor of yogurt per month. It wasn't fine dining, but it was enough for members to grab a little sustenance after a workout or a swim, and the owner had small tables throughout the club so people could sit and watch tennis or just relax. The café had a couple of tables and space for the tennis camp lunch buffet to be set up. From there, glass sliding doors led out to the four outdoor courts: Courts 6 to 9. To the right of the glass doors was the green door that led to the indoor courts: Courts 1 to 4. Just off the café was a narrow hallway that connected the rest of the club to Court 5, which was this big, stand-alone concrete structure. I made a beeline down there and through the door that led to Court 5 and the storage rooms tucked behind it.

I found Evie sitting on a crate full of giant mayonnaise jars in her secret room. This was where they stored all the tennis camp lunch items, along with hoppers full of tennis balls. Evie found solace back there, protected by those heavy plastic green curtains separating the room from the tennis court. Her special hangout was messy and low-lit, and smelled of rubber and feet. But on the bright side, she was safe there—technically, no one under eighteen was allowed inside, but Evie had gotten special permission from the club's owner because she was a staff member's kid, and she'd asked nicely.

When I popped my head in the door, Evie was sucking on a coconut Frooti-Freez bar and listening to that song again, the scraggly end of her side braid resting on her right shoulder. Over and over she'd play that song, and I kept waiting for her to get sick of it. It was the biggest hit of the past five summers combined. "Summer Cool" was taking the world by storm. The words were easy:

> *Summer, summer, summer, yeah yeah yeah*
> *I saw you by the pool and fell in love at first sight*
> *In the summer, summer, summer, cool cool cool*

Let's just say the melody was catchier than the lyrics. Which, by the way, Evie had to listen to on a 1980s boom box. If you've never seen one, this antiquated piece of machinery is basically a radio the size of a small bench with two soccer-ball-size speakers whose sound is far less impressive than their size would suggest.

More *Summer, summer, summer, cool cool cool . . .* And then the harsh interjection: *You're listening to 98.5, the Zoo!* Evie was the only kid within a thousand miles of the club without an iPod—or a cell phone, for that matter. Luckily, the club's owner didn't allow kids to bring their phones in the club, period, so Evie was just like the rest of them, at least by day.

She caught sight of me and put her book down. "Annabel loves—" She took a deep breath. "Annabel *loved* that song," she corrected. She reached over and lowered the volume.

Her voice cracked a little, but she didn't cry. She sat back on her crate and I joined her. She was still reading *A Little Princess*, a book in which terrible things happen to a very nice young girl, from what Evie said. Frankly, it sounded a little dark for a summer read. She smiled at me then, but her eyes were sad and, I swear, a duller green than usual because of it. I had to get her out of here. For starters, it was boiling in this place. Evie had a little row of sweat droplets on her upper lip and her face was a nuclear pink. The air-conditioning did *not* reach the storage rooms, and considering this was shaping up to be the hottest summer ever in St. Claire, it was brutal. I really didn't get how Evie could stand it.

Today she was wearing her trademark gray sweatpants again because she was ashamed of her legs, which she had referred to more than once as *pale, veiny,* and *gross.* She was hidden as usual in her dark blue Reebok T-shirt, a men's XL. She sucked the frozen stump of her melting Frooti-Freez and looked thoughtful for a moment.

"It's scary about Annabel, isn't it?" she asked, licking her lips.

I had to agree. Scary, and sad. I had a feeling the whole thing could get out of control if the police didn't find out *immediately* what had happened. I hopped off the crate. *Come with me.* Evie sighed and looked at the door. I didn't blame her for hesitating—I mean, people were dying out there. But we couldn't hide forever. It was time to show Evie the crime scene, and to let her get a load of this detective they'd sent to investigate. I had a feeling we'd be seeing a lot of this strange-looking fellow in the days to come.

Evie sighed again and said, "You're right, Chels. Let's go find out what's going on around here." We set off together to see what we could learn.

After

Evie blew a stray strand of hair out of her eyes and held a finger over her lips: *Shhh*. Her fine, dirty-blond locks weren't suited for the one braid she insited on wearing since she saw the same look on Serene Cowen-Lynch, the coolest girl at her school and also a tennis prodigy who trained at the club.

We were inside the women's locker room, hunched down against the door that Evie had opened by about three inches so we could see and hear the action. Both the men's and women's locker rooms' main entrances were off the club's lobby, and if you walked through the changing areas, past the toilets, and beyond the showers, you'd hit their back doors, which opened up to a hallway that led to the pool.

We already knew who the big player was in this tragic case: Detective Ted Ashlock, who was currently cornering the club's owner, Gene Hanrahan, outside the men's locker room. Their backs were to us, so we could see and hear them, but for now, at least, they had no idea we were a few yards away, peeking out of the women's locker room.

Ashlock was in mid-threat when we got to listening: "I can shut this place down right now. Is that what you want?"

Gene held up his hands, his wiry salt-and-pepper hair a mess and the bags under his eyes puffier than ever. "Whoa. I'm trying to cooperate here. I can't have this—this terrible tragedy—close me down. I'm a small business. I'm finished if I can't stay open."

Detective Ashlock, a lonesome-looking man whose paleness stood out big-time among the sun worshippers and tennis people who trained here, held his ground. "A girl is dead. That's all that matters to me right now."

That shut Gene up quick. I took a good look at this Ashlock. He wore snug jeans and a canvas belt paired with an azure sports jacket and a white button-down shirt, and he topped off the look with a white fedora that was entirely unfashionable but looked oddly right on him. I didn't know it then, but I'd be seeing a lot of that getup in the weeks to come.

Gene was wearing his usual white tennis shorts and Adidas polo shirt. He crossed his arms over his chest and stared out at the pool, probably thinking about all the paying members who should be out there splashing around right now. In reality, we were watching a swarm of Stormtroopers—that's what Evie and I had dubbed these guys dressed in white, with their strange puffy slippers—hanging around the pool area, vacuuming up bits of fluff or pebbles or blood or hair.

"Of course, that's the most important thing. But it was just an accident . . . a terrible accident. The girl obviously snuck

11

into the club last night and drowned. Or maybe she got sick. It's not like there's any foul play. Not in this town." Gene was talking fast.

Ashlock blotted beads of sweat off his forehead with a white handkerchief. It was the first week of August, and everyone was tired of the steamy New England heat. Ashlock looked like he was in danger of melting, like one of Evie's beloved Frooti-Freez bars.

"Well, we think it's very strange that the upper half of the victim's body was wet, and yet her hair was bone-dry. And styled. Styled like a perfect doll. So I'm not sure how you can assume it was an accident . . ."

The funny thing is that anyone who knew Annabel knew she *never* got her hair wet. She would swim like a Labrador, her head bobbing above the water as she paddled her way across the pool to wherever she was going. Everyone watched her whenever she moved; she knew it, too, and she always planned her migration from the sun lounger to the pool stairs carefully. She was aware she was on display.

I watched her do it so many times, watched her slip her bathing-suit straps back onto her shoulders before sitting up, only the tiniest wrinkles of bronzed skin rippling over her belly. She'd smooth down her hair, and then slowly, slowly she'd stand up while surreptitiously ensuring her bikini area was entirely covered, tucking her index finger under her bottoms to straighten them out. Then she'd stride casually to the edge of the concrete pool stairs and up her foot would come in slow-motion like a crane lifting a girder, and she'd point a dainty, painted toe like a ballerina for a grand dip to test the temperature. You get the idea.

Things were heating up in that little hallway in more ways than one. The smell of chlorine was wafting in from the pool, making Gene's face turn beet red as he fielded the questions lobbed at him by the detective.

"You said Annabel might have sneaked into the club. Who has keys to this place?"

"A few of us," Gene replied. "I'll get you a list. So, um . . . when can we reopen the pool?"

I almost felt sorry for the guy. Gene, who'd been a local tennis star in the 1970s and was slim and sinewy but carried himself with a slight hunch and an incongruous little potbelly, was staring wistfully out at the pool. Evie and I both knew who had keys to the club, including at least one person who routinely used them after hours.

Gene looked like he had something else to say, but at that moment my mom poked her nose into the action. I was surprised it had taken her this long to scurry up to Gene's side, where she commenced speaking sternly to Detective Ashlock.

"Who did this? Our members will be terrified," she proclaimed. "They'll need to be assured the killer is not a danger to them."

Ashlock squinted at my mom, then shot an odd look toward

Gene. I could guess why. It was interesting Mom and Gene had such opposing views of what had happened to Annabel.

"We certainly haven't determined this was a murder," Ashlock said. He wiped sweat off his upper lip with one knuckle. "Our investigation is ongoing."

Ashlock took a long, hard look at my mom. Evie turned to me nervously, mouth open. I could read her mind: We did not want any detectives looking hard at my mom. No sirree.

"Tell me, ma'am," Ashlock said slowly, "what makes you think it was a homicide?"

My mom put her right hand on her chin. She did that when she was thinking about something or when she was stalling. I knew her so well. She recovered after a few seconds. "I just *assumed*, Detective," she said coolly. "I mean, a young, healthy girl is found dead after hours, in her bikini? That screams foul play. The poor kid was only sixteen, for God's sake."

"Mmmhmm." Ashlock was taking notes again. "I'm sorry. What did you say your name was?"

"Beth Jestin. Front desk manager," she replied. I saw Gene raise his eyebrows, but he was too smart to protest. Mom didn't exactly have an official title, but apparently he was willing to let it go. "Word gets around quickly here, Detective."

Ashlock directed his thumb at the owner. "I'm going to need that list of people who hold keys to the club's entrance as well as to this door."

He nodded in the direction of the revolving door that opened up to the pool. Evie and I knew better than anyone how hard that door was to open. Made of steel and Plexiglas, it had several special locks on both sides of the doorjamb. Even people *with* keys had trouble opening it. When summer was over, they would place a great white bubble over the pool, and since the bubble had to stay inflated, there was something about the suction between the bubble and the main building that messed the door up.

Gene nodded, still squinting out at the pool. That rectangular body of water was an oasis during a hot summer, and on a scorcher like today, it gleamed like an Olympic-size baguette-cut diamond that reflected the sun in a million different directions. The pool was surrounded by this fancy new designer caramel-colored pebble decking Gene had invested in, and that, in turn, was bordered by a plush lawn on the back end and the left-hand side. A wooden fence went three-quarters of the way around the whole thing, and at the base of the fence were bushes and flowers. The purple coneflowers and red verbenas were blooming particularly bright these days.

My mom held out one hand and counted off on her fingers while Ashlock made notes on his pad. "Here's your list. One: Gene. Two: the front desk manager—that's me. Three: the pool manager and lifeguard, Harmony Goldenblatt. He's only a kid himself . . . sixteen, I think. Four: the weekend-morning lifeguard, Nicholas Harper, Annabel's seventeen-year-old brother." Her face softened. "Oh, no. Poor Nicholas. Who found her? Who found the body?"

Ashlock said nothing, and Gene, getting emotional, said,

"Harmony found her after he opened the pool this morning. For God's sake, what if one of the little kids had seen her?"

My mom looked shocked to hear this, and if she wasn't such a tough nut I imagine she would've teared up. But not here, not in front of this detective. "How awful" was all she said, her voice almost cracking. Almost.

Evie and I were hanging on every word, and now she looked at me with a frown. It was shocking to hear that Harmony, a pal of ours, had to find Annabel like that.

Ashlock looked up from his pad. "This is just procedure, you understand," he said, "but I have to ask. Where were you last night?"

Gene and Beth each grimaced, and it looked to me like they'd taken the question quite personally. Gene recovered first.

"I was at home."

My mom echoed, "I was at home."

Ashlock appeared to make notes to that effect and didn't bother to question their flimsy alibis further. It seemed like he wasn't nearly finished with them, though. Evie looked at me and shrugged. I had to agree with her assessment. This was getting us nowhere. I mean, did we *really* think my mom or Gene had something to do with Annabel dying?

"Anything else?" My mom had inched closer to Ashlock, almost protectively getting between Gene and the detective. She was nothing if not loyal—if you were on her good side.

"One more thing," Ashlock told her. "I'd like to have a look at your shoes."

"Come again?" Gene said irritably.

"Your shoes. The soles. Let me see them."

My mom huffed but dutifully kicked her right foot up to Ashlock, nearly nailing him. He examined the bottom of her favorite cork wedges. Ashlock dropped her foot with no readable reaction and signaled to Gene, who did the same with his boat-size designer tennis sneakers, albeit with a bit more effort. He wasn't so young anymore. Ashlock took a look.

"Very good," he said. "Don't go too far away from St. Claire. I'll need statements from both of you. No overseas vacations in the cards, I hope?"

My mom and Gene shook their heads. Ashlock blotted his brow again with a handkerchief and nodded a polite goodbye, but it turned out he wasn't actually finished.

"*One* more thing." Gene and my mom looked less than thrilled. "Is there anyone around here you think had a reason to kill Annabel?"

Gene's face remained neutral. My mom's did not. She took a deep breath and opened her mouth as if to speak, but then thought better of it.

"If you know something, now's the time to tell me, Mrs. Jestin."

"It's *Ms.*," she said grouchily. "And I really don't know anything."

"*Ms.* Jestin—"

"Fine. Fine! He would never hurt Annabel, but Harmony Goldenblatt has a key to the club *and* the pool and he was always staring at her. He was pretty obvious about it. But she never gave him a second look."

My mom bit her lower lip. Gene put his hand on her shoulder and spoke to Ashlock.

"Every male with a pulse was always staring at that girl. Beth's right—Harmony's not a bad guy. I hired him because he's responsible and he's the only teenager who doesn't whine about opening up at five thirty a.m. in winter. He did so well as a lifeguard I made him summer pool manager. He and Nicholas Harper are our two senior guards."

"Oh?" Ashlock said to the owner. "So if Ms. Jestin is correct about this being a murder, who do *you* think could have done it?"

Gene's face scrunched up, anguished, almost like he was trying not to cry, though I doubted he was in danger of that. Gene Hanrahan was not what I would call a crier.

"Nobody at this club. No way. This was an accident. Keep investigating. You'll see."

Ashlock nodded slowly and turned in our direction. *Oh, snap.* We had to scramble because it seemed the detective was really done this time, which meant any one of the three grown-ups was about to walk right by us. Before we could move, Ashlock walked by, taking no notice of Evie and me peeking out from behind the women's locker room door. Thankfully my mom was distracted and followed right behind him, passing within a few inches of us. But someone else appeared on the scene who *did* notice us.

"What's happenin', Wonder Twins?" We saw muscular, tanned legs through the crack in the door.

We both leapt up and stepped out of the locker room. That chilled-out-yet-booming drawl belonged to Evie's dad, Lucky. He asked, "How are you holding up with all this?"

"We're fine, Dad," Evie said, looking off after Ashlock, who was no doubt about to investigate something and we were missing it. He squinted as if he wasn't sure whether to believe her. Lucky Clement had shaggy, dirty-blond hair that was similar to Evie's but more spiky than soft, and he never went anywhere without a blue bandanna tied around his head. He wasn't particularly tall, but he was strong: compact, stout, springy, with thick thighs and wide shoulders. Lucky was a summer tennis coach, and like most of the club's coaches he taught both levels of the summer camp—the regular kids, who showed up with money but acutally were kind of average tennis players, and the elites, who had the real, jaw-dropping talent.

"Beth said I should come find you to make sure you're okay." He paused. "So you're . . . okay?"

I thought it was sweet he was checking on us, even though my mom had made him do it.

Evie didn't answer for a second, and Lucky turned to me. "You'll look out for her, won't you, Chelsea?" He looked me

19

right in the eyes. "You're the strongest one of all of us. You take care of my girl."

"We're fine," Evie assured him. "Can we talk about this at home? Later?"

Lucky shrugged, smiled, and patted her on the head, then me. "Sure, kiddo. I gotta go teach, anyway."

Once he was out of the way, we stood watching the forensics team work in the blazing sun at the pool, and I stayed quiet while Evie thought about things. After a minute she said, "Chelsea, we've got to keep an eye on this detective. We have to find out what happened to Annabel. He doesn't have a clue about this place. How will he know where to look, or who to talk to?" She played with her braid and added, "I don't want that detective to miss any important leads. Whenever you can, stay near him, okay? I'll cover the front desk."

She didn't have to say it: *Because that's where all the gossiping gets done.* She also didn't have to add, *Because no one will notice me there.* Well, they wouldn't, and this time it would come in handy. We'd already proved we could overhear the most private conversations without anyone raising a single eyebrow. We could go anywhere in the club. Speaking of which, I was catching a scent that wasn't exactly pleasant. I took a few sniffs. Oh, crap.

"What is it?" Evie took a few loud sniffs herself. "I don't smell anything."

I did. It was faint, but it was there. Every summer, usually when July hit, the county landfill—also known as the town dump, because the powers that be had dumped it on the St. Claire border—behind the club started stinking, and with today's scorching temperatures the rich stench of superheated garbage was wafting our way. Poor Gene. Grumpy members complaining about the reeking landfill was the last thing he needed.

I wasn't surprised by Evie's interest in keeping an eye on the detective's every move. *Harriet the Spy* was, after all, her favorite book (after every single Laura Ingalls Wilder book ever written). I also wasn't surprised because Annabel had been one of the only people around here to ever be nice to Evie. They'd become pals this summer, and I knew this loss would weigh on my friend. Well, maybe the mystery surrounding Annabel's death was a wrong we could do something about. We really needed to keep our eyes and ears open so we would be prepared when Detective Ashlock questioned us. We had to make sure there was justice for Annabel.

Evie put her arm around me and squeezed. "It's all going to be okay, Chelsea."

I felt a little better. I thought it would be okay, in the end.

Before

Evie and I had witnessed some of Annabel's ups and downs that summer. One day in early July, Annabel glided into the club as if she'd hitched a ride on a cloud. My mom was on front desk duty, munching on pistachios while gossiping with Lisa Denessen, who was lining up the shells in the shape of her initials.

Lisa was sixteen and did it all around here: taught exercise classes, worked the front desk, and acted as a roving trainer in the gym supposedly giving fitness advice, but instead spending her shift with members, mostly male, mostly muscular. She tried really hard to be attractive. She had these glints of blond in her shiny brown hair and she had a year-round tan and she was, shall we say, curvy, but her abrasive personality and cutesy-harsh voice—think evil chipmunk—made Evie and me cringe. She had distinctive features that were just short of beautiful: luscious lips, a prominent nose that bent slightly to the right, and wide, innocent eyes framed with long lashes usually weighed down with clumps of blue-black Covergirl mascara.

Anyway, we noticed something different about Annabel that day. For starters, her BFF Portia Belfort, who was glued to her side 99 percent of the time, had recently left for Europe with her family, so Annabel came in alone for once, greeting us with a twinkle in her eye and a smile that flashed two rows of perfect white teeth. My mom offered the simple salutation Gene required of all front desk staff—*Good afternoon, Annabel* (always use the member's name)—and surveyed the girl in her white short shorts, flat leather sandals, and a favorite hot-pink halter top that made her skin glow and accentuated her tiny waist. As always, the golden dog was shining away on her chest. Annabel's mom had given her the solid-gold charm necklace last year after their family pet, Old Fluff, died, leaving Annabel so sad the light had gone out of her eyes for months. She never took that necklace off, not even when she went for a swim. It had sapphire eyes, her mom had explained, to show how special Annabel was, and they were pink to honor her favorite color. I'd heard her call it her lucky charm more than once.

"Hi, Annabel," Lisa sang in a nasal, mocking voice, pretending to do it under her breath but, in fact, saying it loud enough for everyone to hear.

Annabel smiled and wiggled her fingers at Lisa, who was decked out in her full yoga garb of a shiny blue leotard and pink spandex shorts. Evie and I got a special wink. As Annabel continued toward the women's locker room, Nicholas burst out of the men's locker room and bumped into her. His hair was wet, and droplets were falling on his shoulders and down his tummy. Lisa straightened up and smoothed her hair. She'd always had one eye on Nicky.

"Hi, Nicholas," Lisa said, batting her blue-black eyelashes. He glanced over briefly and said, "How's it going?" Before Lisa could tell him how it was going, he turned that smile on Annabel.

"Got my lunch, sis?" He kissed Annabel on the cheek. She put one hand on her hip.

"I most certainly do. And I don't know where you put it all."

She pretend-punched him lightly in his washboard abs, and then reached into her tote to pull out two large Ziploc bags full of meat sandwiches. "Ah," he said, taking the bags. "A veritable feast. See you at the pool?"

She nodded and smiled, and he took off into the men's locker room, drops of water snaking down his back. We watched Annabel walk slowly to the women's locker room, shaking her head and smiling to herself.

"That girl's in love," my mom pronounced.

"What are you talking about, Beth? Why would you *say* that?" Lisa demanded, her hands angrily on her hips. "And, like, with *who*?"

"Because she has that wicked 'in love' look in her eye, that's why," my mother replied, using one of her favorite Bostonflavored terms. *Wicked* this and *wicked* that was all the rage again in Massachusetts these days. "And I don't *know* who, Lisa. I'm just making an observation. If anyone would know who was dating who, I figure it would be you."

Lisa opened her mouth like she was totally insulted, though I wasn't quite sure why. I agreed with my mom. It was the happiness in Annabel's eyes, the way her nose had crinkled with that genuine smile, the joy in her gait. Evie's face darkened, and she played nervously with her braid. She'd been kidding herself all summer that there was nothing serious going on with Annabel and her secret lover, whose identity we were pretty sure we knew. My best friend shot me a look, and off we went to stealthily follow Annabel.

After

Once we'd heard that revealing conversation between Ashlock, Gene, and my mom, the first thing Evie and I did was to try to find Harmony to warn him about those two throwing him under the bus. After an exhaustive search of the club, we couldn't find the guy anywhere. As we huffed and puffed back at the front desk, Mom—who was back on reception duty—put her iced Dunkin' Donuts coffee (extra cream, extra sugar) down and waggled her index finger at us.

"Calm down, girls, and drink some water before you get heatstroke. Sheesh."

We dutifully scampered behind the desk and my mom gave us some water. After I drank enough to satisfy her, she hugged me and sent us on our way. We were close, my mom and I. She'd adopted me about two years ago, and she always made a point of telling me that she never, ever had any doubts about taking me on despite what everyone said.

What did they say? Basically, that the stuff that had happened to me when I was younger might have made me "damaged goods" and cursed me with what grownups called "severe behavioral problems." I'd never be "normal," they explained to my mom. Sure, I have scars, and I have limitations, but Mom says those things make her love me even more. There's one scar on my ear—it's more of a dent, really, a triangular piece of cartilage missing forever—but it's covered by my hair. The ones on my tummy are rarely seen, so the average person would never know they were there; ditto the ones on my ankles. And the scars on the inside of me, the unseen ones, Mom says, make me even more *me*. I like that way of looking at it. I try not to feel sorry for myself, and most of the time I'm just grateful to have her. I try not to spend my time being angry at the people who hurt me. Plus, my best friend was in much more of a crisis these days than I currently was, so I spent more time tending to her and less time worrying that I wasn't exactly perfect.

At this point, I was rehydrated and ready to deal with the crisis at hand. Evie said, "Maybe we should look behind Court 9?"

I agreed. I sure didn't have any better ideas, so we dashed off to find Harmony before the detective did.

It turned out he wasn't behind Court 9, but he was close. Harmony was out by the Dumpster in the far corner of the parking lot, where a dirt path wound around toward the outdoor tennis courts. He was smoking and pacing. I winced. The icky landfill smell was far worse here than at the pool. It didn't really matter in the long run, though; people would keep coming to the club, odor or no odor, because it had cachet. The fancy Long Hills Country Club was twelve miles away and had no dump anywhere near it, but *we* had a summer waiting list full of the richest families in the Boston suburbs because there was *just something about this place*. Everyone said it. I tried not to breathe through my nose as we got closer to our target, who was wearing mirrored sunglasses, a black T-shirt, and baggy olive-green cargo shorts. He had a scraggly mass of hair that was so black it had glints of blue in it, and even when it was scorching hot outside he'd still be dressed in dark colors.

Evie and I stayed out of sight behind some hedges. *What now?* She put on a thinker's face, then focused on Harmony twenty feet away. *Pssst,* she hissed. *Pssssst! Harmony!*

He furrowed his brow and whipped around to look our way. I felt Evie flinch. We wanted to help him, but then again, we weren't sure whether to approach him. What if he had had something to do with Annabel's death? He was strong, with a swimmer's shoulders and muscular legs.

Harmony mouthed, *What?*

Evie beckoned him over. Seeing his face, remembering he was a friend who'd never hurt a soul, convinced us we were safe. *Hurry!* she mouthed.

But suddenly Harmony stopped pacing and looked in the direction of the club's main entrance. We were too late. He ran his free hand through his hair, brushing his feathered black bangs off his face before they flopped right back down over his eyes. He dropped his cigarette and stamped it out with

28

a worn sandal. He leaned back against the Dumpster and put his right leg up, like a stork, and waited.

"Harmony Goldblatt?"

Detective Ashlock came into view. He looked like he was melting again, but he still refused to take off his blazer. He had the handkerchief in one hand, and he extended his other to Harmony. Harmony looked at it like it was swarming with killer germs, but finally took it.

"Gold*e*nblatt."

"I'm Detective Ted Ashlock. I have a few questions for you, if you don't mind." He stuffed his handkerchief in his pants pocket and took his notebook out of his blazer's inside pocket.

"I already gave my statement to your minions," Harmony said. He was still in the stork stance, and his arms were crossed over his chest. "*And* my alibi."

Ashlock didn't have sunglasses, and considering it was sunny and about ninety-five degrees, I thought maybe he should get some. "Oh, right," he said. "Of course. But since you found her body and you're one of the only ones with a key to the place—"

"Whoa," Harmony said, making a face like the detective was a moron. "Who needs a key? You see that fence? A grade-school kid could hop that thing with a boost. A little step-ladder and anyone could get into that pool."

It was true. The pool fence was only about eight feet high and it wasn't like there were any spikes or barbed wire on it.

"That's a good point, Harmony," Ashlock conceded, and

cracked a simpatico smile. "The thing is, we have evidence that indicates someone was in the pool with Annabel, and that they came in through that revolving door." He pointed toward the club's entrance.

This Ashlock guy was turning out to have more gravitas than you could see at first glance. *That voice*, for one. It was like a radio announcer's with a bit of sandpaper thrown in. And it didn't go at all with his other standout feature, which was his smooth alabaster skin. In any case, Harmony was holding his ground against the voice and the questions, and Evie and I were cheering him on silently from our hiding place.

He shrugged at Ashlock's revelation. "Maybe so. But who knows who else could've come in over that fence?"

Ashlock flipped to a new page in his notebook. "Harmony, I want to get your take on what you think happened. Help me get to know the victim."

Harmony kept his sunglasses on so we couldn't read him, but his body relaxed slightly and he moved away from the Dumpster to face Ashlock head-on.

"I understand Miss Harper was the kind of girl who drove the boys crazy," Ashlock said.

Harmony shook his head. "*No.* Who told you that? It wasn't like that. People didn't understand her."

Ashlock raised his eyebrows. "And you did?"

"People mistook her shyness for attitude. She was quiet because everyone always wanted something from her. She wasn't going to give it up for just anyone. It was a self-protection thing."

"By 'it' you mean . . . love? Boys?"

"*No.*" Harmony was gesturing forcefully with both hands. "You're missing the point, like the rest of them. She was a beautiful girl. A work of art. And because of that, no one saw past her looks. Sometimes it was as if who she was and what she had to say didn't matter."

"Mmmhmm . . ." Ashlock was scribbling in his book. He looked back up at Harmony. "So you two were friends?"

Harmony let out a frustrated sigh. "I didn't say that. But I understood her. She spent a lot of time at the pool and so do I. We said hello, she was nice, but I wasn't going to bother her. I wasn't going to be another person trying to get something from her. I respected her for keeping her dignity."

We could see the detective was still unclear about their relationship.

"Well, Harmony, it sounds like she didn't notice you the way you noticed her. Did she look right through you, Harmony? Did she even know you were alive?"

Harmony shook his head. "I've told you everything I know," he said. "I've talked to your cops. I gave them every gory detail they asked for. You know, they even asked me why I didn't give her CPR? Yeah, I'm trained in it. But not on ice-cold dead bodies! Your people knew she was dead for hours when I found her. It's disgusting."

Harmony slid another cigarette out of the pack and lit it up. Finally, he said, "Go check out Patrick. He was one of the people who wanted something from Annabel."

"Patrick?"

"De Stafford. Summer coach at the tennis camp. Check him out, is all I'm saying. Now, I've about had it with your questions. I'm done."

"Okay," Ashlock conceded. He put his notebook away and fixed his gaze on the boy. "But you know, it seems to me you're not too upset about this. That's always something we look at when we're talking to people who were close to the victim."

Harmony froze. After a tense moment, he slowly removed his sunglasses. His face was exposed, and it was a shocking sight. His eyes were bloodshot and the skin around them was so puffy from crying that he looked like he'd had an allergic reaction, and I think he had: to the death of someone too young. Ashlock looked suitably chastened, patted Harmony kindly on the shoulder, then turned and walked slowly back toward the club, wiping his brow again. He was going to need a bag of handkerchiefs if this kept up.

Well, Evie and I were none the wiser as to who Ashlock suspected in Annabel's death. We watched Harmony for another minute, watched him wipe still more tears from his eyes. I couldn't tell what that detective was thinking, but I think he was barking up the wrong tree with this kid. The thing about Harmony was that he was weird in a good way. I always thought what you saw was what you got with him.

It was the people who pretended to be perfect that scared me.

Before

Among the many moving parts at this place, the tennis people, who came from all over New England to train here, were the beating heart of the club. It was quite a cast, and the club's lobby, with its great glass wall overlooking indoor Courts 1 through 4, was their stage.

It was the second week of June, the official kickoff to the summer tennis season, when Evie and I had to walk through the lobby during lunch, which was the buzziest time of day. Evie stared straight ahead as we shuffled across the worn maroon StainMan 5000 carpeting Gene really needed to replace. Our first hurdle: the world's most arrogant regular campers, who thought they owned the place because they were signed up for tennis camp for the whole summer. Their leader: twelve-year-old brat Tad Chadwick, who was busy mocking another kid's "lame" sneakers while his minions laughed at everything he said. He was Evie's most dedicated tormentor, having bullied her relentlessly for the nearly two years I'd known her.

The cool kids were up ahead. These were the elite tennis players and camp counselors (some were both) who hung out near the far end of the lobby at two round pine tables in front of the club's old, clunky TV that Gene stubbornly refused to replace with a flat-screen. A group of them were stitting with their feet up and rackets strewn haphazardly around them. One of the coolest kids gave Evie and me a wink— seventeen-year-old Patrick de Stafford, the regular camp's assistant director and coach during the summer *and* an elite tennis player. Despite some seriously average looks, he was catnip to the girls. According to my mom, he wowed them with his charisma. *That smile*, they said. One dimple, a deep crevasse in his right cheek, a twinkle in his otherwise unre-markable eyes, and that Cheshire cat grin. As we approached, we got a friendly "Hey, girls!" from the the camp's blue-blooded elite Celia Emerson, a sixteen-year-old who also coached in the tennis camp for extra pocket money.

And then there he was, in all his imposing Czech glory: our resident god of the fuzzy yellow ball, the elitest elite of them all, seventeen-year-old Goran Vanek. Evie started breath-ing faster. I thought she was going to pass out when he trained his eyes on us—and he wasn't smiling.

After

The day after Annabel's body was found, Detective Ashlock was back at the club first thing. Evie and I met at the front desk at precisely eight thirty a.m. and he strolled up minutes later, his white fedora marking him a mile away. He seemed to be making people nervous.

Patrick de Stafford caught sight of him from the door of one of the coaches' offices that were off to the right as you entered the club. Patrick watched with narrowed eyes, gripping the doorjamb until his knuckles turned white, as the detective walked toward the front desk. My mom was fiddling with the radio while Evie and I played it cool over at the far end, trying to appear nonchalant.

"Can I help you?" Mom asked the detective, pretending like she actually thought this strange, pale man was hitting her up for something mundane like, *Hey, where can a guy get a cuppa coffee around here?*

He cleared his throat. "I need to speak with Gene, please,"

the detective said politely, arms stiff at his sides, posture ramrod straight.

"He's not here," my mom informed him.

"Fine. I'll wait." He added, with a tip of his hat, "Thank you, *Ms.* Jestin."

My mom sighed. She was *not* amused. Ashlock turned away from the desk and surveyed the lobby buzzing with its usual morning chaos, full of campers and counselors waiting to be called out to the courts at nine a.m. sharp.

"Hey, Detective," my mom called. "You know people are talking around here, right? Shouldn't you make a statement or something? Call a town hall meeting? I mean, people are *scared.*"

She wasn't kidding. Since everything that had happened yesterday, there was talk of a serial killer and fear was rippling through the club. Gene had called an early meeting this morning for all staff, held in the privacy of cavernous, echoey Court 5. Everyone said the same thing: *We're in shock. We're scared. How could Annabel be here one minute and then just . . . be gone? How?*

Gene said anyone who needed to should take the day, the week, the month off. Then he'd explained it was okay to have all sorts of different feelings, and that sometimes it helped to get back to normal right away. Turned out none of us wanted to go home *just to sit around freaking out*, as someone put it. So for now, everything was routine, at least on the surface.

That was an hour ago. Now, Ashlock took a step closer to my mom. "Oh?" he inquired.

"It's the only thing people can talk about," she said, hopping off her stool, her curls tumbling over her shoulder as she laid her elbows on the desk, a shiny black slab of granite nearly fifteen feet long with white-swirl accents. "I'm surprised you haven't been talking to a *certain person*."

I shook my head and closed my eyes. What was she *doing*?

Ashlock was nonplussed. "I assure you we have things under control."

She narrowed her eyes and tried harder. "A lot of people think Annabel was killed for one time-honored reason." She waited for Ashlock to whip out a notebook and start scribbling furiously. When he didn't, she upped the conspiratorial tone. "Some believe a *certain person* killed her," my mom pronounced, "for love."

I tried not to look at Evie because I imagined she, like me, was beside herself. *Who* killed her for love? And what did my mom know about it?

And there it was—Ashlock kicked into detective gear. Suddenly she held a little more interest for him. "Who killed her for love, Ms. Jestin?" he asked.

My mom beckoned him closer. He leaned across the desktop and she met him halfway and whispered something in his ear.

"Okay," Ashlock said, stepping back. "We'll need an

official statement from you ASAP. The department will be in touch."

My mother couldn't stop her mouth from hanging embarrassingly open as Ashlock, who didn't seem remotely wowed by her whispered theory, turned on his heel and strode away. Only then did Evie and I make eye contact. What had just happened? We thought we'd known who Ashlock was here to talk to, but maybe we'd been wrong.

The lobby was still packed with dozens of loud campers awaiting their court assignments, so we could follow him at a safe distance, no problem. Evie put an orange back in the fruit bowl and off we went to see the club through Detective Ashlock's eyes.

Before

As Evie and I walked through the lobby on the summer tennis season's kickoff day, we saw our resident tennis god, Goran Vanek, wasn't smiling—but then again, he was a serious guy. I mean, he'd been stuck at number three in the New England eighteen-and-unders for over a year, and was determined to be numero uno by summer's end. When he zoned in on us standing awkwardly off to the side, I thought Evie was going to hyperventilate. When he gave us a curt yet respectful nod, I worried she'd pass out.

The rest of the elites were sitting at their table watching him practice his strokes, whooshing his racket through the air. He demonstrated his backhand a few times, fast and then slow, and said in his thick Czech accent, "You see? It is all in the wrists. The *wrists*."

Evie was mesmerized. Goran was basically the love of her life, the man she planned to marry (a dream I supported because it was, at least, more realistic than her backup plan to marry Simon Pertwee from her favorite British boy band, Hot

Minute), even though we weren't positive Goran knew her name. Anyway, the joke of this scene was, you couldn't teach Goran's backhand. It was known in the New England tennis world as the Missile. He never missed, and he could angle it like nobody's business, and he hit it so hard sometimes you could barely see the ball flying from his racket and skidding off the court before it jerked up and curved away with crazy topspin. And then everyone would try to work their wrists like him, and their balls would end up in the bottom of the net.

But the elites each had their own strengths. They were— in Evie's words—*annoyingly good-looking, incredibly cool,* and *ridiculously talented.* I watched them sitting there, tanned and beautiful and basically extra special, and I had to admit Evie was right. Take Serene Cowen-Lynch, with her perfectly swishing lavender tennis skirt, who at that moment decided to join Goran. Half the lobby was now watching their impromptu tennis demo.

"Check out my forehand." Serene winked to her elite pals. While Goran nodded seriously and let her take over, she swung her racket back, stepped sideways with the proper footwork, and brought her oversize Volcano X right smack into Goran's butt.

The lobby erupted in giggles and a few hoots, and Goran pointed his racket like a lance at her. "You're dead meat, Cowen-Lynch. Watch your back."

She pretended to gasp in fear, but it was all good-natured; pretty, twinkly eyed Serene could get away with anything. She was thirteen years old and really, really awesome at the game. We were about to move on when, suddenly, there she was: our poolside goddess. Annabel Harper was walking toward us, on her way to the women's locker room. Daisy Dukes showing off tanned, toned legs—check. Aviators on her head, holding back perfect blond hair—check. Laser-blue eyes on a blemish-free face—check. Patrick's eyes almost popped out of his head. Annabel wasn't a "tennis person," but she was friendly with the gang, as was Nicholas.

Patrick leaned back coolly in his chair, held out his hand, and said, "Hey, Bella. Give me some love." Those eyes were playful, his voice husky.

I saw Annabel's eyes flash for the quickest second. She didn't like that nickname. Anyway, she dutifully slapped his hand and said, "What's up, Paddy?" *Ha.* He hated that nickname. *Touché*, my friend.

Annabel gave Celia Emerson a hello squeeze on the shoulder and Celia, the tennis person who probably knew her best, said, "See you after work?" Annabel nodded.

The elites waved to Annabel. All but *one* elite. I hoped Evie didn't notice, but tall, brooding Goran—who'd never, ever dated a girl at the club despite having tons of females swooning over him—couldn't take his eyes off Annabel. In the midst of greeting her friends and fans, including Evie and me, who got a special smile and a wave, Annabel pretended she didn't feel his eyes on her. But she couldn't help it in the end. Before she turned to go, she raised her head and shot a shy, under-the-eyelashes look at Goran and nervously fingered her cherished dog charm. The electricity nearly made me jump out of my skin. I don't know when or how they'd gotten together, but yep, it was a fact: our tennis Adonis and our sun-worshipping Venus were having the romance of the century. And for some reason, they were trying to hide it.

Teenage boys aren't always so perceptive, though, and I don't think Patrick noticed his best friend, Goran, had a budding relationship. Patrick stood up, stretched, and stared shamelessly after Annabel sashaying into the women's locker room, no doubt to change into her bikini for an afternoon in the sun. "Yes, boys," Patrick pronounced. "It's gonna be a great summer."

After

The first thing Evie and I noticed as we skulked in the detective's wake the day after Annabel died: he either was a tennis fan or would be by the time he was done with this case. He'd stopped in the crowded lobby, and as Evie and I jockeyed for position, we could see he was staring at the elites. They were out on Court 1 early today, practicing their short balls. They moved in a rhythm as if choreographed, one after the other, never missing a shot. Sure, Ashlock could've been eyeing a potential suspect out there, but I could see he was fascinated.

Goran ran up and slammed the ball crosscourt, smoothly turning and jogging back to the line afterward; Serene, long black ponytail flying behind her as she came up right behind Goran, was already nailing her forehand down the line with one silky stroke before Goran was back in line; and the rest of the kids followed.

"*Go! Go! Go!*" The elites' head coach, Will Temple, was

feeding them balls as fast as he could. After they each went one more time, he shouted, "Okay! Volleys!"

And so the elites had to move faster, running closer to the net, crouching, and lunging to pull off crisp volleys from Will's feeds. The three of us, with twenty feet separating Evie and me from the detective, stood behind the glass and watched them play like they were zoo animals. They were exotic, youthful, and full of promise. Special and elusive and rare. All of them—only five to ten at a time trained during a given week in the summer—held high rankings in their age groups in the New England junior tennis world. Today, their play, while perfect as usual, felt robotic and joyless. If you'd watched them enough over time, you could just tell they were rattled by Annabel's death.

Pretty soon Ashlock snapped out of it and weaved his way through the packed lobby. We scurried behind him, dying to know who he was looking for at the back end of the club. It wasn't a manager at the front desk and it wasn't a tennis player, because he'd just passed them all by.

Before

I headed for the café to find Evie. She should be grabbing lunch right about now, while the campers were munching on their first helpings. Evie's M.O. was to hit the buffet when the fewest number of people were around to see her eat. And yep—I found her there alone, building a yummy-looking sandwich. She often helped out in the mornings by setting up the lunch spread, chopping tomatoes and onions into stackable rings, organizing bottles of mustard and piles of bread, and spreading it all out over three oblong folding tables. The lunch lady knew Lucky never packed Evie wholesome meals, so she let her slip into the line in exchange for a little light labor.

Evie practically lived at the club because there was no one at home to watch her. Her mom packed up her yellow Hyundai almost two years ago and took off. She avoided telling Evie she was going until it was too late to protest. This terrible event happened after an awkward meeting only one year before, when Evie's mom first told Lucky he had a daughter. Up until then, Evie had been told her dad lived in Europe and simply "couldn't be found." Basically, Evie had explained to me later, her mom had lied to her for nine years. "Eh." Lucky had shrugged when Evie's mom dropped then-ten-year-old Evie off at the club for her new life. "How hard can it be? She's a mini-adult by now. Practically old enough to take care of herself. We'll have a blast."

Evie explained to me that her mom was just tired. She needed a break. She'd be back. I never met her, but from what Lucky said it didn't really sound like her mom had wanted kids at all. I think she went to Oregon or someplace that was far away from St. Claire.

I hung back while Evie began to load her plate. Right then, tennis camp villain and little twerp Tad Chadwick decided he needed seconds. He and his crew—Marcus Reilly and Fat Stan, who wasn't overweight but whose nickname lived on because he'd been chunky in third grade—fell in behind Evie, which was bad news. I moved closer to eavesdrop.

"What do you *do*?" Tad was saying. "You're here every day but I never see you *do* anything." *(Cue loud, cackling laughter from Marcus and Fat Stan.)*

Evie said nothing. She was tensed up, turning red. She reached for a carrot stick, bypassing the crinkle-cut potato chips. Tad was on a roll. "Well, I guess you do *something*. All I see you do is eat and stare at people! Evie *skeevy*."

He laughed hysterically at his own brilliant rhyme. Tad

was the son of Boston Brahmin, old money whose ancestors had allegedly come over on the *Mayflower*. He had the arrogance and self-assuredness that came with that privilege. He had curly brown hair, shocking blue eyes, and was, annoyingly, very good-looking and probably always would be.

I wished there was something I could do, but Evie told me a long time ago that when anyone made a big deal out of Tad's harassment, even to stick up for her, it only made things worse. She finished creating her ham and cheese on rye and we walked toward the little eating area in the pool lobby where there were a few tables—when summer tennis camp wasn't in session, parents could sit and watch their kids taking their swimming lessons or members could relax with their coffee—but it was packed, so Evie had to sit on the steps that led up to the pool lobby. I sat with her while she ate. Normally she'd slip me some potato chips—she always got extra for me, because my mom was on a health kick and wasn't exactly handing out delicious snacks to me on a regular basis—but thanks to Tad she only had carrots today. She gave me one and I munched on it as she ate her sandwich. Things were going okay until Tad finished his latest sandwich and tried to get down the stairs we were sitting on.

"Thar she blows!" he shouted, making sure the campers and counselors, who were still picking at their lunches, were listening to his clever little take on a literary masterpiece. "We've got ourselves a big one, mateys."

I turned to see him standing one step above us, holding his arm up and pointing an air spear at Evie. "Get out of the way, Moby, or I'll have to harpoon you."

Marcus cracked up at that. As if that moment couldn't get any more hideous, Serene was watching, too, and while she didn't step in, I saw a flicker of sympathy on her face. I saw Will, the senior coach, tense up like he was ready to intervene if necessary. Tears were welling up in Evie's eyes as she scrambled to get away, upsetting her plate and dropping the uneaten crusts of her sandwich on the floor. I fought every instinct I had to take Tad Chadwick down. I was younger than both of them, but I'd been called scrappy more than once and I didn't give up easily. I didn't know if Evie would ever eat lunch again after this.

The thing is, Evie is fat. That's what everyone said. She would be tall when she grew up, and she might be beautiful, according to my mom, but only if she quits eating. I didn't really see her eat that much except for the occasional Twinkies binge when things get really bad, but something must be going on for her to be that size. That's what the grownups said. For the two years she'd been hanging around here with Lucky, she'd stayed plump.

My mom and her dad agreed we were a good pair. *It's been so great for Chelsea to have a friend like Evie*, my mom had said to Lucky one night when he was staying late and she was closing up the club. *Someone to keep her company. They're like two peas in a pod, those two. It's sweet, really.* Even Lucky, the

48

most absentee parent ever, had to concur. *Chelsea has saved Evie's life this summer,* he said. *I think she's the best friend my daughter's ever had.* My heart soared when I heard that, because it meant we could hang out all summer, and maybe even have a sleepover or two at my place.

Now, it killed me that I couldn't back Evie up, but I had to respect her wishes to stay out of it. Tad never bullied me, and aside from a few snotty remarks here and there to various other kids, he saved his ire for Evie. I walked with her as she retreated back to her safe place behind Court 5, and I thought about how I could possibly soothe the feelings in her that had just been scraped over with a cheese grater. It was going to be a long, hot summer.

After

We were hot on Ashlock's heels as he continued to move through the club after watching the elites. Evie and I caught up to him as he reached the end of the lobby, when he stopped again to survey the café area below. Off to the left was the pool and the aerobics-floor-slash-basketball-court. Speaking of which, we could hear the thumping of house music coming from an exercise class. Ashlock walked down the stairs, following the sound, and we followed him. We hung back to see where the detective was heading, which was straight to the scene of the crime: the pool. This was devilishly good news for me and Evie; we could sit on the pool lobby's comfy sofas and watch what the detective was up to without raising a single eyebrow. We perched on the gray love seat and, as we gazed out over the pool area, we were presented with an interesting sight.

Ashlock was on his hands and knees at the deep end of the pool, looking more wildly out of place than ever among the crowd of half-naked kids, moms, and a few teens. This was where Annabel's body had been found. The Stormtroopers had combed the deck forever, so I couldn't imagine what he was looking for.

Evie agreed. "What does he think he's gonna find?" She was leaning forward, elbows resting on her knees. "Man . . . this is surreal."

Ashlock crawled along the pebbles on all fours, rubbing the deck with his fingers every few inches. His white fedora stayed firmly on his head, like it was glued on. Evie yawned. I yawned. This was like watching paint dry or grass grow— whatever works for you in terms of imagining how boring it was getting. Evie poked me a few moments later as I started to nod off. Ashlock was in the grass now, picking through what looked like one blade at a time. He started rubbing the ground with his fingers and then began digging one finger into the grass. We stood up and pressed our noses against the glass. I realized then he'd snapped on some rubber gloves, and he seemed to be working something out of the ground. After a minute he rose and walked slowly, deliberately, along the pool's edge, toward the exit. He was holding something in one hand, and covered that with the other, like a big clamshell.

I turned to Evie. *What the heck?* She shook her head and widened her eyes, like, *I don't know!* When Ashlock got close to the revolving door, Evie and I hightailed it back to the café to act like we couldn't care less about this detective.

51

We stood casually by the counter, pretending to check out today's yogurt flavor, which was still boysenberry, whatever a boysenberry was. Evie reached down and tugged at the bottom of her oversize black T-shirt, making sure it was covering her belly.

We sensed Ashlock pass by us so we waited a few beats, then turned and slowly headed up to the lobby behind him. The detective was still carrying the mystery item, and he was getting some odd looks. He paused in the lobby to check out the elites again as they pounded tennis balls on Court 1. Goran was still out there, now hitting with Will.

Evie didn't just adore Goran. She loved his skill, too, loved watching what he could do with that ball. It could be very hypnotic, if you appreciated the game of tennis. Nobody cared about what was happening on Court 4, where a handful of regular campers—including Tad—were training. They were clunky, flawed, hapless. See, the tennis class system is absolute. You'll get along fine if you play by the rules. You're either elite, or you're not. Someone once asked head coach Will Temple what separated an elite from a regular player. Will, who was about twenty-eight and resembled a nerdy male model with glasses and a physique that was more Statue of David than lean-and-wiry tennis machine, had replied, *A champion is born, and then made. You can't be an elite without both the talent and the training.*

The champions at our club were currently sweating it up. I couldn't prove it, but I swear I saw that detective paying particular attention to Goran, and a burning question began to nag at me: Could Goran know something about what happened to Annabel? Evie noticed too, and I caught her looking terribly sad. I worried this awful thing might turn out to be too much for her to handle.

Before

As June got under way, it was time for the annual staff pool party—one of my favorite nights of the whole year. From the minute Lucky pushed through that revolving door carrying his guitar and Patrick followed grasping a big blue cooler, it was all fun and laughter and sultry air. By the end of the night, someone would inevitably get crazy and gallop to the pool, usually fully clothed, to perform a klutzy cannonball.

This year's bash was held on a Friday night during the second week of the season, and when I burst through that door onto the pool deck behind my mom, the smell of summer was so pungent it was like you were inhaling a whole season floating on a gust of wind. As dusk turned to night, an old U2 song in which Bono was screaming out about the streets having no name was playing on Harmony's iPod.

Patrick was holding court on the lawn, perched on the edge of a lounge chair, still in his tennis shorts, laughing at everything Will said but never appearing to really listen; his eyes kept flitting to the door. My mom made a beeline for the other side of the pool, where her friends were hanging out. We doubted Nicholas Harper would be here tonight; he had too much going on to find time for a staff party. Gene always said Nicholas was "going places." People loved him, even though sometimes when he was really tired he could be snappy. But that was rare. He always had a smile and a hello, and was wicked good-looking, a trait that no doubt contributed to his popularity.

So where was Evie? I scanned the pool area and finally found her. She was sitting on the long cedar bench along the back wall to the right of the pool entrance; the wide bench doubled as storage for the lifesaving equipment and pool cleaning stuff. Nearest the revolving door, the bench was bathed in light from the pool area's overhead lamps. The far end remained in the shadows, and Evie was sitting there alone. Lucky happened to be sitting six feet or so away from his daughter, chatting with an aerobics instructor.

Evie was sitting on her hands, staring out at nothing, swinging her legs. I was going to go over and say hi, but Celia called to me then, coaxing me over to the grass with the rest of them. The crowd greeted me, and Patrick gave me a squeeze. Yeah, I got along with the cool kids, but it bothered me that Evie felt so excluded. It's not like I didn't have to work at it, though. I mean, my mom didn't exactly trumpet my life story around here, but people knew what had happened to me. The basics, anyway. Sometimes new people would try to press my mom about my case, because exactly what had happened to me was still a mystery that had shocked St. Claire and surrounding towns, and remained unsolved. But my mom would always say, *We've moved on. Next question.*

Anyway, when my pals started debating who had the best serve at the club, I wandered over to Evie. I was about to greet my best friend, but that was the moment Lucky finally noticed his daughter.

"Hey, kid. What are you doing in the dark all by yourself?" he asked.

Evie looked at her dad and shrugged. Lucky sprang from his seat and walked over to her. He held out his hand, and she looked at him, her eyes shining as he pulled her up. "Come on. Let's go over and hang out with the gang."

He put his arm around her and sort of pulled her with him, and Evie nestled against him, and I saw her inhale her father's smell and then exhale a long breath of contentment. I went along, and Lucky easily broke into the circle on the lawn.

"Hey, Lucky," Patrick said, and grinned.

Lucky looked down and nudged one of the girls sitting on the cooler. "Move over and make room for my daughter."

The girl shifted a few inches and Evie barely fit in the space the girl left her, but she managed to get one butt cheek on. It didn't look very comfortable, and yet my friend appeared so happy to be included I think she would've sat on a rusty nail if they'd asked her to. I found a spot on the grass next to the cooler. Everyone greeted Evie like they were old friends.

"Well, well. Look who it is," Patrick exclaimed, giving Evie his best Patrick de Stafford dimple.

"Hey there," Celia said.

They were all drinking from those big red cups, and Lucky raised his, chugged, belched, and amid the groans of protest announced, "This, my friends, is going to be the summer of our lives. Chug if you *belieevveeeee!*"

Everyone yelled "I believe!" in unison, then whooped and chugged, and Evie was giggling as she drank her Sprite. She crinkled her nose at me. It was a great start to the summer, and things were looking up for my friend. Alas, it wasn't to stay that way for long.

After

Detective Ashlock came for Patrick on a steamy August morning three days after Annabel's body was found. Thanks to Harmony Goldenblatt, we thought Patrick might be one of the St. Claire PD's prime suspects.

Patrick was a sitting duck teaching on Court 1, but he kept his cool. Ashlock, in his usual outfit, stood a foot away from the glass watching intently as Patrick yelled and did torture drills, which basically entailed throwing ball after ball in quick succession all over the court while the kids scrambled and worked on their reaction times, speed, and footwork.

Evie and I were in a prime location on one of the love seats facing the courts, thanks to her mad crush on Goran, who was playing on Court 3. Lucky, teaching on Court 2, soon called time for morning snack, and Patrick waved his kids toward the exit. He met Ashlock in the café as he headed for the stairs to the lobby.

"Patrick de Stafford?"

"Yeah," Patrick answered, wiping his brow with his T-shirt sleeve. He knew exactly who this guy was.

"Is there somewhere we can talk?"

They settled in the tennis coaches' office, which had a window overlooking Court 1. Detective Ashlock was sizing up Patrick, who said nothing for a solid minute or so while he studied the top of his Gatorade bottle as if it held the answers to many secrets, then smoothly loosened the cap, threw back his head, and took a long, loud gulp of the fluorescent liquid.

Then Ashlock went in for the kill.

"Where were you Monday night, Patrick?"

They had the office to themselves, with Patrick in his favorite soft swivel chair and Ashlock relegated to a stiff wooden chair. Evie and I had gotten lucky—they'd left the door cracked open, so we'd sidled up and sat down with our backs to the wall outside the door as if we were just chilling out. When we swiveled our necks as far as they could go, we could just see Patrick through the crack, and Ashlock's shins. I knew our luck would run out at some point. But for now, we were eavesdropping with impunity. Patrick set down the half-empty bottle on the hideous gray linoleum desktop, wiped his mouth with the back of his hand, and leveled his gaze at the detective. "I was asleep. In my bed at my parents' house in Natick."

We heard Ashlock let out an *mmmhmm*, which actually came out as a half grunt, half sigh. "And what time was that?"

"I don't know. About eleven until eight in the morning, when I dragged my butt out of bed to come here." Patrick stared at the tennis courts, which were empty during snack time.

"Uh-huh," the detective said, and I pictured him writing everything down in his notebook. "What were you doing *before* eleven p.m.?"

Talk about pulling teeth. I was starting to think Ashlock's strategy was to bore his subjects into confessing. Like, just for something to do, they'd give it all up: *Okay, okay. I did it, man. I killed Annabel. Now, like, stop annoying me, please.* It was, interestingly, the same way Patrick beat his opponents on the New England tennis circuit. He had no distinctive serve, no killer forehand; he didn't have Goran's natural gift. He'd just keep hitting back, over and over, until his foe made an error or grew exhausted. Until he beat them down.

"I was at the movies." *Pause.* "By myself." Patrick leaned forward. "Let me ask you, Mr. Detective: Why are you hassling a guy who's never had so much as a parking ticket? I mean, give me a break, I'm not a *murderer.* I'm a *tennis player.*"

He was holding his own. Patrick definitely had some suburban-style street smarts. He'd been around here most of his life, and we all knew his story. Patrick came from a family with something like six kids. Rumor had it his dad spent what savings they had on Patrick's tennis training before he turned ten. So, as soon as Patrick was old enough to work off his tennis fees at the club by teaching at various camps and clinics, Gene put him on the payroll.

Patrick shook his head angrily and continued, "I'm not the person you should be worrying about. There's a murderer running around St. Claire and you're not doing a thing about it. When are we going to know what happened to her? The cops are a joke."

The detective stayed silent, but Evie and I had now confirmed something we'd been led to believe by Harmony: Patrick had some sort of passion for Annabel, though I didn't think either of us knew exactly what it involved or how it had played out.

"Here's the thing," the detective said when Patrick finished his rant. "I never said anything about murder. I am investigating every angle—and that includes you. Are you aware that the majority of females in these cases are killed by someone they know?" *Pause.* "No? You didn't know that? Well, believe it."

Patrick shrugged as if to say, *You don't scare me.*

"I've been told by a reliable source that you and Annabel had an unpleasant encounter back in June. In the women's locker room. In fact, I was told it was more than just unpleasant. Did things get physical that night in June, Patrick?"

Evie and I gasped as quietly as we could. Luckily, Patrick gasped louder so no one heard us (we hoped). "So, Mr. de Stafford," the detective continued coolly, "before we start talking about serial killers on the loose in St. Claire, why don't you tell me what happened in the locker room between you and Annabel that night?"

Before

The pool party was in full swing. My mom was shouting something to Lucky about a bet going on across the pool over what burns more calories, eight hours on the tennis court or one hour of running. Lucky agreed to go over there to settle the bet, leaving Evie with one butt cheek on the cooler.

The older kids started talking around Evie and basically ignoring her, and eventually the other girl slid off the cooler and closed the circle on the lawn, leaving Evie alone and excluded. Again. It wasn't a calculated move, aggressive as it felt. It just *was*. As I got up to go to her, I watched Evie's face collapse. But then she seemed to make some sort of decision. She stood up, held her head high, and said, "Come on, Chels." She walked with her chin up back to the bench. Celia, I saw, noticed this a little too late; her mouth was open as if to say something, but Evie was already gone. That was the night the temperature turned brutal enough to peel paint off the walls, as my mom put it, and stayed that way for weeks. I loved the heat. It was as if summer temperatures brought out all the scents around us, from the grass to the hydrangea bushes planted along the fence, to the people, to the aroma of hot chlorine. I had to admit I didn't love when the air got too damp, though. The power of New England humidity is hard to understand unless you've felt it envelop you like a warm cloak—a heavy, claustrophobic cloak you can't take off until Mother Nature herself sees fit to lift it.

Evie and I sat silently together on the dark side of the bench, checking out the pockets of people around the party.

Lucky was back on the bench now, too. He drained his red cup and picked up his guitar, hunching over it, studying the strings, his fingers going berserk up and down the neck. No one gave him any notice until he'd finished warming up and turned the iPod off, and then the opening chords of Girl Gang's "Summer Cool" pierced the night. There was a hush as Lucky told us, "They say this is the song of the summer. Here's my acoustic take on it."

Lucky's gravelly voice, staying beautifully in tune, sang the upbeat lyrics with a haunting slowness: *The sun got hotter, and you showed your face / I saw you there, in that same place . . .* And then, when he got to the chorus, Harmony started singing, then Lisa, then my mom, off-key and louder than anyone, then pretty much everyone.

Summer, summer, summer, yeah yeah yeah
I saw you by the pool and fell in love at first sight
In the summer, summer, summer, cool cool cool.

I was watching Evie as Lucky sang, and I saw a tear roll down her cheek. As her dad made faces of longing and feeling, his daughter was sitting just feet from him, weeping. Lucky finished his song and smacked his guitar, closing his eyes and biting his bottom lip as he did. He raised his head to absorb the whistles and applause, while Harmony fiddled with his iPod and joked, "Let's cleanse our palate with the *real* singers, shall we?" On came the actual "Summer Cool" and a few of the guys groaned, but I hoped Evie's favorite song would cheer her up. She had tears pouring down her face, and her eyes and mouth were twisted in pain. I didn't know how to help her, so I touched her leg and stayed with her. She was stifling sobs, crying as silently as she could while everyone else laughed and chatted.

"I just want to go home," she said. "Lucky doesn't get it. No one wants me around."

I looked over to see Lucky, in Levi's 501s and a purple tie-dyed shirt with his dirty-blond hair flopping around under his blue bandanna, gyrating to the music.

Evie said to me, "Your mom's always telling me I have to *be friendly to make friends*. But if no one wants to be my friend, how can I be outgoing?"

I couldn't argue with that. I mean, the girl wasn't whining—she truly didn't understand why she was invisible. I sat and listened to her, and I totally got why she was so sad. Bullied by day, ignored by night. It wasn't easy. She seemed to feel better the more she talked, and in the end she hugged me. "At least I have you," she said, "the best friend I ever had." My heart swelled with happiness.

Will was first in the pool that night. After Patrick dared him, he ripped his shirt off and ran to the water in his shorts, forgetting to take off his shoes. After two weeks on the outdoor tennis courts, Will had a pinkish-brown tennis tan, which meant he was darkening on the arms and neck but maintained a pasty chest and back. As Will trudged up the concrete steps out of the water, his soaked shoes making hilarious gurgling noises as he walked along the deck, Lucky was shouting for Patrick. But no response came.

"Where the heck is de Stafford?" Lucky yelled to the guys still hanging on the lawn.

Harmony shouted back, "Dunno! He said he was going to the men's room and never came back." I watched Harmony slip through the revolving doors as Lisa was busy showing the group how many cartwheels she could do in a row.

A minute later, Lucky said, "Now where's Harmony? Where's everyone going?"

Celia piped up from across the pool, "Hey, Lucky! Harmony went to look for Patrick. He'll be back."

Lucky nodded back to her. "Okay. Throw me a Bud, will ya?"

Celia did. And then everything went ballistic.

Before

This year's pool party was going south—and fast. The full can of beer Celia attempted to gently lob to Lucky missed badly and thwapped a staff member smack on the side of his head. As my mother attended to him on one side of the pool, I saw Harmony frantically pushing through the revolving door to get back into the pool area, his party face deflated.

His eyes darted around, and then he beckoned silently for Lucky to follow him. I ran to Evie, who was watching Lucky with concern.

"What's happening?" she asked no one in particular. Then she said to me, "Stay by me, Chels. Something's going on."

She was hugging herself as if it were freezing, though it had to be at least eighty degrees. Lucky and Harmony raced to the men's locker room, quickly disappearing from view. Everyone else was focused on the injured staffer. My mom was calling for a first-aid kit, and Lisa was wondering loudly if we needed an ambulance.

"He's gonna be okay," I heard my mom say. "But he'll need

stitches. I'll drive him to Margot General. So where the heck is Lucky? I need him to bring Chelsea home with him so I can take this guy to the ER."

Evie smiled at me. We were having a sleepover! I loved staying at Evie and Lucky's. There weren't a lot of rules at their two-bedroom bungalow in St. Claire. It was a nice break from my mom, who had rules all over the place, including taped to the refrigerator. Half of them were rules for herself like, *Buy diet soda* and *Lose five pounds.*

By now someone had turned off the music and the party was pretty much over. I looked at a few of the kids on the grass and saw Lisa staring at the pool hallway like she was really mad at it. *Ah.* I then saw the kerfuffle through the glass in that pool hallway. There were three very upset-looking males: Lucky, shaking his head and gesturing; Harmony, gripping Patrick by the shoulder, getting in his face about whatever was going on; and Patrick . . . *wow.* Patrick was as pale as his tennis sneakers. Lucky finally threw up his arms, said something to Harmony, and took off, jogging back toward the pool door. Lucky headed straight for our bench, grabbed his guitar—not five feet from Evie and me—shouted a general goodbye to everyone, and took off, lost in thought. His bandanna was still firmly on and his head was down. Evie looked shell-shocked, paralyzed, as if she expected him to come back and get her. As if maybe he was just putting the guitar in his rickety Oldsmobile Cutlass and would be right back.

My mom saw him leave and shouted in disbelief, "You've got to be *kidding* me." She yelled over to Evie, "Sorry, kid, but your dad needs a good talking-to. This is *not* acceptable parenting."

My mom asked Harmony to drive the injured guy to the hospital, and Evie and I had our sleepover with my mom's tedious rules firmly in place. But hey, at least we were safe at home, tucked into bed together.

The events of that night started a lot of rumors, but as far as I knew at the time, only Patrick was aware of what had really happened. All we knew was that none of us saw Annabel that night—but some were adamant that she was in that locker room with Patrick.

After

Patrick was suitably indignant at the detective's blunt accusation. "I would never—*never*—lay my hands on a girl! How could you even say that?"

He jumped out of his chair and banged the wall with his fist. Ashlock stayed put.

"Hey," Ashlock said. "I get it, kid. I do. I'm only following the evidence. Why don't you tell me your side? Did she lead you on? Pretend to like you? That would've made anyone mad."

Patrick ran his hands down his face, rubbing his eyes and his cheeks and his mouth.

"Tell me how this girl ended up in the women's locker room crying and bruised, with you in there with her."

Evie looked shocked. She blew some hair out of her eyes and mouthed to me, *Bruised?* I was as confused as she was. Who had Ashlock heard this from?

Patrick, suddenly looking exhausted, collapsed on his seat and put his head between his knees before looking up at

Ashlock. "It wasn't like that," he said. "You've got everything wrong."

"I'm all ears," Ashlock said before ratcheting up his tone. "But don't lie to me again. If what you tell me doesn't match what I already know, we're going to have a problem."

The great and charismatic Patrick literally gulped. I'd been watching Ashlock for a few days now, and I loved how he played good cop *and* bad cop. He didn't need a partner.

"Literally the only thing that happened was I saw her in the pool hallway during the summer kickoff party, and then I went to talk to her, but she was gone by the time I got inside."

"Interesting," Ashlock said. "Because my information is that you followed Annabel around like a lost puppy, but she wasn't interested."

Patrick glared, drained his Gatorade, and slammed the empty bottle down on the desk. "First, she *did* like me. Okay? We'd kind of dated earlier in the month. We were both at the club late one night—I'd been working out and she'd been soaking in the hot tub. We got to chatting in the lobby. We talked for hours, Detective. We had a connection. So I asked her out, and she agreed to go to the movies with me."

"Except the date never happened, did it, Patrick?"

More glaring from the suspect. "We could never find a night when we were both free—that's it. We still talked all the time." The smile was back. *All girls adore me*, it was saying. *All the time.*

There was a pause, and then Ashlock said provocatively,

"I'm not so sure about that, Patrick. I think you were obsessed with her."

Silence, then Patrick sighed. Finally, he admitted, "Okay. I had spoken to her earlier that day, and she told me she was going to be at the club late working out. I invited her to the party, but she didn't want to go. She said it wasn't her style."

Whoa. Evie poked me. I don't know what Patrick thought he was doing, but everyone knew Annabel didn't work out. Ever.

Patrick threw up his hands. "That girl was an enigma. She says she doesn't want to go to the party, and yet I catch a glimpse of her peeking out of the women's locker room, checking out the action."

"Wait a minute," Ashlock said. "She wasn't a staff member. How could she have been there if, as you say, the party didn't start until after the club closed?"

"Easy. She was one of the people Gene gave a key to."

Ashlock cleared his throat, to stall I thought. I exchanged glances with Evie. I don't think any of us knew about Annabel's key. "Why were you so upset that night, Patrick? Something must have happened to get you riled up."

Patrick snapped, "I was upset because she blew me off, okay? Happy now? She totally dissed me and I was . . . annoyed. That's it. There's always another girl, Detective."

I imagined Ashlock rolling his eyes. "Fine, Patrick. So tell me: Who do you think we should be looking at for this?"

Patrick looked startled. Ashlock did the silent routine

again. I pictured him skeptical this time, raising his eyebrows as he leveled one of those cool gazes at Patrick.

"Well," Patrick said finally, "I don't want to get anyone in trouble, but . . . you should be talking to Goran Vanek. He had a major crush on that girl."

Evie squinted at me. *What the heck?* I had the same exact reaction, because one thing was clear: Patrick was lying his butt off. Why was Ashlock letting him get away with such a weak explanation? What was his game?

Before

"Isn't he beautiful?" Lisa swooned one day in late June, elbowing my mom. They'd stopped in the lobby to watch the action on Court 1 on their way back from grabbing some coffee at the café.

Goran had one arm in the air, biceps curled, fist shaking in victory. He'd just hit a winner down the line that his opponent and best friend, Patrick, barely got a look at. My mom was way too old to moon over Goran, but Serene, nursing a can of cranberry juice with other elites taking a break, admitted of Goran's legendary backhand, "That Missile is pretty hot."

Serene, an exotic beauty with thick, jet-black hair Evie coveted, had some hot shots of her own, notably her serve, which was one of the fastest on the girls' tennis circuit and better than many of the boys'. Tennis is a great equalizer for age and gender—girls beat boys in the sport all the time. In fact, Serene had beaten Patrick in a practice set last winter.

Not everyone was impressed with the clash of our two

tennis titans. Nicholas and Harmony walked by on their way to their afternoon lifeguard shifts at the pool, and Nicholas guffawed. "Please. Tennis is for weaklings."

"Try competing in a hundred-meter butterfly. *That's* athleticism," Harmony agreed.

Evie and I were standing alongside my mom and Lisa by the plate-glass windows overlooking the courts. Annabel walked into the lobby then, and with everyone focusing on the tennis match, she caught my eye and sidled up to me. "Hey, Chelsea." She smiled, giving me a hug. I felt the dog charm on her necklace gently knock me in the eye as she embraced me. She gave Evie a squeeze on the shoulder before turning to her brother, who had made yet another anti-tennis crack.

"Stop it, you two," Annabel said to Nicholas and Harmony. "There's enough testosterone to go around. Why must you boys make everything a competition?"

Goran and Patrick whaling the ball at each other was always quite a sight. They'd had an intense-but-friendly rivalry practically since the day Goran stepped off the plane from the Czech Republic with his bowl cut and orange pants six years ago. Legend has it (i.e., Gene's version of the story) that Goran's parents brought him to the club for a tennis evaluation even before they signed him up for school.

Celia, sitting with Serene and hearing Annabel behind her, turned and said, "Hey, girl. What happened to you Friday night? I thought you were coming out with us."

Annabel opened her mouth and stuttered something like, *I—I, um, I was—um . . . I—*

"She had a *daaattte*," Nicholas interrupted. He worked his eyebrows like Groucho Marx and looked at his sister. "But she won't say who the mystery man is."

Celia said, "Ooh. New guy? You'll have to tell me *everything* when these clowns aren't around," then went back to watching the tennis match. "He's looking good," Celia observed of Goran. "I bet he makes number one by Yale."

Ah, the Yale Championships. The big end-of-summer event in Connecticut included boys' and girls' competitions in every age group, and whoever won their tournament almost always rocketed to number one in New England. As for Celia, she'd been teaching more than playing lately, so she was expected to stay put at number five in the eighteen-and-unders. And she was right—Goran had been training like a madman and was in fine form. He was clad in full Volcano gear again today because they were his sponsor. Far as I could tell, this meant the company shipped him all the newest stuff for free before it was even in stores, including these oddly shiny sneakers he'd been sporting lately.

Oof. Goran aced Patrick, and Patrick fell into the court's side netting trying to get to it. Goran, with his white shorts and jaunty ice-blue T-shirt, tendrils of sweaty hair clinging to his neck, jumped up and down in place. He jabbed an index finger in Patrick's general direction and yelled loud enough for us all to hear, "Try again, loser!"

Then Goran focused his eyes on one person behind the glass, a girl standing there in jean shorts topped off with a fitted turquoise top and matching flip-flops, her cream crocheted beach bag slung over her shoulder. Annabel. The energy was zinging between the two of them. I saw Evie's face fall and thought, *Who did they think they were kidding?*

By the time Patrick bounced back on his feet, he glanced at the crowd, too, then shot a look straight at Annabel, holding his arms out and mouthing, *I'm letting him win.* She smiled and shook her head.

Meanwhile, *oof* was right. Patrick's tennis wasn't beautiful, not by a long shot. *I have to work ten times harder than Goran to get the same result,* he'd been acknowledging matter-of-factly for years. Goran, on the other hand, swaggered onto the court and his body naturally knew what to do, like he'd been born with a tennis racket in his hand. But the difference in their talent hadn't mattered. They had a bromance for the centuries, and I hoped their mutual attraction to Annabel wouldn't come between them.

Goran and Patrick always practiced together after school and spent weekends at tournaments around New England. Through it all, Patrick helped Goran learn English. They'd come off the court for frozen yogurt and Gatorade, draping themselves over their table next to the TV and talking loudly about boy things. Goran had always kept his love life outside the club, which only added to his air of mystery. Until now.

*　*　*

The lobby fell silent at match point. **Goran dove for a ball**
and flicked it back to Patrick, who watched the ball fly over
his head, then ran back toward the curtain and performed a
backward through-the-legs shot that sailed over the net. The
lobby was in an uproar as Goran went for it, set up, and whaled
the ball—straight into the net. It was Patrick's game, set, and
match, and Goran ran and leapt over the net like a racehorse,
and the two sweaty players embraced in a quick hug. Goran
rubbed his palm hard on Patrick's head, and the lobby went
wild. Annabel cheered the loudest, with Lisa a close second.
I noticed Gene was now hanging in the background, smiling
as his flock filled his club with laughter.

Before the boys could come off court, Nicholas turned to
his sister and offered her his arm. "Shall we?"

"We shall." She grinned and tucked her arm in his, getting out of Dodge. I think Annabel sensed both boys would
run straight to her and she wanted to avoid that scenario.

I loved seeing Annabel and Nicholas together. They were
so beautiful, like stars that only got brighter when they col-
lided. They walked through the lobby, turning every head that
saw them coming, oblivious, as always, to the effect they had
on the common people.

That included the effect they had on Lisa, who was staring
after them, her mind working on something that didn't appear
to be very nice, and it was pretty obvious why: *she* wanted to be
princess of the club. But unfortunately, Annabel was in the way.

After

Lisa was supposed to be helping my mom run the front desk, but instead she was sitting there explaining her favorite new smart phone game to Patrick. Because of Gene's insane no-technology-during-club-hours rule, she had to show him on a piece of old-fashioned paper.

"See," Lisa was saying as Patrick leaned in close, "you slice 'em off. *Whack*." With her purple pen she slashed a line through what was supposed to be a chicken's neck. Then she scribbled in flourishes around the "chicken," which looked more like a giant artichoke. "And blood goes everywhere."

"That's twisted." Patrick screwed up his face. "Seriously, Lisa."

"Whatever," she retorted, eyes at half-mast, leaning into him. Always the flirt. "Talk to me when you're a vegetarian."

"Lisa," my mom chimed in from her stool, "don't you have anything better to do than play a disgusting game like Chicken Heads? Like address those envelopes Gene gave you for the membership mailing?"

"Sure," Lisa said. "But I'd rather hang out with Paddy." She twirled her hair and rubbed his upper arm.

Patrick, who'd had a fling with Lisa last summer that she never quite got out of her system, pulled away and said, "I gotta go. And don't call me Paddy."

"Whoa. What's *his* problem?" Lisa squeaked as he slouched off into the lobby.

"What do you *think* his problem is?" Mom quizzed her. "We're all upset, Lisa. You're the only one pretending nothing's happened."

Lisa shrugged. "I'm as upset as anyone," she said. "But people are acting like she was this perfect angel when she was—and I'm sorry, but it's true—a *snob*. She thought she was better than everyone else. You're all afraid to say it, but I'm not."

My mom grimaced while Evie, sitting next to us, was turning purple with anger. "That's not fair, Lisa," my mom said, tucking some curls behind her left ear. "You ever heard of karma? You keep saying stuff like that and you might find yourself in some trouble of your own. The universe has a way of evening things out."

Evie glared at Lisa, who was now doodling over the dead chicken-slash-artichoke.

Mom asked, "Have you cried yet? Even once?"

Lisa's pen froze. Then her face morphed from bitter to, well, kind of sad. My mom saw this and closed her eyes for a second. I guess she'd underestimated Lisa, which was funny because Mom also avoided letting her real emotions show around the club. She'd done her crying at home—and there had been a lot of tears for Annabel, and "for all the violence of the world," as she put it between blowing into her Kleenex.

Lisa said, "I guess not. I guess I'm evil, right? Mean old Lisa. Never as sweet or pretty as the rich St. Claire princesses."

My mom closed her eyes again. "I'm sorry," she said. She was surely thinking what I was: Lisa lived in the less affluent Margot, two towns away, and had what Gene called "a troubled home life." Hers made Evie's situation with Lucky look like a trip to Disneyland. "I'm sure you're grieving in your own way, but you need to be careful about what you say."

Come to think of it, there hadn't been a lot of dramatic displays of grief around here in the days since Annabel died. Goran would come in with red-rimmed eyes. Nicholas, for his part, hadn't been seen since that first day. Only Gene and Harmony were happy to let the tears flow. Everyone else seemed to be in a state of suspended shock. Also, most of them were irritable as heck—when they weren't terrified about a possible serial killer on the loose. A few members had stopped coming altogether and demanded full refunds, which Gene would refuse, then look up to the heavens and moan that giving back even *half* a year's membership could kill his profit margin.

We sat quietly for a moment—and then suddenly I felt a chill in the air. There was a big-time member walking through the front door. Joe Marbury, fifty-something, ruddy faced, slightly sinister. He was rich, hideously unattractive, and basically leered at every female under forty. He set off my creep-o-meter something fierce.

"Good afternoon, Mr. Marbury," Lisa said with a big smile. "How are you today?" I guessed she hadn't gotten the memo about how icky Joe Marbury was.

"Special delivery," he said in his gravelly voice that sounded like he smoked five packs of cigarettes a day. He threw a folded newspaper down on the desk in front of my mom. It was the *St. Claire Bee*, our twice-weekly afternoon paper. My mom gave Joe a tight, fake smile and flicked the rubber band off the paper.

Joe put one meaty palm on the granite and told Lisa in that raspy voice, "I'm hearing members are asking for refunds." He smirked at my mom. "That's gotta be bad for business."

I watched my mom's expression as Joe lumbered toward the men's locker room, his khaki pants sagging and revealing a part of his rear end I did not need to see. Anyway, something had dawned on my mom, and on me, and by the look on Evie's face she got it, too. After all, Joe Marbury did a lot of business with another local rich guy: Herbert Harper, Annabel's dad. Only Lisa didn't seem to realize that among the suspects around us, Joe Marbury suddenly felt like an interesting possibility for someone who might've hurt Annabel.

After

About ten days after Annabel died, the tennis people got
ahold of the new *St. Claire Bee*, and Lisa passed it along to
Celia. Their reaction was about as extreme as my mom's had
been when she read this week's shocking exclusive half an
hour ago.

"Good God," Celia breathed, the broadsheet newspaper
shaking in her hands. "Have you seen this?" she asked Patrick.

A bunch of counselors were lounging at their table in the
main lobby while Lucky led the regular camp in suicide sprints
on the outdoor courts. The elites were about to head out for
drills, but sensed something was afoot. Patrick grabbed the
paper out of Celia's hands and everyone went quiet. Goran
hugged his tar-black Volcano Onyx racket to his chest, and
Will looked at the floor.

Celia, somber and pale, stepped forward. "Read it aloud,
Patrick."

Evie and I, sitting quietly a few feet away on the sofa that faced the tennis courts, were in the dark as much as anyone. My mom had freaked out and run off to show Gene when she saw the story. Patrick took a deep breath and started reading. Serene was sitting next to him looking stricken as he began.

"In the midst of an historic heat wave, local teenager Annabel Harper was laid to rest Tuesday in a private funeral at St. Claire Cemetery. Her family was joined by a handful of mourners, all dressed in black, for the forty-five-minute ceremony."

Patrick paused to clear his throat. He was trying not to sound choked up, but failing.

"The popular teen, who was voted prom queen at St. Claire High School last year but famously turned down the crown because 'it objectifies girls,' would have been a junior this year. A source told the *Bee* of the secretive funeral, 'The Harpers are in shock. They couldn't bear the media circus a public memorial would bring. They want to be left alone to grieve.'"

Patrick brought his fist to his mouth. "Ms. Harper's cause of death is still unknown. Police tell the *Bee* they concluded the autopsy and are waiting for test results."

Patrick attempted to put on a casual expression, dropped the newspaper on the table, and shrugged. "That's it." Serene, who'd hung out at the pool with Annabel more than once, wiped away tears. *Tuesday*, the story had said. Yesterday.

Evie hugged me, I think to comfort both of us. So many

had loved Annabel. The whole town of St. Claire would be going nuts over this abrupt memorial. Why couldn't we *all* have had a chance to say goodbye? I know a lot of Annabel's club friends had been waiting for the closure of a funeral to make sense of our grief. Now that chance had been taken from us.

"I can't believe it," Celia said, her voice sticking in her throat. "Why would her family do this? Why?" She shook her head and looked at Goran, but he was no help. His eyes were wide, like he'd just gotten the shock of his life, and he was clutching that racket like it was going to break his ribs.

Will reached out and touched Goran's arm. "Let's play some tennis. We've got Yale coming up. You can do it, buddy. Win it for Annabel."

I realized then that Patrick had been seething quietly. He said to Goran through gritted teeth, "Well. It looks like you missed your little girlfriend's funeral. Yet again, *you weren't there for her.*" Patrick was shaking, in body and voice.

Patrick and Goran's off-court rivalry had been simmering over the summer, and now it exploded in a cloud of fear and grief and hate and love, all mixed together to make a dangerous brew.

"What are you talking about?" Goran shoved his Volcano at Celia and approached Patrick, who rose from his seat. "You never had a chance with her, man. You killed her. *You* killed her," Goran cried, his voice cracking.

Patrick's face twisted in rage. "You—*you*—" he shouted at his friend, drops of spit flying from his mouth. "You knew

84

about me and Annabel and you went after her anyway. For all we know, *you're* the killer."

Patrick lunged at Goran, pushing on his chest with both hands, and then shouts and screams of "Hey! Hey! Save it for the tennis court!" rang out in the lobby as a scuffle ensued. Will stepped in and held Goran back while Celia tried to soothe Patrick. Evie and I stayed low on the sofa, and as I peeked over the cushion, I saw one person off to the side doing something extraordinary: Gene had come upon the drama and was watching with concern, but showed no sign of intervening. Patrick and Goran were staring each other down while being kept apart.

My mom left the desk and came running. She saw Gene and ordered, "Eugene Hanrahan, get a grip on your people! They're out of control. *Do* something!"

Gene, though, was as calm as I'd ever seen him. He had one hand on his chin, and looked thoughtful. "Finally," he said.

"*Finally* what?" my mom shrieked.

"It's what should've happened days ago," he said to my mom. To the rest of the lobby, Gene boomed with authority, "Everyone—and I mean everyone—be at the pool at five fifteen today." A bunch of them swiveled in his direction, surprised to hear his voice from out of nowhere. "Five fifteen on the dot. Spread the word."

"For what?" Patrick dared to ask, wiping sweat from his brow with his free arm.

"You know for what," Gene said to the ragtag pack of

emotionally overwrought people. "And don't look at me like that. This is happening. Deal with it."

At precisely five fifteen that evening, people began silently filtering through the pool's revolving door, converging from all over the club. Swimmers emerged dripping from the pool, wrapping themselves in towels. Members were invited, too. The club regulars knew what to do and showed the way to those who didn't. Amid a dusky haze, we formed a tight circle, standing shoulder to shoulder on the lawn. Harmony flipped the music on, handed out tissues to everyone, and fell in between Serene and Celia.

"Welcome," Gene said, "to the Love Circle."

Nope, he wasn't kidding. He'd invented the Love Circle two years ago, after he fired the club's twenty-year-veteran racket stringer for embezzling. No one could believe dear old Herman would do such a thing. The staff had started bickering nonstop, so Gene came up with a peacemaking plan. He was mocked mercilessly for his weird idea and for the New Agey music he played, but you know what? Everyone felt better afterward. *The Love Circle, with all of us in it, gives us closure by literally closing the loop on our grief,* he'd explained. He told us now, as flutes and harps and strings harmonized with the buzzing cicadas around us, "Funerals are for the living, not the dead. While it is not for us to judge why this poor family chose to keep Annabel's funeral private, it is also important that we have our chance to grieve. She was a part

86

of the club's family, and make no mistake, she is with us now. We miss her, and and we always will. She was a ray of sunshine and we were lucky to have her for as long as we did."

He took a breath in through his nose and let it out loudly through his mouth. "This is a safe place to grieve. Cry, don't cry, laugh at a special memory you have of her, smile at the thought of knowing her. Only two ground rules: respect everyone in the circle, no matter what, and don't break the chain. Stay connected to one another until I toss the tissue. Now," he said, closing his eyes and hanging his head, "let us be quiet and think of Annabel."

Evie stood between Lucky and me, and my mom was on my other side. This was the only funeral for Annabel we'd ever get, and the floodgates opened. Evie, then my mom, then I began crying audibly, while Celia and Serene were flat-out bawling. I sneaked a look at Goran, who was contorting his face every which way so as not to cry, but failed in the end.

After exactly five minutes, Gene wiped his eyes one last time, held up his tissue, and tossed it in the middle of the circle. A few blew their noses one last time and threw theirs as well. Some tissues caught the wind and didn't make it to the center, but that was okay. When everyone had let go of their grief in the form of soaked tissues that dotted the lawn with white blobs that looked like doves in the dusk, Gene broke the circle and put one arm around my mom, and the other around Lisa, and hugged them both tight.

Then, silent but for some sniffling, we all filed back across the lawn and out of the pool area while Gene and Harmony stayed to retrieve the snotty tissues. I have to say, the Love Circle did its job that day. We got to say goodbye to Annabel, and we were together, which was the most important thing. I looked back on my way out, and as Gene bent down to pick up a tissue, a gust of wind picked it up and it flew away, taking our Annabel with it.

Before

First thing on the Monday morning after the disastrous pool party, Evie and I were sitting on the stoop outside the club's main entrance, killing time until tennis camp started so we could avoid navigating the packed lobby. Lucky finished up a cell phone call at the back end of the parking lot and bounded toward us.

"Dad, you're late for your staff meeting," Evie said. Lucky waved his hands at us as if to say *Hey, isn't life great?* and smiled.

"You girls be good today," he said. "Keep out of trouble, okay?"

He gave us one last wave, and off he went into the club without a look back at his daughter, or a thought as to how a twelve-year-old girl would spend her day without structure, activities, or adult supervision. As Evie watched Lucky go, I watched her, and I wasn't sure how this family dynamic with just her and Lucky was going to work in the long run. Without her mom, I mean. That morning was kind of depressing.

It was a harbinger of things to come, as it turned out, because Evie's melancholy got worse after that.

In the following days, she refused to hang outdoors with me. I dutifully spent time with her in the back room, and I found myself in her dingy bolt-hole behind Court 5 on another beautiful day in late June that happened to be Cookie Wednesday—the one day each week when, instead of orange slices and fruit salad, the camp snack was, you guessed it, fresh-baked cookies. I watched Evie unwrap her second packet of Twinkies of the day. She peeled one of the long sponge cakes out of its wrapper, the moist brown part of the cake sticking to the plastic. Snack time was in an hour, but I suspected she wasn't going to show her face anywhere near the cookie platters.

She broke off a piece of Twinkie for me. As I chewed, I was thinking of ways I could coax her out of there. She ate her third Twinkie in three bites. She laid the fourth one, still in the wrapper, on the crate next to her. Then she went back to her book. I took a gander at the cover. Man, this was dire: the girl was reading *The House With a Clock in Its Walls*, a book supposedly for kids but with a dark, superspooky cover that gave me the creeps. I looked around the place. The camp lunch ladies must have gone on a shopping spree at Big Bob's Warehouse, because boxes full of chips and grape juice towered over us. The industrial refrigerator was buzzing annoyingly, and the hot air in there was stagnant and putrid.

This was bad. At the best of times, Evie's routine included

at least *some* socializing. Sometimes, in the afternoons, she and I would take a walk around the building, looking for little chameleons behind the club, by the outdoor courts. Occasionally Evie would take time to watch some tennis while pretending she didn't care about the game. But now she'd started skipping more lunches, and instead of eating a healthy sandwich and salad, she'd head out to the Cumberland Farms mini-market down the road and use the spare change Lucky gave her to buy Ho Hos or Twinkies.

Evie turned a page crisply and loudly. I was bored. I was worried.

I took a swipe at her book.

She gasped as it flew out of her hands and onto the floor with a *thud*. "What are you *doing*?" She had to smile, though, and then she couldn't help but laugh, and that was a start.

"Okay," she said. "Fine. I'm being antisocial. You want to talk?"

Duh. Of course I did.

"All right. Let me offer you a simile about my life. You probably don't know what that is, but let me give you an example." She adjusted her rear end on the hard crate and tightened her ponytail. "If Celia is like a forehand winner," she said, "then I'm like . . ."

She looked off into the distance, and I followed her eyes to a mass of cobwebs up in a corner of the ceiling until it came to her: "I'm like . . . a defensive lob: slow, round, and desperate." She looked at me with a satisfied expression.

I wasn't amused.

"Okay," she tried again. "Look, Chelsea. It's not your fault everyone loves you around here, and that you've got Beth, and that my parents are total losers who don't want me."

Whoa. That was *not* true.

"It's a fact, Chelsea. God, how many times has Lucky left me here—totally forgotten about me—since my mom went out west?"

Okay, that was true. But to be fair, Lucky had been coming here for, like, fifteen years and it had been only a couple years that he'd had a kid to think about. Lucky was a longtime fixture at this place, having started his tennis career here at sixteen. He disappeared after college when he'd gone on the pro circuit and traveled to exotic places to play tournaments. He made it to number one hundred ninety-nine in the world, which is actually quite impressive, contrary to what tennis novices might think of that number. And then he quit. One day he walked through the club's front door again, and Gene hired him on the spot.

Evie continued trying to explain her philosophy to me. "It's not that I expect my parents to *change*," she said. "It's more that I want different ones entirely. In fact, I want to get out of my life. I want to be someone else *so bad*, Chelsea. Have you ever felt that way? No, you probably haven't . . ."

I had to admit I hadn't. It's weird, but even though I retained clear, terrible memories of what had happened to me when I was younger, I was still okay with being me. As my mom liked to say, *It's your entire story that makes you who you are, not just the happy things.*

"I'd love to be anyone but me," Evie said wistfully, reaching for that last Twinkie. "Anywhere but here."

I took that in and realized I'd failed this time. I hung my head and sighed. I wasn't equipped to talk her down from this one. But we'd get there. I wasn't giving up on her.

Before

So Evie and I were secretly following Annabel on the July day when my mom figured out Annabel was in love with a mystery man. Annabel was easy to spot in her hot-pink halter top. After she'd handed Nicholas his lunch of meat sandwiches, Annabel glided toward the women's locker room. Evie and I picked up the tiniest hint of a hum coming from her, a happy tune I couldn't place. But just as Annabel was about to enter the locker room, Evie touched my shoulder and froze. We weren't the only ones tracking her.

Patrick was perched on the back of the main lobby's big sofa, which happened to be directly across from the entrance to the women's locker room. Annabel swanned into the locker room, and Evie and I pretended to walk on by Patrick, eventually settling about ten feet away from him at one of the tables in front of the TV.

The expression on Patrick's face as he watched Annabel disappear into the locker room was indescribable, but I will try: picture love, plus anger, plus longing, plus sadness, plus . . . a dash of hatred. In that order. Annabel hadn't acknowledged him when she passed by, so we couldn't be sure she'd even seen him. That was the thing with Annabel. She didn't show her cards or let on what was really happening with her. You just caught glimpses of who she might be, of who you thought she was, of how she was willing to portray herself on a given day. In any case, I didn't think Patrick would've noticed Evie and me if we'd started juggling kittens with a clown chorus singing behind us. This was another one of those times Evie's social invisibility worked in our favor.

She whispered to me, "We should follow her in there."

I thought about that, but before we could make a move, Annabel stormed out.

We were shocked. We'd never seen Annabel storm anywhere. "How the—" she seethed at Patrick. "*How* did you do this? How did you get into my locker?" She was spitting mad. She shook something at him: a piece of notepaper folded perfectly down the middle. "You're sick, you know that?"

Patrick looked at her with ice in his eyes, a closemouthed, self-satisfied smile on his face. I'd never seen him like this; I'd never seen anything sinister from him.

"This kind of stuff is why—" Annabel shook her head, and again refrained from finishing the thought. "You'll never be the man he is, and you know what? You can say what you want, write what you want, think what you want. I guess I can't stop you." She crumpled the paper in her hand and jabbed her index finger at him. "But the next time you touch anything of mine, I'll call the police. You got that?"

Before

I couldn't sit in that storage room with Evie for another day. Sure, I'd still hang out with her as I always had, but I couldn't stay cooped up in that room *all day long* like she'd started doing. Nothing I did was helping get her out of there, so one day I just hit the wall; I had to skedaddle. It was so hard, leaving her behind. It went against everything I stand for. My protective instinct is fierce for Evie; it had been that way since we'd met.

July was around the corner, and it was going to be a scorcher today. I walked with Evie toward Court 5 and back to her hideaway after Lucky dropped her off at the club's front door, and sat with her while she got situated with a can of Cran-Apple from the vending machine and her latest tome, the one about the scary doomsday clock. She was slogging through dark novels when it seemed to me she'd be a lot happier reading *Summer Cool: The Book*, obsessing about boys, and splashing in the pool like the other girls her age I'd seen around the club.

But I knew it was hard for her. Things were getting worse. Tad and his cohort had been working really hard this summer to find new fat-related insults. She'd tried out a few comebacks on me, such as *I won't always be fat, but you'll always be a moron*, and *I won't be fat forever, but you'll forever be stuck with that ugly face.*

They sounded pretty good to me, but it wasn't the same when it came time to make a stand, mostly because Tad never confronted her by himself. It was always in a crowd, always when he had reinforcements, while Evie stood alone. The one time she did summon the courage, during a rare assault when no one else was in earshot, she snapped back, "God, Tad, can't you think of anything more original? That doesn't even make sense."

"Yeah!" He cackled. "It doesn't make sense because you can't hear it. All that blubber is blocking your ears."

Evie didn't talk back after that. It was so stupid because I didn't think she was fat. Just bigger than some other people, and so what? The girls were mean, too, but mostly behind her back, pretending like they weren't talking about her when clearly they were. For the most part, their cruelty lay in excluding Evie—like she was a terrible person who smelled horrible.

But even with this awfulness, I didn't want Evie throwing her summer days away over those dopes. So on that day when I'd had enough, I let her know I was taking off. She squinted at me, looking a bit lost and definitely surprised. We'd spent practically every hour of every day together for the past two summers.

Well, she was welcome to follow, but I couldn't take it back there another minute. I wandered up to the front desk to see my mom. I'd go back and check on Evie later, of course.

This happened for a few days. I spent more time at the front desk than ever, and one day my mom finally said it.

"Why aren't you with Evie? She still hiding away in the storage room?" She hopped off her stool. "Look, Chels," she said. "No one can make a person do what they don't want to. The kid drew a crappy hand in life, I'll give 'er that. But only Evie can make the choice to come out of her funk. Everyone makes a choice."

I felt really sad hearing that, because I didn't see Evie making a different choice anytime soon. My mom saw my distress and her voice softened. "We'll make sure we stand by her, support her, and do our best to make up for that father of hers. Okay?"

She squinted at me, then pulled me in for a hug and a kiss. I got it, I really did. But it didn't seem fair that Evie was punished every single day simply for being who she was. It seemed to me it wasn't *Evie's* funk. It seemed to me the world had put its funk on her, and she was having a hard time standing strong because she was alone. If she was supposed to be facing life by herself, where were Evie's weapons? Where were her instruments for fighting?

I didn't have the answers. It was one of the hardest things I had to do that summer, to leave Evie alone with her pain. If Evie wanted to hide in a musty old room all day when the sun was shining and there were a million corners to explore and no one to stop us from exploring them, I had to let her. I had to give her the gift of tough love.

After

Nearly two weeks into the investigation, Evie and I were tired, hot, and a little irritable after another day of trying to keep up with the detective. We found the lobby empty and plopped down on the sofa. Evie laid back and closed her eyes. It was so quiet . . . and then—

"Hello, girls."

Evie's eyes flew open and she found herself looking directly at Detective Ted Ashlock's white, upside-down face as he leaned over her. She scrambled to sit upright, tighten her ponytail, and pull her shirt down over her tummy.

"You've been quite the little detectives lately."

I looked over from my perch and smiled, and he smiled back at me. I didn't think we had too much to worry about from him, but Evie's eyes were the size of tennis balls. Ashlock stood there calmly. He said, "What exactly do you think is going on around here?"

That question could be mildly scary to kids at the best of

times, but said in that Ashlock voice, coming down like a hammer out of his pale, thin frame, it was paralyzing.

"Annabel's dead," Evie said. I think saying it out loud made our loss more real, and I thought I caught a tear or two welling up in her eyes.

"That's right," the detective said. "And I'm trying to find out what happened, but my work has no room for kids. This isn't some TV episode where everything gets solved and wrapped up in an hour. This is a real person, and another real person may have done this terrible thing to her. Do you understand?"

Ashlock slid into the matching chair to Evie's left. He put his elbows on his knees and leaned forward. "What's your name?"

"Evie." She pulled at her T-shirt again, stretching it over her knees.

"Lucky Clement is your father?" She nodded. "And your friend here?" He tilted his head my way.

"My best friend. This is Chelsea. Her mom is Beth Jestin—"

"Nice to meet you, Evie and Chelsea," he said. "Come to think of it," he added, putting his hand to his chin like that famous statue, "if you're *the* Chelsea, you've made quite a name for yourself around town."

I knew what he meant—it was this thing that happened earlier in the summer—but I wasn't a hero or anything. I was glad I could help. But Ashlock's face changed as he checked me out. He knitted his brow and took a harder look. *Ah*. He thought he knew me for reasons other than my "heroism." My case had, indeed, been quite a big deal back in the day.

He quickly got down to business. "So. You know a few things about what I've been doing. Do you have any theories about what happened?"

Evie paused and I watched her gauging him, wondering how much to trust him.

"It's okay," Ashlock said. "No one will ever know it came from you . . . It'll be our secret."

He took out that ever-present hankie and blotted his upper lip, and Evie blurted out, "How come you never take off your hat or your jacket?"

I thought that was gutsy considering she wore sweatpants even when it was hotter outside than the center of Earth, but Ashlock didn't seem offended.

"I have a condition," he said. "I'm allergic to sunlight."

Evie was immediately fascinated. "Really? So do you burn up if the sun's rays touch your skin, or—?"

He smiled. "It's not really that dramatic," he said. "Some people with this condition do have to stay indoors their whole lives, but I just have to be very careful. I break out in a terrible rash if I'm outside for too long, and sometimes, even with my hat, I won't know the sun's hit me until it's too late and I get a bad burn like if you spill hot coffee on yourself. Sometimes, I even have to wear gloves in the summer."

Actually, I had noticed how his shirt was buttoned up to the base of his neck. Now his diabolical wardrobe choices were starting to make some sense.

Evie nodded her understanding. She said, "I guess we do have a few suspects in mind . . . Some of the same ones you do."

"How do you know who my suspects are?"

"Because we heard you question them."

"Just because I question someone doesn't mean they're a suspect. Sometimes we have to shake people up so we can get to the truth."

"Like you're doing to us now?" Evie asked.

"Maybe." He smiled at us, a mild, weary upturn of the corners of his mouth. I could see him doing that classic Ashlock mind-reading thing with Evie, and it was clear he liked what he saw. I thought they had a lot in common: authentic and kind, but not very popular.

He took out his notebook and stared at Evie. She sat up straighter and unhooked her shirt from her knees. She said, "I don't know who did it, and that's . . . scary."

Ashlock nodded his understanding. "You don't need to worry about that. I'll tell you a little secret, but you have to swear you will never, ever repeat what I'm about to tell you to anyone. Do you understand?"

Oh, man. We were on pins and needles. We were finally going to get some answers.

"If this was murder, and I'm not saying it was, it was about

Annabel. It wasn't about you, or Chelsea, or anyone else at this club, or in this town for that matter. Whoever did this is not a danger to either one of you," the detective said gravely.

"Okay . . ." Evie said.

"But I have one condition if we're going to get along," he added. He leaned in closer. "You can't go poking around trying to find out who did this. Because then, and only then, would this person become a threat to you. Do you understand?"

Evie looked at me, and we both understood. If the perp thought we were onto them, we could be next. We'd have to be more careful with our snooping.

"Now, I'd like to hear what you think."

Evie took a moment, directing her eyes up and off to the right as she contemplated the weighty demand. "Well," she said finally, "I don't think Harmony had anything to do with it. He wouldn't hurt a fly." Ashlock didn't let on whether he agreed with that or not. "Other than that, I really don't know." Her voice cracked. "No one I know is a . . . killer."

He nodded, and didn't press her anymore on that topic; he seemed to remember she was only twelve. Evie regarded him for a moment, then decided to go for it. "Everyone's saying Goran did it," she said. "That he's going to be arrested any day now. You know, because he was"—oh Lord, I knew she'd choke on these words—"totally into Annabel. Like, it was a lovers' spat that went bad or something."

Ashlock didn't look convinced. "You knew they were

dating? My understanding is that they never told anyone about their romance."

Evie shrugged. "They didn't have to say anything. I think a few people saw them . . . hanging out at one time or another."

"You and Annabel were friends?" he asked gently.

Evie was choked up and could only nod. Ashlock said softly, "She was a nice girl, wasn't she? But Annabel was a very private girl, too. Even her best friends didn't know everything about her, so we're doing a lot of work to get to know her."

Ashlock reached into his pocket and gave her a fresh hankie folded into a triangle. "It's clean, I promise," he said when she hesitated to take it. "I have to carry a whole bunch of them around with me."

Evie smiled politely and wiped her eyes, but was too shy to blow into the cloth, and handed it back. Then she looked away and quickly, as if we wouldn't see, wiped her nose on her T-shirt sleeve. She forged on. "I'm sure he didn't do anything to her, but Patrick really liked Annabel, and when Annabel didn't like him back, he got mad."

Ashlock raised his eyebrows—I was learning how valuable that move was to his interrogation technique—and got his pen and pad ready. Evie told him about the last time we saw Annabel, about the confrontation with Patrick and that mysterious note, about how we'd never seen Annabel show emotion like that, ever.

Ashlock gave her a nod of respect and said, "This is very helpful, Evie," he said. "Thank you for sharing with me."

I thought that was a sweet way of putting it. Evie nodded and said in a grown-up voice, "You're welcome."

As he tucked his notebook away, Evie said, "Detective? Did Patrick do this?"

The detective didn't miss the frightened look on her face. "I want you to remember something as the investigation goes on," he said. "People aren't always who they seem to be on the surface."

He was right. Things around here were definitely not always as they seemed.

After

My mom spit her coffee out on the shiny granite. It wasn't long after dawn the next morning, maybe six thirty a.m., and she and I were alone at the front desk. She'd just gotten hold of the latest *St. Claire Bee.*

"It's about time!" she exclaimed as she wiped up the coffee with a paper towel. She read aloud the front-page headline: "Cops: Annabel Harper Was Murdered."

The real bombshell was in the second paragraph: *"Police said the victim appeared to have drowned in chlorinated pool water, likely from the pool she was found next to, although tests are still being conducted."*

"I would've sworn that poor girl was strangled," Mom said. "I would've bet the house on it."

I knew what she meant. I remembered what Ashlock had said that first day about how Annabel's hair was dry and perfectly styled when she was found, and how could a person drown without getting her hair wet? But Ashlock—all of us— had been wrong.

* * *

Later, Lucky walked up to the front desk where Evie, my mom, and I were hanging out. He leaned on the countertop with his chin resting on his folded arms. "What do you think the mystery item is?" he asked my mom.

"What?" she responded, not bothering to look up from changing the radio station.

"In the *St. Claire Bee*. The 'item' they mention."

She reached under the desk for the newspaper, incredulous. She checked the front page again, then flipped to the jump page.

"It's terrible," Lucky said. "I have a daughter myself, you know? It really makes you think."

"Oh, *I* know you have a daughter," my mom said, briefly meeting his eyes. "I'm just not sure *you* know."

Lucky almost looked hurt.

Suddenly my mom's eyes went silver-dollar wide. "How did I miss this?"

I had a peek. I could see how it had gotten past her— strangely, the *Bee* had put the detail in question in a separate box with just two brief sentences, below the main story about Annabel's death. Maybe the editor was out sick that day.

My mom read aloud: "A source close to the investigation into the death of local teen Annabel Harper tells the *Bee* that police are focusing on a 'missing mystery item' that could lead investigators to a suspect in her killing. No further details were available at press time."

Mom squinted and read it again, then looked up at Lucky, who was now yawning. "So? What is it the cops are looking for?"

"I thought *you* might know." Lucky shrugged. Then he wandered away, leaving us to guess into the wind about the *Bee*'s tantalizingly vague clue.

Before

"Come *on*," Evie said, brushing her hair vigorously again. "Why is my hair so *flat*?" She bunched it up with her hands, but it went dead and fell unevenly past her shoulders.

She looked at me. "I need a haircut."

I agreed. She really did. We were hanging out in the locker room while Evie got ready. Lucky was taking the older tennis camp kids to the movies and Evie was allowed to join them because he was her dad, and plus the movie was rated PG, so it wasn't just for the older kids—thus the hair drama. She sighed and combed her hair back up into a ponytail. I knew she was nervous about tonight. As she wrapped a scrunchie around her hair, she said to me, "You're the only real friend I have, Chels. But sometimes I need more, you know?"

I knew. My feelings weren't hurt because we were the best of friends and always would be. But man, was I worried about her. On top of everything else, her mom had skipped calling this week. It wasn't that Evie had illusions that she was going to come rushing back to St. Claire and move them into a house with a white picket fence and start taking her to dance classes, oboe lessons, or what have you, but a phone call now and then wouldn't have hurt.

Evie checked herself in the mirror one last time, sighed, and then we headed out to the lobby. We ran smack into the tennis people sitting around the elites' table waiting for Lucky, who'd be driving them to the movies in the club's beat-up old white utility van. They were all freshly washed and could've posed for a J.Crew catalog. Nicholas appeared and walked up to the table in vintage Levi's.

"Where's your sister?" Patrick asked him. I noticed that in the face of a six-foot-one protective older brother, Patrick acted like he was inquiring about a library book, not like he was flirt of the year.

Still, Nicholas bristled. "She's not here," he said testily. Patrick put his hands up defensively. Mr. Perfect, Nicholas Harper, was not in a good mood. It was rare, I had to admit, but he had his moments, like anyone else. He took a seat and there was a tense silence. Perhaps that was the moment more people started to *get* it. Because here's the thing: Who else was missing? That's right: Goran Vanek.

Celia noticed us then and beckoned us over. "Hey girls, come on over here."

I smiled and went over to her. She put her arm around me and squeezed. "Where were you all day? Your mom asked me to keep an eye on you, but you were running all over the place."

Patrick leaned over and said to Evie, "Sorry about tonight. I'm afraid you're a little too young for this one."

Evie shook her head. "No. *Jump Town*'s only rated PG. I checked."

"This is true," Patrick admitted. "But we're seeing *Die, Die, Die*. It's an R."

Lisa, sitting as close to Patrick as she could get, said to Evie condescendingly, "It's *way* too old for you. You can stay here with Beth and Chelsea."

Ouch. Evie would be so hurt to be left out—again. But at least now we could hang together tonight until Lucky got back from the movies. I wasn't invited, of course, because they'd never let me in to see *Die, Die, Die*. Celia was hugging me a little too hard, so I pulled away. She was checking Evie out with concern. She was one of the few people who treated my friend like a normal person, and she happened to be a legend around here. Nine out of ten tennis experts agreed: Celia Emerson could have been the next Martina Hingis. Celia was classically pretty, delicately slender, and moved like silk on the tennis court. But to the extreme consternation of her coaches, her ambition had never matched her talent. They'd winced when she talked about applying to Princeton next year instead of going pro—without so much as a blink. Now, not *everyone* loved Celia. She had no time for fake people, the type who happened to be drawn to her. Some believed she was a colossal snob; I would say she had a silence about her, and when you wrapped that in a package as attractive as Celia's, you were going to get misunderstandings. I always thought that was one reason she and Annabel had become friends.

Celia put her arm around my friend's shoulder. "Come with me."

I went along because I wanted to know what the deal was. We followed Celia, who was now locking eyes with my mom as she approached the front desk. Celia gave her one of those knowing looks grownups are always exchanging, and tilted her head subtly in Evie's direction. Mom seemed to get it right away. Her face went from confused to—*bam*—wide-eyed, and then she grimaced.

Celia brought Evie back behind the desk. "Doesn't she look nice all dressed up?" she said to my mom.

"Absolutely," my mom said, nodding energetically.

Evie looked to me for help, as if *I'd* know what the heck was happening here. Celia led us into the glass office behind the desk and slid the door shut.

My mom cut to the chase. "Evie, kid, let's take a little field trip tomorrow, okay? I'll take you shopping at Macy's. Say, lunchtime?"

Evie was as confused as I was. "What for?"

"Honey," Mom said with as much subtlety and gentleness as she was capable of, "it's time you started wearing a bra."

Celia broke in. "You know, I was your age when I got my first bra. It's kind of fun . . ."

Evie crossed her arms and hugged herself. A slow wave of burgundy crawled up her face. They were right, though. My friend was growing into a woman before our eyes, and she needed some support—*stat.*

I could see Evie thinking. The girl wasn't stupid. She'd read *Are You There God? It's Me, Margaret* a bunch of times. She said, "Um, Beth . . . I don't have any mon—"

"I'm paying, don't you worry," Mom said, waving her hand as if to shoo away a fly.

She winked and went back to her stool to monitor the comings and goings of the club. Celia waited a sec with Evie. "You know what? Don't worry about tonight," Celia told her conspiratorially. "There are lots of good movies coming out this summer. I'll make *sure* you get to come with us next time."

Evie smiled. "Thanks, Celia."

We looked up as Lucky bounced over to the desk, clearly unshowered. His blond hair was sticking out from under the bandanna, but at least he'd had the decency to change into jeans—and the same purple tie-dyed shirt he'd had on at the pool party. He dangled the van keys in front of my mom and Evie.

"Let's move it out, people!"

Evie, arms still crossed over her chest, said, "Dad, you told me we were going to see *Jump Town.*"

Lucky put on a sympathetic face, as if he had no control over anything, and wasn't it awful his daughter would be left

115

out yet again. "Hey, the gang wanted to see *Die*." Lucky shrugged. "What was I gonna do? I'm outnumbered."

Although it shouldn't have, Lucky's cluelessness shocked us yet again, and Evie's mouth was agape, while Mom had steam coming out of her ears. He seemed to pick up on this and added, "Another time, okay?"

Evie shrugged. "I don't mind seeing *Die, Die, Die*."

"Mmm . . . Sorry, honey, you know what your mom said. Absolutely no R-rated movies or it's my butt in a vise."

"Yeah, well, she said a lot of things." Evie frowned. "You've ignored most of it."

Lucky looked at her sharply. "What was that?"

"*Nothing* . . ." Evie gave in and accepted her fate for the night. She watched them file out the front door, and then she turned to walk back to the smelly storage room to sulk, and I went with her.

After

Something was afoot. Evie and I were following Ashlock again, and he'd slipped into the men's locker room. He *had* to be cutting through to get to the pool. We hotfooted it to the women's locker room, zipping through to the other side. Yep. The pool.

Luckily, our pal Harmony was on duty this evening so we could *easily* have a legitimate reason to be out there. It was that quiet time of day; the sun was on its way down.

We saw then exactly what Ashlock was up to. He was standing over Joe Marbury, who was in the steaming hot tub, which was sunken into the ground off to the left of the lifeguard's perch. We slipped in next to Harmony on the bench. He greeted us with a distracted hello because he was busy guarding the pool like a hawk.

Evie elbowed Harmony and pointed toward Ashlock. Harmony mouthed *Wow* to us, and quickly turned his iPod off. We all sat there like robots, not moving, not making a sound, staring at the pool and trying to pretend like we couldn't care less about the hot tub.

"You're a hard man to find," Ashlock was saying. "We've been leaving messages at your place of work for over a week."

"I don't like to stay in one place for too long," Joe Marbury told him. "I'm like a shark." He flattened his palms together and made a swimming motion in the air.

Marbury smiled, his smoker's teeth stained and oversize and off-putting. Joe was a fixture around here, a longtime club member who was also an investor, so we couldn't really get rid of him. He'd made his fortune in land development or construction or some such.

"So I'm here now. Shoot," Marbury said to Ashlock.

Not everyone knows this, but water carries sound like nobody's business. So while those two clearly thought they had the bubbling water to mask their conversation, they actually had nature's own amplifier. Ashlock was on his haunches. He adjusted his fedora, which was in danger of slipping back on his head. The steam from the tub was making his already shiny face positively nuclear.

"Mr. Marbury," Ashlock said in a measured tone, "you can either get out of the hot tub now, or we can bring you down to the station for questioning."

Marbury shuddered with mock fear. "Well, if you put it *that* way." He stepped out and grabbed his towel off a nearby sun lounger. It was about time Joe Marbury was questioned.

*   *   *

The first and only time Evie and I ever saw him interact with Annabel gave me the creeps. She'd headed over to the hot tub one day in July for a relaxing soak. I'd seen her nose wrinkle as she stepped in and adjusted to the heat, her eyes closing slowly as she sank down and lay back against the tub. When Joe walked into the pool area and caught sight of her in her modest pink bikini, he whipped off his T-shirt and splashed into the tub next to Annabel in two seconds flat, leaving only about three feet between them. Her eyes flew open and her peaceful expression evaporated.

"Hey," he said. I wasn't even sure they knew each other. She'd given him a tight smile in return and shifted another foot away from him. He sidled closer to her. "Your dad should be very proud to have a daughter like you. You sure are a pretty thing." When I saw her clutch her dog charm as if it could somehow protect her, I went over and sat on the edge between the two of them. The look of relief on Annabel's face when she saw me told me how ill at ease she'd been. "Hey, sweetie," she said to me, her eyes thankful. "Of course I'll come hang out with you." With that, she'd sprung out of the hot tub, wrapped a towel around herself, and walked out with Evie and me.

"I understand you're acquainted with the victim's father?" Ashlock was wiping sweat off his forehead. Marbury's hairy gut was spilling over his trunks as he slouched with a towel

119

around his neck, water still dripping off his body onto the deck. We could hear easily now, as Harmony had shut off the bubbles when Joe got out.

"We did some business together," Marbury confirmed.

"What kind of business?"

Marbury gave him the stink eye. "We both have an interest in real estate," Joe finally replied when Ashlock didn't flinch. "He sells, I buy. We know each other peripherally."

Ashlock flipped open his notebook, which was growing fat with dog-eared corners. "How well did you know Annabel Harper?"

Joe thought that was hilarious and broke into a smoker's laugh, all choky and coughy. "I knew her from around."

"You ever harass her? Try to get close, maybe?"

"Of course not. Next question." His tone suggested he was possibly lying.

Next to us, Harmony's jaw clenched and his fingers were digging into the wooden bench. I was equally tense. Besides Marbury's obvious offensive characteristics, something else about that guy, something less tangible, gave me the willies.

"You don't believe me?" Marbury babbled. "Please. That brother of hers would kill anyone who touched a hair on her head."

"What would you say if I told you we'd found a very distinctive button from a pair of men's jeans at the crime scene? We found it in the dirt right near the body."

What? Evie raised her eyebrows at me, like, *Get it?* I got it—*Of course!* The item Ashlock had carried like a baby chick out of the pool area that day. It had been a button.

"And what if I told you there were only a few pairs of these very expensive designer jeans sold in the state of Massachusetts this summer?"

Joe said, "Then I would tell you I haven't worn a pair of jeans since 1972. In my line of business it pays to dress to intimidate. Ain't nothin' intimidating about jeans."

Ashlock abruptly stood up to leave. Marbury looked confused. "Thanks for your help," the detective said, clearly not meaning it. "Don't leave the area without letting the police department know."

After

We held our breath when Nicholas came back to work for the first time since his sister died. He walked into the club just before nine in the morning and people parted for him like the Red Sea, if the Red Sea had been made up of nervous human beings clustered together in a health club lobby. With each step he took, people moved, in sync, farther away from him, clearing his path to the men's locker room.

They were looking up, down, away—anywhere but at Nicholas. My mom, who was at the front desk, had no choice but to face the music. She blurted an overly chirpy, "How's it going, Nicholas?" then picked up the phone to make an imaginary call.

Wow, I thought. Gene was right with his whole Love Circle thing. People really didn't know how to handle grief, or grieving people. I came out from behind the desk and greeted him with the same big grin I always had. He hugged me, and I swear I felt some of his pain transfer to me. And I could take it; I was strong, and Nicholas was carrying too much.

He whispered in my ear, "You have the world's best smile, you know that?" And he let go of me.

Lisa chose that moment to run up to him, apparently oblivious to any sense of occasion. You would've thought she was meeting him for a big date from the way she was staring at him and playing with her hair. "Hi, Nicholas," she said in this sultry voice I'd never heard her try before.

He looked startled, but said stiffly, "How's it going?"

She smiled. "It's nice to have you back. I'm so sorry about . . ."

"Thanks," he said. "Thanks a lot." He looked longingly toward the locker room. "I better get going. I'm guarding in, like, five minutes."

Lisa nodded, and then reached out and did that thing she does with men's biceps, a lingering touch or even a squeeze. Slowly, Nicholas looked down at her hand on his arm, then again, very slowly, he looked right at her. She smiled up at him flirtatiously. Nicholas's expression changed then, and it was like he became a different person at the snap of a finger.

"Please get off me," he growled, and those of us who could hear it were shocked. Now the people who'd avoided his gaze were watching him. Lisa recoiled and scurried back behind the front desk. He stalked off, head down, scowling.

"Poor Nicholas," my mom said under her breath.

Poor Nicky, poor Lisa, poor Annabel. It had been a strange reentry for our golden boy. I started to think maybe we'd lost Nicholas, the club's bright star, with this tragedy. It was still early, but it wasn't looking good.

* * *

The days were passing quickly now, and there was a prevailing sense that the cops were flailing—and failing—in their investigation. Evie and I, however, knew the detective wasn't letting up. I mean, the guy was here constantly. Like at snack time a few days after Nicholas returned, when Ashlock stopped by to grill Lisa. She got a soft tap on the shoulder from behind while she was taking a break from front desk duty with Celia, Patrick, and Serene at the elites' table. She turned around slowly when he said her name: "Lisa Denessen?"

"Yes," she said, rapidly blinking those heavily mascaraed eyelashes.

Ashlock said, "I'm investigating the death of Annabel Harper. Come with me, please."

Lisa got up as instructed. Patrick, sitting there with his light brown hair casually ruffled, was trying to pull off the lovable rogue look. His hands were clasped behind his head and he was leaning casually back, legs open. But you could see he was strung about as tight as his racket, clenching his jaw and shooting a make-me-look-good look to Lisa.

As luck would have it, Evie and I were hanging out just down the stairs in the café area. She was sucking on a banana Frooti-Freez pop and gave me a knowing smirk. Ashlock would now have to learn about Lisa the hard way.

"Let's talk out on the patio," Lisa suggested to Ashlock.

Yay, the patio. This meant all Evie and I had to do was stay put at the café counter and we should have a good vantage point—as long as someone, which was the usual practice around here, left the sliding door open. Not that we expected to hear anything good. Considering Lisa had had a brief romance with Patrick in the past and seemed to still have a crush on him, we suspected she wouldn't spill much to this detective. The girl had never been cowed by authority, and I had a feeling she could match Ashlock's plodding manner with her own fearless attitude until he gave up and went home.

They settled into the white metal chairs, your standard lawn furniture, with Lisa facing Court 6 and Ashlock to her left. He took out his notebook. As predicted, the door had been left half-open so Evie and I could see and hear everything.

Lisa crossed her right leg over her left, and spoke first.

"So, Detective," she said. "What took you so long? Everyone knew Annabel. I'll tell you what I know—as long as you swear it won't go any further."

Ashlock refused to commit. "I promise to be discreet, but I expect you to be entirely truthful with me—with no exceptions."

Lisa took a few moments to squint at him. Maybe it was the long arm of the law hovering over her, maybe it was something in the air. Whatever the reason, she started spilling like Niagara Falls. She told that detective everything about Patrick: how she'd caught him red-handed in a compromising situation earlier in the summer around Wimbledon time; how, in Lisa's opinion, he treated girls like pieces of meat; and how Patrick resented his best friend, Goran, for his tennis talent.

Lisa didn't seem to care that she was saying all this in public. For all she knew, Patrick—or even a reporter from the *St. Claire Bee*—was lurking in the bushes around the patio, listening. Then again, maybe that's how Lisa wanted it. Either way, Ashlock seemed as surprised as we were by the flood of new information spouting from her mouth, and we could see him scribbling frantically to keep up.

"I want to ask you about a note," he said during a rare pause. "It—"

Lisa inexplicably started cracking up before he could finish. "Let me stop you there," she laughed. "I know the note you're talking about." She caught her breath. "And let me tell you, Detective, you've never seen something so messed up in your entire life."

Before

July was ticking along, and one of the most important tennis tournaments on planet Earth was about to be shown on the clunky old TV in our lobby: Wimbledon. In St. Claire, a torrential summer rain was hammering down, which meant the tennis camp's rain-day rotation was in effect since we were four courts short. It was bedlam in the lobby, with a herd of campers and counselors—elites, regulars, Pee Wees, you name it—milling about. Lucky was sitting at a table scribbling down a schedule. I was sitting against a wall facing him, with Evie next to me on the floor, her legs stretched out in front of her. She was out of sorts today because the storage room was unavailable. Workmen were behind Court 5 doing maintenance.

Enter that walking snot rag Tad Chadwick. "What's *she* doing here?" he said, pointing at Evie. Marcus guffawed and Fat Stan cackled. But then, thank goodness, Evie was saved by the bell when Lucky stood up and shouted that it was time to get moving. The chattering Pee Wees came trotting by with one of the new junior counselors. The little ones were beyond adorable. One boy was asking in his nasally, gulpy voice, "Why do tennis balls smell like magic markers? What if dogs could play tennis? Will tuna be available at lunch today?"

Everyone who wasn't a Pee Wee, about twenty-five of us, moved to crowd around the TV in its pine box, and Will opened the cupboard doors to flick the set on. We were treated to scratchy old video of a long-ago tennis game. A collective exclamation of *"What?"* erupted.

Will let out a frustrated growl. "The match is postponed. It's raining in England, too," he grumbled.

Lucky spoke up. For once he was actually firm and, in an even more shocking twist, organized. "Okay, everyone! Time for the rain-day rotation," he shouted, scratching his head. "Group A on the tennis courts. Group B out on the basketball court doing sprints. Group C in the lobby taking a break. We do forty-five-minute intervals."

"Sprints?" Serene jutted her right hip out and refused to move. Her white tennis skirt and her ponytail moved with her.

Lucky sighed and rubbed his eyes as more whining and complaining wafted from the crowd. Will surveyed this congregation of grouches. He wasn't the most intuitive guy when it came to anything that took place off the tennis court, but he was the first to figure out what was going on that day. Will bounded out of his seat and said, "Everyone, up! No more slumping around. Let's go."

No one moved. "Everyone, *uuuuup!*" Will boomed again, and this time everyone jumped. "You know what we need?" he asked the lobby.

No one ventured a guess.

"We need a big game of Relay 21. *Everyone*—let's go. Advanced camp. Summer camp. Counselors. Kids. All of you."

When Will said *everyone*, he meant everyone who played tennis. Evie would be left behind again. Or so I thought. Will made it to the front desk, then came back through the lobby and saw Evie and me. "Get up. Come on, let's go! *Everyone* out on the court." Will even managed to get Lisa to play. Due to her history of pining after tennis instructors and campers, she could hit a ball or two. Out she went in her aerobics outfit, her wiry hair held back by a shiny gold scrunchie. Evie had perked up and was looking at me with nervous energy. She had never been invited to join in on anything around here before, but Will was an equal-opportunity whip-cracker. I swear Evie was about to get to her feet and find a spare racket, but Lucky came up then.

"Don't even try with this one." *Ha-ha.* Lucky smiled and looked kind of like a dopey sheepdog as he ruffled his daughter's hair, messing up her ponytail. "Give 'er the choice and she'll always rather sit on her butt and read a book."

And the crowd left us in the dust. Evie was frowning. Had her father meant to hurt her, or was he really that clueless? I'm not sure anyone knew the answer to that question. Personally, I didn't have to worry about being excluded. It was a given I wouldn't ever play tennis. The regulars around here knew at least a version of my backstory, and they also knew I wouldn't be able to play the game even if I tried. I'd never really minded, because my mom always reminded me there was a lot of other stuff I could do in life. Plus, regarding the tennis thing, I could always watch, cheer on, and help out.

I decided to watch the Relay 21 game live, and Evie smiled goodbye to me. As she buried her nose in a philosophical novel called *Tuck Everlasting*, I went out onto Court 1. As always, I was blasted with the unique smell of the game, one that's impossible to label or convey in a neat descriptor. I was struck again by how every single one of these kids had dreams. Tennis wasn't just a game at a club like this. It was a way of life and had its own culture and hierarchy.

Half the crowd lined up on one side of the court, half on the other. Will started the first rally, hitting it to the kid in line on the other side. You didn't want to be the one who ended the rally—trust me. The first boy got the ball over the net and you could see the relief on his face as he ran around the court to the other side and got in that line. Next up was Tad, who slammed the ball into the bottom of the net. I looked through the glass and winked at Evie, who grinned evilly. They played for the next hour, and I had a blast watching. All in all, it was a good game, and calmed the kids down.

Afterward everyone piled back into the lobby and Patrick went straight for the TV. The rain had stopped in London but not in St. Claire, so we got to watch Roger Federer play in Wimbledon. Evie stood behind the group and took in every point.

A few games into the first set, Lisa mumbled absently, "Where's Paddy?"

Someone remembered he'd gone off to get an orange juice from the vending machine, but he never came back. I was getting a bit antsy sitting in front of the TV, so when Lisa slipped away, I tagged along. The club was a big, sprawling place, and Lisa and I searched everywhere for Patrick. She even checked the parking lot for his silver Acura. It was parked in the back, drenched in summer rain.

We ran back in, Lisa's hands futilely hovering over her head, and shook ourselves off in the lobby. She came up with one last idea. I followed her as she sneaked around the back of the crowd around the TV, moving stealthily through the café area and opening the door to Court 5. Evie's place. Maybe the workmen were on a break, because all was quiet. Lisa turned to me and put her finger over her lips. *Shhh.* We tiptoed to the entryway and she peeked in; I poked my head in under hers.

What we saw was bizarre. Patrick—Mr. Cool, number nine in New England, best friend of Goran—was *crying*. And he wasn't alone. His arms were crossed over his chest, his head hung like he'd been a bad boy, and there, arms crossed to mirror his, was Celia.

"I'm sorry," he blubbered. "I'm so sorry. I just want things to be like they were."

Celia seemed unsure how to handle seeing the guy she'd known since they were both Pee Wees breaking down like that. He looked up to see how she was reacting; she was chewing the inside of her cheek. "I want to believe you," she said. "I really do, Patrick. But I'm not sure we can turn back the clock." He looked at the ground again; he seemed broken to me.

Lisa and I stayed silent and pulled back out of the doorway. She had a faraway look in her eyes. If I didn't know better, I'd say it was a look of satisfaction. We walked back to the café area, and as we went, I tried to figure out what that scene was all about.

After

Evie and I could see Ashlock's profile from our position inside the café area, and he appeared pretty shocked. His pen was hovering over his notebook. "You've *seen* this note?"

The crisp *whack* of rackets on hollow balls served as background music as Lisa, still on the patio being interrogated, told more of her story. "Let's say I, like, saw enough." She put her foot up on the empty adjoining chair. "Specifically," she said, "I saw Patrick hanging out in the coaches' office after hours, hunched over the desk looking superserious. I asked him what he was doing, and he got weird and covered up the paper he was writing on. But it was too late. I never got close enough to read the actual note—there was typed writing, like, ten lines or something—but I could totally read Patrick's additions."

I could swear Lisa was enjoying this. "He'd covered the note with these insults in red marker: she was a loser, scum, her reputation was trashed, stuff like that. It would have been funny if it wasn't so pathetic. So later, when I saw him walk into the women's locker room, I followed him and caught him coming out. You know what he said? That it was none of my business. *Ha*." I translated the *Ha* to mean the note was, in fact, totally Lisa's business.

Ashlock made a *whew* sound. "That's a pretty aggressive thing to do to a girl he liked. What do you think prompted something so . . . extreme?"

"Oh, that's easy." Lisa grinned. "I know *exactly* what prompted it. Patrick flipped out after he saw Annabel and Goran together. And P.S.," she added, shaking her head, "who sends paper notes anymore—what is this, the Stone Age?"

Lisa chuckled evilly. Ms. Glamour Girl About the Club was going to bury Patrick if it was the last thing she did. I just didn't understand why. A lot of us were worried sick about him, because who wanted to believe one of your own, a guy we'd cheered on since he was a kid, had drowned our Annabel?

Ashlock prompted, "Go on."

"Well," Lisa said, smoothing her hair and then leaning back in her seat. "It happened over there"—she pointed back to the far courts—"behind Court 9. They thought they were being so clever, waiting until after camp ended, but I saw Goran take Annabel back there. Since that girl didn't know a tennis racket from a lipstick, I knew they weren't going to practice her serve. So I followed them. You should have seen them. Like, gag." She jabbed one finger into her big mouth. "They were disgusting. Goran was acting shy and *aw shucks*, kicking at the gravel and like, 'Your tan looks good . . . Did you have a nice day at the pool?' And Annabel was like, 'Yeah, you have to come hang out with me there sometime' with this breathy voice. It was nauseating."

Ashlock cleared his throat. "I'm confused. What does this have to do with Patrick?"

"Well, Detective, after seeing their secret meeting, I went and got Patrick and, of course, he wanted to see for himself." She appeared to relish the memory. "He was *livid*."

Ashlock seemed taken aback by her twisted ploy. "He *needed* to see what was really going on," Lisa said. "He was obsessed with that girl, and it wasn't working for me. *Or* him."

Ashlock said, "I was told by many people here that you and Patrick got close. That you're good friends. Right?"

"Past tense," she said. "He doesn't know it, but I hate his guts."

Her upper lip curled in anger. "Patrick thought he could use me. I used to think he was different from other boys," she continued. "I thought he would realize someday that we were meant to be. That's how it was supposed to be with me and him."

She made the shape of a smile with her mouth, but it was no grin; it was an angry face. "But ya know what, Detective? The jerk dumped me out of nowhere and said he just wanted to be 'friends.' Ha."

Evie frowned. I hadn't realized how stuck Lisa was on Patrick. Suddenly, I felt in my gut that she, out of everyone in the club, could've killed Annabel.

"To your knowledge," Ashlock asked, "did Patrick and Annabel have a romance of any kind?"

"Ha." Lisa snorted again. "He wishes. I mean, he tried, but—"

Evie and I heard something then. Suddenly, Nicholas was running toward us from the pool, barefoot and wearing those red lifeguard trunks, soaking wet, announcing himself.

"Detective. Hey, Ashlock," he called out. "They told me at the pool you were here. Please tell me what's happening with the investigation?"

Nicholas was about to burst onto the patio, but he stopped right outside the door, because Lisa's voice was carrying perfectly. "I don't know why people don't just *say* it," she sneered. "I mean, God. Annabel was not that special. Pretty, sure, but not too bright."

It happened so fast. Ashlock saw Nicholas and sprang out of his chair, but he was too late. Nicholas was standing on that patio with his arms at his sides, dripping from head to toe, like his whole body was crying. Water was pooling on the stones. Evie and I saw Gene mosey down to the café then, and he quickly picked up that something was going on. Nicholas burst back inside, his face like thunder.

Gene reached out to stop him. "What is it? Nicholas, what happened?"

Nicholas's eyes were flashing, and he silently shook his head. "That—that girl," he said. "That horrible, awful Lisa . . . What she *said*—" His voice cracked. And then he ran off.

"I'll take care of it, Nicky," Gene yelled after him. "Whatever it is, I promise you—I'll fix it."

But Nicky was gone.

Before

One day when Evie was engrossed to distraction in yet another book, I felt like hanging out with the Pee Wees. Celia was on duty and was thrilled to have me on the court with her. I had some energy to burn, so I ran around the court gathering the balls the kids hit and brought them back to Celia's ball hopper. I loved it, and so did the Pee Wees. Whenever I'd bring them a ball when it was time to practice serving, they'd whoop with excitement. It wasn't often they got butler service. After an hour, the kids were getting tired and Celia announced snack time. As the junior counselor corralled the group, Celia was stuck with little Justine tugging on her shorts.

"Please, Miss Celia," she begged. "Can I do some more forehands? *Puh-leeze?*"

Justine's sweet voice, silky smooth ratcheted up to Munchkin speed, always cheered me up. When she giggled, she emitted a tinkling sound that Evie always said reminded her of baby angels laughing; it was guaranteed to lift your spirits.

Celia couldn't turn her down, and shouted for the junior counselor to head out with the rest of the kids. I wasn't going anywhere until the last Pee Wee had been shepherded inside. I watched Celia toss Justine a gentle ball to her forehand. The little girl flailed about and managed to get her racket on it, but didn't quite lift it over the net. Celia said, "That's okay." Then—Justine didn't swing at the next ball. She was staring into space, glassy-eyed. "Justine?" Celia walked to the net. "Kiddo? You ready for the next ball?"

I perked up.

"Justine? Justine!"

Justine had dropped her racket, and Celia was sprinting to get to her, but I was already there. I couldn't get into position in time so I dove, and when the little girl crumpled, she at least found a soft landing on top of me. It killed my elbow, but I didn't care.

"What's wrong?" Celia shouted when she got to us.

I didn't move, and she knelt and gently maneuvered Justine, who was half on me, half off, until she was lying flat on the ground. Justine started jerking, her eyes open but empty, as if she was not really with us, and Celia put her hand under Justine's head to stop it from knocking on the court surface. She took stock, quickly realizing there was no one around. We were alone on Court 9. Everyone was at snack time, so no one could see or hear us. Celia looked at me, met my eyes, and told me what to do.

"Chelsea," she said. "Go get your mom. *Go get her.* Run as fast as you can. *Go!*"

And I did. I ran faster than I'd ever run before, my hair blowing behind me, my mind cleared of everything except my task. I made it across the courts in about two seconds flat, but I didn't run to the lobby toward my mom. Instead, I ran straight back to the pool. Nicholas could save Justine. I knew it. It took me only another few seconds to get there; it was like I was possessed by the soul of a cheetah. I stopped at the plate-glass window in the pool lobby, banging and hopping up and down to get Nicholas's attention because I couldn't open that heavy revolving door by myself. It took a few seconds, but Nicholas caught sight of me and looked at me questioningly at first; then panic filled his eyes.

Good old Nicholas. He immediately knew something was wrong. He forced open the revolving door and shouted into the echoey hallway, *"What is it? What's wrong, Chelsea?"*

I ran to the mouth of the hallway and when he saw me waiting for him, he gave one quick nod, dashed back through the door, shouted something to Harmony, whipped out the first-aid kit, and joined me in the hallway.

"Where?" Nicholas asked, and he took off after me as I led him to the tennis courts.

"Thank God," Celia cried when we arrived. She was still cradling Justine's head, hunched over, like she hadn't moved an inch since I left them.

139

Nicholas dropped to the ground, shoeless, his bare knees on the hot court, and assessed Justine's condition. He brought the ever-present scent of coconut oil with him. "How long has she been seizing?"

I stayed back, giving them room, wishing I could take Justine's pain away.

"About three minutes," Celia said, checking her watch. "We need an ambulance."

"Harmony called 911," Nicholas said. "In the meantime, the best thing we can do is keep her from hurting herself and let it pass. She's epileptic?"

"No, no. She's not." Celia shook her head, her porcelain complexion looking paler than usual. "Nothing was reported on her health form."

Justine arched her back, and I thought she'd snap in half. She flung her head down on Celia's hand. "It seems to be getting worse," Celia said. "She's burning up."

Nicholas, who'd done junior EMS training when he went for his lifeguard certificate, observed, "This seizure may be a symptom of something else." His jaw was clenched. "Where's that ambulance?"

It was torture. Then, in another minute, it appeared Justine was getting better. The twitching slowed down. But then, suddenly, she went limp. Celia slipped her hand out from under Justine's head, massaging her scraped knuckles.

"She's not breathing," Nicholas said sharply, gently tilting Justine's head and commencing CPR. I heard distant sirens as Nicholas kept pumping, breathing, counting. He took a quick break to listen for breath, and we saw her chest heave on its own once, twice, three times. But she was still unconscious. He shook his head. "There's no time to waste."

The sirens were getting louder, but we'd still have to wait for the paramedics to navigate through the club and then run across four tennis courts. Nicholas scooped up Justine, held her tight, and took off running in the smoothest gait he could manage. He was superhuman then, taking all forty pounds of that girl out the back way, behind the courts, toward the parking lot, and Celia saw what he was up to and sprinted ahead to hold the net curtain open so he could slip out to meet the paramedics. I stayed out of the way after that. I walked pensively back to the club, praying for Justine. I didn't even see until I was one court away that everyone was lined up on the patio, having watched the drama unfold. My mom hugged me.

"Good girl," she said. "You're a hero, you know that? You did everything right. I'm so proud of you."

My heart swelled with optimism, even as I worried for Justine. But something told me we'd saved her. Celia came back after the ambulance had screeched away with Justine and Nicholas on board. Nicky had refused to let Justine go by herself, leaving Harmony to cover the pool.

We later learned Justine had been felled by an aggressive case of meningitis, and that her life had very possibly been saved by the minutes Nicholas gained for her by carrying her to the ambulance. He was a hero.

I frankly thought he deserved all the congratulations, but he wouldn't hear of it. He kept saying to everyone, "If Chelsea hadn't been there . . . If Chelsea hadn't come to me for help . . ." And then he'd shudder at the thought. Everyone loved Justine, and that turned out to be a good day because she survived.

After

Lisa Denessen, who was staffing the front desk on her own while Evie and I kept an eye on her, jabbed her index finger toward the back of the club where my mom had gone with her exercise ball.

"I wouldn't bother Beth during her workout," Lisa warned Detective Ashlock.

I'd left Mom only a few minutes ago on the aerobics-floor-slash-basketball-court huffing and puffing away with abs and thigh exercises. Detective Ashlock thanked Lisa and took off to find my mom anyway. Evie and I pretended to be interested in a member walking through the door, but thirty seconds later we fell in behind the detective.

When we got to the aerobics floor, which was directly across from the pool lobby, I could hear my mom's voice behind the privacy curtain Gene had put up so members could jump around during exercise classes without being watched. This was too easy. Evie and I stood outside the curtain, where Mom and Ashlock couldn't see us, but we could hear them. I had to admit I had the beginnings of a tight little knot in my tummy that was threatening to grow out of control if I didn't keep calm. This was my mom, after all, and I was worried sick for her. I happened to know she'd left out some pretty important details in her chats with Ashlock thus far, and I suspected he might catch her out today. He'd show no mercy if he discovered she'd lied to him. Not surprisingly, my mom started off on the defensive.

"I gave you a statement on the day it happened, Detective," she said. "Why do you feel the need to grill me again?" You had to hand it to my mom. She had some nerve copping a 'tude with such an important guy.

"Perjury is a felony," Ashlock informed my mother. She started to protest but he broke in and said, "Let me stop you there. Lying by omission is still lying."

"Fine, put me in jail," my mom snapped. "But honestly, I assumed Lisa would put everything about what happened in *her* statement. Certain things aren't my business."

"Perhaps," Ashlock admitted. "But it *is* my business. And no—I don't believe Miss Denessen revealed everything she knows in her statement. I think you also left out some details about the night it happened. Call it a gut feeling."

I felt a sharp pang of fear. Evie sensed it, and put her arm around me. I couldn't calm myself, though. *If anything ever happened to her . . . If she was taken from me . . .*

I didn't know anyone who would take someone like me

on. Would I be sent to live with strangers again? Strangers who could do anything they wanted to me . . . again?

Evie whispered, "Your mom is innocent, Chels. That's what matters. Nothing's gonna happen to her, okay?"

Her words calmed me and reminded me of something very important: Ashlock was smart—he'd figure out soon enough that my mom wouldn't hurt a fly. I let out a sigh, and with it some tension. My mom was quiet, mulling things over.

"Okay," Ashlock prodded. "Let's say you're sticking by your story: you closed the club the night of the murder and saw nothing unusual. But did you *hear* anything unusual?"

"Yes," my mom admitted softly.

It was about time. Evie ruffled my hair and whispered her support directly in my ear: "Don't worry. She's not going to get in any trouble. I promise."

"I was supposed to close up the club," Mom said, "but three hours before my shift was due to begin, Lisa called and begged me to let her take it, crying about how she needed money. I said no because I could use the paycheck. So I worked the shift. But Lisa stayed around, which was weird because she'd been there the entire day—she'd worked that morning in the fitness room, she'd done her exercise, gone for a swim, the whole nine yards."

"When did she leave?"

Mom paused. I imagined her looking at the floor. "That's just it," she said. "I'm not sure Lisa ever left that night."

Ashlock cleared his throat, probably to stall at this bombshell, but *I* wasn't surprised. A lot of us now believed Lisa was still hiding something.

My mom continued. "Lisa had stayed at the club that night, even though I was on front desk duty and she had nothing to do. You know . . . it was dead summer. The place is like a tomb once the after-work crowd leaves."

"And what time is that?"

"About nine," she said. "I started my rounds about ten thirty. The receipts and all that junk was done, and the place was quiet. So I headed back to the front desk so I could lock the doors right at eleven."

"But . . ."

"But," she said, her voice growing softer, "when I walked back through the lobby, I heard yelling in the women's locker room. I hadn't seen anyone around, yet there were two voices in there. Whoever it was, was angry, and—it wasn't like I was eavesdropping or anything—it was so quiet in the club that I could hear most of it."

"Who was arguing in there, Beth?" Pause.

"I can't be sure, but it sounded like Lisa and . . . Annabel." My mom took a deep breath and exhaled slowly. "They were screaming at each other. Annabel was angry, saying things like, 'It's *you*, I knew it was you.' That kind of stuff. Then Lisa called her something horrible, and Annabel threatened to tell everyone about whatever Lisa had done, and to get her fired. Then Lisa said something like, 'If you don't want to believe me, that's your problem. You're a phony and everyone around here knows it.'"

I cringed. I hated to think Annabel had to hear those words only hours before she died. Shame on Lisa.

"Do you know what the fight was about?"

Mom replied, "I don't know what started it, but Lisa was talking about Annabel stealing every boy she ever liked . . . Patrick . . . Goran . . . even Nicky, which of course is ridiculous." She sighed and seemed to measure her words carefully for once. "I knew Lisa didn't like Annabel," she said slowly, "but they're teenage girls. Competition comes with the territory. Lisa's had a hard time in life. Things came easily to Annabel."

"I'm not happy about you leaving this out of your statement. You've cost us valuable time," Ashlock said sternly.

"I'm sorry about that," Mom admitted. "It's just that a part of me thought I'd imagined it. Like I said before, I didn't see Annabel come into the club that night, and I even checked the membership card records, but she hadn't swiped her card that day. Only Lisa was still around. She has her own key, so I knew she'd let herself out. The pool was pitch-dark when I left, and I never heard anyone go out there."

At that point things got even worse. "It bothers me that you were one of the last people to be around this girl when she was alive, and then you lied about it. We might have to take another hard look at *your* movements," Ashlock finished ominously.

147

My eyes widened. Evie turned to me and whispered soothingly, "It's okay. Detective Ashlock is only covering his bases."

When she smiled reassuringly, I almost felt better. But my emotions had been yo-yoing and I was scared again. A trickle of cold fear had been building up inside me, and I was starting to shake now. I was strong; oh, I could handle so much. But I got overwhelmed sometimes, and when someone messed with my mom it got to me. The club's maintenance man, Roberto, walked by us and waved, a bunch of tools clanging on his tool belt. Then I saw a white rope slung over his shoulder. That did it. I had to get away, and I took off running as fast as I could. Evie didn't even try to stop me, and instead went straight to my mom, pushing aside the privacy curtain as I took off.

"Beth! Beth, hurry. Something's wrong with Chelsea. *Hurry*—"

In the distance I heard the grown-ups' footsteps clunking after me and yells of *What? What happened? Wait, Chelsea!*

But I was already gone.

I guess one of them had called the reception desk after I took off, because when I made it to the front of the club, Gene was there to catch me. He was one of the only people at the club who knew my entire story, according to my mom. As much as the police had revealed to my mom, anyway. He was squatting, his arms open, his eyes tired, as they always were these days.

"Chelsea," he sang. "Chelsea. Stop. It's okay. Slow down . . ."

But I was crafty and I was quick. I slipped past him, turned around, and ran again through the lobby. I wasn't sure where I was going to end up, but I needed some space. It took Gene a second to get his age-fifty-something legs going, but I heard him—and a few others—behind me when I was half-way back to the aerobics court. I had a head start, but I knew I was running on borrowed time. Everyone turned their heads as I ran through the lunch area and through the pool lobby. I wanted to hide. So I ran past the basketball-court-slash-aerobics-floor and into the weight room.

A couple of guys appeared startled at my racing into the room as they lifted their dumbbells, I guess because I came out of nowhere. A second later Gene, my mom, Ashlock, Roberto, and Evie—in that order—blew in. I was sitting on the floor breathing heavily and looking around at everyone. I felt nauseated and pretty freaked out.

My mom came and knelt next to me. At that moment, I almost didn't remember how I got there. She tucked a curl behind her ear and said, "He doesn't have the rope anymore, Chelsea. See? Look at Roberto."

Roberto was a little shaky, and he tried to smile. "It's gone. See? Gone." He added, "I'm sorry. I'm so sorry. I must go back to work." He strode off as fast as he could.

My mom helped me up, and together we walked out of the weight room. When we were standing in the pool lobby, she fixed her gaze on Gene, Evie, and Ashlock, who had been silent. "It's the rope," she said quietly. "She saw the rope and it—she's having a bad day. That's all. She'll be okay."

I guess the men took that to mean they should leave us be, so Ashlock and Gene walked off, whispering and gesturing. Evie sat down next to my mom and let us have our moment, but she wasn't gonna leave me. I felt better with her there, and with my mom cuddling me. It wasn't only the rope that upset me, like she thought. It was my mom's role in this Annabel thing—I had this feeling of doom growing in the back of my mind, and I couldn't snuff it out. It was also the physical pain that was nagging at me. Some old injuries had been acting up, and I was finding it harder than usual to run and play, but I didn't want my mom to know—she'd force me to *slow the heck down* or, worse, get a sitter and make me stay home when she went to work.

Mom let go of me for a moment and took my best friend by the shoulders. It was only then I saw Evie had been crying. "This has nothing to do with you, you understand me?" Mom said to Evie. "There's nothing you could have done. You know what happened to Chelsea when she was younger. Sometimes it gets to be too much for her. She has things called triggers, and that rope was one of them. Okay? It's not your fault."

Evie nodded, tears rolling down her face. I wasn't the only one who'd felt the threat, and I had to remember that. Evie and I couldn't lose each other. That wouldn't be acceptable.

Later, I overheard Gene telling my mom that maybe it was time for me to go back to "that woman." *Puh-leeze.* My mom had promised to get me professional help along with medical attention when she adopted me, and she'd stuck to her word. But after three sessions she put a stop to it. She said I always came home totally hyper after seeing this lady, who my mom called "a loony-tunes nut job." All the rich St. Claire families swore by this woman, whose name escapes me now. In the end my mom said her method of "tough love" was baloney. "We're doing fine on our own," she said. "We'll get through this together, Chelsea."

And we *were* getting through it, even if we had to roll over a few bumps in the road along the way.

Before

As it turned out, my mom was a genius. Based on her sage advice, I had let Evie stew in her own juices for a while, trying once every day to coax her out of the stinky back room before finally leaving her to her misery when she didn't respond. Each day, her eyes stayed on me for another second longer as I left.

I was worried the day would never come, but one evening Evie finally reached her breaking point. Tad Chadwick had been on her case, this time with Goran in earshot. On top of everything else, Evie had to go without dinner again. Lucky had started dating someone, a bank teller he'd met while cashing his paycheck, and he was seeing her tonight. Which meant Evie was stuck at the club until the date was over. I was there when he broke the news just before camp ended for the day.

"But, Dad, if I stay here, what am I supposed to do for dinner?" Evie said, her face falling. I really didn't think her angst was only about the food, though.

Lucky had fished around in his pockets and checked his wallet. He'd frowned, shrugged, and handed her eighty cents. "Get some corn nuts or something," he said.

"But, Dad—"

"You'll be fine for one night, kid," he told her, and patted her on the head. "I'll swing back and pick you up as soon as we're done."

I know, I know. To any normal person it would almost sound like child abuse. To Lucky, the fact that Evie would certainly survive without one meal was a simple fact no one could argue with, and it was not a cruel thing to say, but rather a given. These moments made me angry for Evie, but also grateful. God knows my mom would never, ever leave me without food. I mean, when she hired sitters for me she gave them three pages of instructions about what to feed me and when and all that. Corn nuts for dinner did not enter into the equation.

And so, a few minutes after five on a gloomy July evening, I found Evie tearing up her storage room. I was nervous, but also prepared. My mom had explained to me that Evie might have to get lower before she could rise up again. I watched as Evie turned out her sweatpants pockets, found only lint in the little pink coin purse she kept back there, and scrabbled around on her hands and knees along the cold concrete. I knew what she was looking for; she was desperate for spare change. Eighty cents wasn't buying anyone a pack of Twinkies, and she had no one to ask for money without getting the third degree about why she wanted it. I watched her try, and fail, to find any coins. She even checked the refrigerator. As if, magically, cash would be hanging out under the carrots or something.

"This is *ridiculous!*" she cried when she knew she was beaten.

She froze in place for a moment, thinking. I was quiet as a mouse. Then she started breathing heavily, and the heaving grew louder and louder until I thought I'd have to run and get my mom to give Evie a paper bag or something for her hyperventilating. Then, inexplicably, she slowed down. She got a strange look in her eye. And then she made a move. I followed Evie as she stormed out of the back room and stalked up to the front desk, where Mom was killing time until the end of her shift.

"What's eating you?" my mom asked Evie.

Evie ignored her, and kept glaring at no one in particular. I watched my mom's attitude change from mildly curious to slightly worried. We could now both see Evie was angry, and she was up to something. She still had that strange expression on her face, one I hadn't seen before. Kind of like a demented version of the otherworldly focus Goran showed when he was heading out to the tennis court. Evie slipped behind the desk and before we knew it, she'd reached into the loaner bin under the desk and was rifling around with *thud*s and *bang*s. She finally withdrew a racket, an old graphite Wilson with a massive head.

"Those are three bucks a day," my mom told her, tucking a bit of errant hair behind her right ear. Evie paused. The girl

couldn't even raise the money to buy a Twinkie. My mom offered a magnanimous smile. "Oh, all right. Bring it back
when you're done."

I knew my busybody mom was happy to see Evie doing
anything new. I, however, was slightly concerned. I mean,
clearly the girl wasn't going to play *tennis*. More likely she was
going to bang the racket against something to let out her frus-
tration. I followed her, and wasn't surprised to see her head
for Court 5. I sighed. Back to the smelly room we'd go.

Oh, but how wrong I was. She walked through the door to
Court 5, but instead of going straight behind the curtain, she
went left, out to the court. She grabbed a few stray balls and
stood in front of the imposing wall, a monstrosity made of
cinder blocks painted a drab olive green. It went as high as
the start of the pitched tennis roof, twelve feet at least. I
couldn't believe it. Was my Evie going to attempt tennis?

She tucked two balls in the waistband of her sweatpants
like she'd seen the elites do, and gripped the racket as if she
was shaking hands with it, like the counselors always instructed. She stood ten feet away from that wall, held a ball
in one hand, dropped it, and whacked it as hard as she could.
She was shocked when the ball came right back to her at a
softer pace, and she hit it again easily. Her first time, and she
was already a pro. I literally jumped for joy as she smacked
that ball over and over and over. She was on fire. She just
kept whacking that fuzzy yellow ball. I was mesmerized by

the unusual sight of her holding that racket, of her moving from side to side with urgency to get the shot.

By the end of the session, she'd kept a single ball going for about twenty hits in a row *on her first day*. She seemed to take to the game immediately, her ease with the racket and her ability to control the ball surprising us both. I watched Evie come alive, even if it was in secret, even if only for a brief moment, as she wielded that racket and bossed those balls around. I could see in Evie's eyes what she was thinking: *this is even better than Twinkies*.

That day began a tradition for Evie and me. We named the great wall on Court 5 the Green Monster. Despite his scary name he was a perfect addition to our partnership. When camp ended at five every day, there was a good hour before the staff remembered to turn the court lights out. That's when Evie had her chance to slip in and play some tennis. Sometimes she lasted ten minutes, and other days I swear she was on the court for an hour. I'd sit there and watch her whack the ball at the great green wall, her fine, dirty-blond hair held back in a long ponytail with wispy bangs. I'd help her fetch the balls if I was in the mood.

The Green Monster was the perfect hitting companion. It was a very forgiving partner and *always* hit right back to her. By the end of her first week, she'd taught herself a rough facsimile of a forehand, a backhand, and an underhand slice. All from watching other people.

Considering it was dead summer and the club's air-conditioning could only do so much on the cavernous indoor courts, she'd be boiling hot in her sweatpants and oversize T-shirts, along with extra support from the bra my mom had bought her. It was kinda sad because she had her eye on a white collared Ellesse shirt with pink trim, but Lucky couldn't afford a seventy-five-dollar tennis shirt, and anyway it didn't come in Evie's size. I could see how much she wanted it, and also Serene's lavender tennis skirt, but same problem.

The whole time she played, my eye was drawn to the Wilson graphite in her hand. Such an unusual sight, and yet it looked like it was meant to be there, her fingers wrapped tightly around the leather grip. I had to ask myself: Would that racket turn out to be Evie's instrument, the weapon she needed to face the world? Maybe, I thought, just maybe, my friend had finally found a cure for her melancholy.

Before

One day in late July, Evie overheard something she shouldn't have. Annabel's BFF from St. Claire High, Portia, was speaking in hushed tones to Celia as they freshened up in the women's locker room.

Portia was saying that Annabel was upset about something. And that it was big. Evie recalled it vividly because it was such a surprise to her that someone like Annabel even *had* problems. *I don't know what's wrong with her,* Portia said, standing in front of a mirror, brushing her long brown hair over and over. *She's been my closest friend since we were in kindergarten. I can tell when something's up.*

Celia had piped up with teenage-girl platitudes: *She's probably PMSing. It's just a bad day. She seems fine to me!* But Portia had shaken her head "in a foreboding manner," according to Evie.

That's not it, Portia had said. *I'm worried, and I'm going to Europe with my parents tomorrow for the rest of the summer.*

Evie had walked away from that with a sixth sense that something was very wrong.

Later that same day, with this encounter weighing on her mind, Evie bumped into Annabel herself. It was an odd twist of fate that the beauty happened to stay extra late on a day when Lucky had completely forgotten about Evie again. My mom was off duty, so I wasn't even around to keep her company. Evie ran into Annabel in the otherwise empty ladies' room.

"Hey," Annabel had said to her.

"Hey," Evie said back coolly, as she relayed it to me later.

"How's it going?" she asked Evie.

"Good," Evie said. "How about you?"

Annabel hesitated. "I'm good," she said finally, and smiled at Evie, who later described it to me as a sort of *hungry* expression.

Annabel moved a few feet away from the sinks to the full-length mirror and started examining herself, turning sideways, sucking in her nonexistent tummy. Annabel hadn't looked quite so perfect then. Her hair, usually straight and shiny, was mussed just the smallest bit, and then Evie saw why. Annabel was playing with it obsessively, brushing it behind her ear every few seconds. The sparkle seemed to be gone from her eyes and her skin looked more pale and dry than tanned and robust like it usually did. She was fidgeting like crazy: fingering her hair, tugging at her shirt, fiddling with her beloved dog necklace.

Evie took a deep breath, turned her back on the sinks to face Annabel in front of that mirror, and mustered up the strength to ask shyly, "Are you sure?"

Annabel froze. "I'm sorry?"

She looked quickly at Evie and then back at the mirror. She started tugging on her pink cotton midriff-baring halter top, staring into that mirror again. Evie had never seen her do that before, not in her bikini out at the pool, not in the lobby, not anywhere.

"Is something wrong, Annabel?"

Annabel faced Evie. Something about the confidence in how Evie spoke got through to Annabel. Her eyes teared up, and the fact that Evie had been right, that Annabel had responded to her, emboldened my friend to actually carry on a conversation with her idol, listen, and ask questions. Annabel cleared her throat and composed herself.

"Do you know how many calories fidgeting burns? It's ridiculous. I can burn off half my calories while playing with my hair." Annabel was looking for approval in Evie's eyes. "It's pathetic, isn't it?"

"No," Evie said. "It's not pathetic at all."

My friend later told me she felt like she was out of her own body in that brief moment when she was the strong one in the face of this tortured beauty.

The tears came back and Annabel said, "I don't know what's wrong with me. I can't tell anyone. No one will understand. *I* don't even understand it."

She sat down on a wooden bench in the changing area and Evie stayed where she was, to give the girl space. "I understand," Evie said. She said she'd never forget the smell of Annabel: it was the smell of flowers and elegance.

"Everyone tells me how happy I should be. What a perfect life I have. But I don't feel perfect—and I don't know what's wrong with me."

"You're not crazy, Annabel. Lots of girls feel that way," Evie assured her.

Annabel asked, "What're you doing here so late? Aren't you in that tennis camp?"

Evie shook her head. "My dad works here. I only watch."

Annabel crinkled her nose. "I happen to know the camp gets out at five on the dot. Come on now. What are you still doing here?"

Evie, in the spirit of sharing and honesty, admitted her father's deadbeat behavior.

"My dad kind of, like, forgot about me. He's so busy and sometimes he—"

"Forgets." Annabel nodded. "That sucks. But no biggie. I'll drive you home. You're really easy to talk to, you know," she said, rising and smiling at Evie for real this time.

They walked through the lobby together, so close that every few steps Annabel brushed against her, and to Evie's dismay not a single person who mattered saw them begin their friendship. In the car, Evie told me, Annabel had shared more with her than any girl ever had, and she'd talked and talked, and Evie listened. Two things Annabel *didn't* mention were Goran and Patrick. Evie learned a few things that night, but not about Annabel's love life.

After

Goran was not doing well. His tennis game was on the fritz, and the Yale Championships—his last chance to hit number one this year—was coming up fast. Evie and I winced as he shanked another backhand into the net. Will shouted from across the court: *"Concentrate!"* Youch. If the Missile was misfiring, we knew Goran was in trouble. You didn't need a psychology degree to see he was grieving for Annabel; his looseness was gone, his legendary confidence shaken.

He slammed a down-the-line forehand so wide of the line Will couldn't get to it, oblivious that Detective Ashlock, who'd just breezed by Evie and me sitting on the lobby sofa during afternoon camp session, was heading his way. We tiptoed behind him, keeping our distance as he cruised through the café doorway and took a sharp right—straight to Court 1. We were hot on his heels and managed to plant ourselves in the walkway behind the green curtain, peeking through a crack after he'd disappeared onto the court.

Goran ended another rally with a net ball. Thoroughly irritated, he tossed his Volcano Onyx high in the air. When he turned to catch it, he saw the detective—and didn't miss a beat. He caught the racket and said, steely eyed, "I do not have time to stop. You may talk to me while I practice." He fed a ball to Will, bouncing on his feet waiting for the return.

"That's okay," Ashlock boomed from ten feet behind the baseline. He seemed startled by his own voice; I don't think he realized how much it would echo under that cavernous roof. "This won't take long."

He looked wildly out of place, and for the first time since we'd been spying on him, he wasn't in charge. Or so it seemed. "Your shoes," Ashlock yelled over the sound of slamming balls and squeaking footwork.

Goran lunged for a wide forehand from Will, and proceeded to nail it out of bounds. Will yelled, "Focus, Goran. Keep your eye on the ball."

Goran said nothing and started another rally.

Ashlock tried again. "Nice sneakers. Are they Volcano exclusives?"

"Of course." Said sneakers squeaked against the green surface as Goran nailed a shot. I remembered Goran showing off the new, experimental shoes the company had sent him, and Will shaking his head about style over substance.

"I notice you wear them a lot. In fact, every time I see you," Ashlock said.

"Yeah. They're kind of helpful (*grunt, thwap*) for playing tennis." He was in a killer rally with his coach now.

"I also like the little decoration on the right shoe."

Goran huffed and puffed and hit a down-the-line forehand humming with topspin, his stylishly longish dark hair whipping as he did.

"I asked myself," Ashlock yelled, "why is this tough guy wearing a heart on his sneaker? Is it a good luck charm? A mistake at the sneaker factory?"

Will hit a mid-court shot right to Goran, but our handsome tennis machine, clad in black-and-white Volcano gear that day, didn't even swing for it. The ball died and rolled into the curtain. Goran turned around slowly to face the detective, hugging his shiny Volcano Onyx tightly to his chest. "Say what you need to say so I can get back to my training."

Ashlock crouched and, kneeling before our god of the fuzzy yellow ball, examined Goran's right shoe. "This little pink heart," Ashlock said, peering closely at the sneaker's instep: "Annabel drew this on your shoe for good luck during one of your meetings behind Court 9, didn't she? And despite knowing there will be evidence on this shoe because it—and you—were with her the night she died, you keep wearing it because you feel like you have to honor her somehow. Am I getting warm?"

Evie mouthed to me, *Oh. My. Gosh.* I knew this would be almost too much for her to process. I, too, felt the revelation like a punch to the gut. I mean, this put into astonishing perspective Ashlock's demanding to look at Mom's and Gene's shoes that first day.

Will took off jogging from the other side as the detective rose and leveled his steely gaze at Goran. "If I look under your shoe right now, I'm going to find microscopic flakes—flakes you would've missed when you scrubbed them—that we can match to the vomit at the pool. More to the point, we will match an imprint we found in that vomit with your exclusive, one-of-a-kind, not-available-in-stores sneaker with a very distinctive pattern on the sole."

Goran was not cowed. He stood tall, with a firm set to his jaw. "There is nothing I can say to the evidence," he replied in thick-accented English. "I was there. I did not kill her."

Will slid up to stand next to his student. "I don't believe you have to talk to the police if you don't want to, Goran," he said with narrowed eyes.

Goran spoke anyway. "I will tell you this. This has killed me, do you understand? I might as well be dead myself. You are right about one thing. It is my fault this happened."

I could practically hear my—and Evie's—heart thumping.

"You found her body, didn't you?" Ashlock confirmed quietly. "Why didn't you call the police if you had nothing to do with her death?"

Goran laughed sardonically. "In my country, you do not call the police. Look, sir, I was at the club for a date with Annabel. Things were finally perfect with us. There are always rumors about me in the tennis world, and she'd started to believe them—until I proved to her they were lies. I'd promised to meet her here after a dinner with my parents and we were going to make a fresh start. Annabel was going to sneak out, and we were to meet at midnight, but my car broke down. I called and called, but she never picked up. Then the phone went to voice mail. I didn't have enough cash for a cab and I didn't want her to think I stood her up, so I left my car and walked six miles home, took my dad's car, and drove here."

"Let me guess," Ashlock said. "You have your own key."

Goran looked confused. "Of course."

That was the joke of this whole investigation. See, my mom and Gene had given Ashlock the answer they believed to be true back when he'd asked who had keys to the club. It was a short list. But it was inaccurate. The truth was, everyone and their uncle had a key to this club. Patrick had gone out and copied the master key years ago when Gene had loaned it to him for some after-hours tennis training, and over the years keys had been copied again and passed down to junior staff, senior staff, and even members.

Now Goran had a lump in his throat. "And so I went out to the pool and saw her there. I—I—didn't know what to do. I don't know what happened. I was three hours late; it was three a.m. Because of me, someone killed her." Goran looked on the verge of a breakdown. "If I'd been there, no one could've hurt her. But I swear: she was dead when I arrived, and I knew the lifeguard would come very soon. I did not think it would do any harm if no one ever knew I was there."

It broke my heart to hear that Annabel was waiting for the love of her short life to come and meet her, but evil came instead. I figured Ashlock had to give Goran a big hug now. Instead, he said, "Mr. Vanek, I'm going to have to take those shoes with me. You are officially a person of interest in the murder of Annabel Harper."

Goran didn't flinch. "My parents have hired a lawyer, so from now on you must speak to her. And check Annabel's texts, her phone records. You will see I am telling the truth."

"I will," Ashlock promised. "But I still need your shoes. And by the way, her phone was found destroyed in the pool. We can get phone records, but no texts."

With that, he left Goran on Court 1, shoeless, looking devastated and silly at the same time in his white tennis socks, Volcano Onyx racket drooping at his side. No one won today, I thought. Certainly not Annabel. I would never, ever believe Goran could hurt her, not for all the tennis balls in the entire club. Meanwhile, I wondered why Ashlock hadn't asked the question that I, for one, was dying to know: What "rumors" were going around about Goran?

Before

As July steamed along, something strange started to happen: Evie was shrinking. Everywhere she went, she was awkwardly hiking up her sweatpants. I noticed it in her cheeks—they were more angular and less *juicy*, for lack of a better word. I hoped she wasn't sick.

One Cookie Wednesday not long after she first picked up that racket, she came to the club looking . . . well, *fresher* is the best word I can come up with. She was slimmer than ever, made evident by a shocking new outfit. She still wouldn't risk shorts, but she'd teamed a new, more fitted pair of lightweight navy blue bottoms with a girlie (though only slightly less oversize) hot pink T-shirt. I wondered what she'd had to do to get Lucky to take her shopping.

She greeted me at the club's entrance with a smile, which was rare, and that made me happy. We ran inside, where Evie deflated the littlest bit. I stayed glued to her side, and we made it through the lobby without incident. I don't think she noticed what I saw—Tad Chadwick and his minions Marcus, Fat

Stan, and a redheaded new kid were checking her out, not with disgust or annoyance, but with interest. I took note, then followed Evie through the café before realizing she'd veered off to the left toward the pool, *not* to Court 5.

"Harmony said we can hang out at the pool when it's not too crowded," she told me excitedly. "Of course, absolutely no lounge chairs for us. They're for members only."

Hallelujah! It was about time she ventured out of her hovel. Evie pushed open the revolving door and we were greeted by a blast of morning sunshine. Harmony held out his hand for a low five, and we each obliged. His eyes were hidden behind mirrored sunglasses as he watched two senior citizens doing laps, ready to dive in, in the event they needed saving.

The grass was soft and warm. Evie got comfortable on a towel, then took out her latest book. I eyed it, and she explained, "I thought I'd try something a little more fun."

Ah. *A Wrinkle in Time.* I was glad she was lightening up a bit. I had to give credit to the Green Monster for this change. Goodness knows Evie needed an outlet that involved swatting at objects as hard as she could. Her mom's "weekly" phone calls were now down to about one every ten days, and last time they'd spoken, Evie's mom had told her how she was really "getting to know herself" for the first time and how beautiful the mountains out West were. She hadn't asked Evie a single question aside from *How are you?*

So Evie now whacked away at that wall whenever she got the chance. She'd even taught herself how to serve, contorting her body while managing to get the ball in the right box five times out of ten, and with some good power on it. The Green Monster was a friend. It would never judge her or blow her off—kind of like food, but cheaper and with less calories. Evie never beat the Green Monster, but she never gave up, either. Anwyay, we had the lawn to ourselves so early in the day, our own little piece of heaven, at least for the time being. Goodbye, stinky Court 5 back room. I stretched out and took a nap.

We hit the camp buffet at lunchtime, at which point Marcus, who very well might be cute one day but for now had that weird fuzz above his lip and a rather lumpy gait, ambled up to Evie as she was putting together a ham sandwich. She handed me a carrot. I crunched away as I observed Marcus, wondering what he was up to.

"Hey, Chelsea," he said, and elbowed Evie awkwardly. "Hey, um, Evie?"

She wrinkled her nose upon being addressed directly. *Ugh*, this could get ugly. Marcus swiveled his head back and forth to be sure no one was listening.

"You know that new kid Ronnie? The redhead?" he asked. His eyes were shifty but I thought it could be because he was nervous, not necessarily because he was up to no good. Evie nodded.

"Mmmhmm."

"He, um . . . he likes you."

Evie suddenly wasn't so nervous anymore. She gripped her

paper plate, weighed down with a half-made sandwich and a bunch of red grapes, until it shook.

"Shut up, Marcus," she said.

I was braced for a fight. I wasn't going to keep quiet if this got bad, no matter what Evie had said in the past about me staying out of it.

"*No,*" he said earnestly. "I'm serious. He thinks you're cute."

My mom had been saying for a while now that someday Evie would be pretty or cute or even beautiful, in between calling her chubby behind her back. So I could see how the new kid might actually think that right now, in the present. Evie had color in her cheeks and she was looking really healthy. Of course, this Ronnie was hanging out with Tad Chadwick, which was bad news. Unless . . . maybe he had a particularly strong backbone. Hey, stranger things have happened. Marcus grabbed a handful of barbecue Lay's out of a bowl and said, "He wants to talk to you. Meet him out behind Court 9 at snack time, okay?"

Court 9 was not exactly make-out ridge, but it *was* known to host the occasional tryst simply because it was out of sight. Evie was sizing him up, testing her instincts and scrambling for a response. "Out back?" she repeated.

Marcus nodded and scurried away. I very possibly saw sincerity in his eyes. After the morning we'd had in the sun, it would be one more nice thing to happen to Evie, to have a boy actually like her. She looked at me. I was on the fence. I thought it was sweet, but I also wasn't naïve, and neither was

Evie. I wasn't sure what she should do. Tad and his crew had tormented her all summer, but then again, Evie had transformed recently, and redheaded Ronnie had only arrived at camp last week, and maybe he hadn't been poisoned by Tad yet. If Tad knew nothing about this, perhaps it was real. We took our food out to the pool to think about it. We had a few hours until snack time. Personally, I thought it was worth a shot.

Normally at snack time, Evie's biggest concern was nabbing some of the white chocolate macadamia cookies while they were still warm, and before anyone in the camp saw her. You couldn't have a fat girl scarfing down cookies in public, she'd explained to me. Too much ammunition. This time, of course, she had too much on her mind to think about cookies. She was hyped-up and nervous, but I did my best to keep her calm. We decided it would be uncool for me to tag along and would make her look like she couldn't do anything by herself. But if she thought for one second I wouldn't be watching out for her, she was crazy.

Precisely at three p.m., she headed out the glass patio doors by the café and picked her way across the gravel strewn at the back of the four outdoor courts. Her arrival would be announced long before Ronnie saw her because the back passage was a five-foot swath of deep pebbles. She crunched along, slowly but surely, her footsteps in concert with the popping sounds of three different tennis matches going on at once.

I watched from behind the Dumpster. Ronnie was there, fidgeting, looking around like he was waiting on a drug deal.

"Hey," he said when she got there. He couldn't muster a smile—too nervous.

"Hey," Evie said. Same deal.

He looked down and kicked some stones. The town dump loomed in the distance behind his shoulder, set against a beige sky. A haze had moved in since morning, and they were predicting rain in the early evening.

"What's up?" he said.

"Not much," she replied. "So . . ." She looked up at him expectantly.

"So," he said. "Um . . . Marcus talked to you?"

Evie nodded and cleared her throat. "Sort of."

"I've seen you around. You really like to watch tennis."

She nodded. "Yeah. You're new, right?"

"This is my first summer. I signed up for two weeks but now my mom said I can go for a full month. I'm totally psyched."

This was not only awkward and boring, but painful, too. But it was safe, so I relaxed a bit. She wasn't going to get into any trouble. Marcus took a deep breath and managed to make eye contact with her. This kid was a bundle of nerves. He held out his hand. "Want to try?"

Evie's eyes lit up. He handed her a brand-new, shiny little tablet of some sort. This was mega contraband—Gene did *not* allow campers to bring cell phones, computers, or anything electronic, for that matter, into the club. She put on his blazing-green headphones and said, "What's on here?"

"'Summer Cool,'" he yelled, but she hadn't turned it on yet so she winced. She pressed Play and nodded along with the music.

Evie was totally starting to get sick of that song, but she yelled back, "My favorite song!" As she was listening, Ronnie took a step closer to her. They were still about three feet apart, but it felt intimate. Oh, God. I felt it, and Evie felt it. Her face looked like she was bracing to become a victim of a chain-saw massacre.

He was going to kiss her. But then something stopped him: the sound of people coming toward them. Tad, Marcus, and Fat Stan were sneaking through the parking lot. They were going to ruin everything, and there was nothing I could do. Evie's first kiss was now or . . . who knew when. If Tad found out Ronnie liked Evie, he'd tear them both to shreds. Within seconds the three boys came around the Dumpster, and suddenly they were there and grinning, and Tad slapped Ronnie on the back. I hated to give any of them credit, but Ronnie looked mildly uncomfortable, and even Marcus looked like he wasn't entirely on board with what I now realized was about to happen.

"Whatcha doing back here, Ronnie boy? Going elephant hunting?"

Evie held her ground and didn't crumple, and we were both trying to figure out if Ronnie was in on it or not.

Then Ronnie laughed. "Yeah. God, it totally worked! I can't believe she fell for it!"

This kid didn't even have the guts to look his victim in the eye. Evie glared at them. No tears. I thought it was her new tennis hobby. Strong body, strong mind.

She finally said, "So you said you liked me because?"

Ronnie snorted and looked at the ground.

Tad cackled and doubled over at the hilarity. "Ronnie doesn't like *whales*. Give me a break."

Then the absolute worst thing that ever could have happened to my friend happened.

Evie farted.

It came out forcefully, one little *parp*, and the boys couldn't even laugh at first because they couldn't believe their luck. Within a few seconds, though, they were buckled over, guffawing and pointing and laughing. Tad screamed, "Nice fart!"

Evie was purple and breathing hard. Enough was enough. She turned to run back in, but then Marcus took a step closer to her, and Tad came up on her right. She was surrounded by the laughing boys.

"Hey, fatty. Fatty farty. Someone should drive out to the country and make you walk back. Ever heard of exercise?"

Evie stood frozen in the spot. She couldn't outrun them, and if anyone else saw this, the humiliation would be complete. The thing was, I knew Tad was capable of hurting people. Last year he'd forced a kid to eat a whole packet of Pop Rocks and wash it down with a can of Coke, knowing full well the combination could make the kid's stomach explode. Thankfully, it hadn't worked.

"Hey, do you think her blubber would explode if we lit it on fire?" The redhead was carrying a lighter for some reason and he pulled it out, stepping toward Evie.

That was it for me. I took one step out from behind the Dumpster. Tad saw me and seemed a little thrown by my expression. Oh, I was irate, and he was starting to get that. Lucky for Tad, I didn't have time to make a plan of attack, because around the corner came Harmony, cigarette out and ready to be lit. He saw our unlikely gathering and stomped on over, a scowl on his face.

"What's going on here?" he boomed. "Evie, are you okay? Are these boys bothering you?"

She nodded, too choked up to talk.

"Look, you little worms, get lost," he said. "And if I catch you anywhere near this girl again I'm going to rip your tongues out and stick them up your butts."

The boys looked frightened and scurried away like roaches toward the parking lot, but Tad put on a bit more of a show of bravery, stopping and turning back to throw one more insult our way. "Freak," Tad yelled. "We're not afraid of you."

But I noticed he put many lengths between himself and Harmony before he said it. Harmony took one long, strong stride toward Tad, and the boys jumped at the sound of his shoes stomping the ground. Tad turned and ran with his gang, which was way ahead of him. Harmony winked at us, lit his cigarette, and leaned up against the building doing his stork thing with his right leg. With the butt dangling from his mouth, he said in a cool Elvis Presley side-mouthed way, "They won't be bothering you again."

Then he blew some smoke and looked off into the distance, thinking about something deep, I was sure of it.

Evie's chest was heaving by the time she made it back into the café, not caring who saw her. The only variety ever left over on Cookie Wednesday was oatmeal raisin, which Evie couldn't stand, but she grabbed every last remaining one. There had to be three or four in each hand. She took those cookies and ran to the back room, bingeing and crying, both of which ultimately sedated her and, for those few minutes, took the edge off the pain.

Afterward she'd be worse off than ever, and I'd be there to catch her fall. Even so, I couldn't *fix* any of it. I knew then that our short, happy time out at the pool in the grass might be over. I stayed with her that day, and for the first time, I was getting truly panicky about her. Evie cried longer than ever, and nothing I did to comfort her could stop her bawling.

Before

Evie did eventually stop crying on that fateful Cookie Wednesday. I was with her when she finally shuddered to a stop. Later, when she was good and sure every single camper was gone for the day, she ran as fast as she could to the front desk and grabbed the first racket she saw. She headed back to Court 5, with me alongside her. But when we got there, the court was taken by Celia giving a post-camp private lesson to an old lady. I heard Evie's sharp intake of breath, which usually preceded tears, but I guess she was all out of water because she switched gears and galloped away without another crying jag.

I followed her back toward the main lobby, where she soon came to an abrupt stop and took stock. The indoor courts were empty and still lit, and no one was in the lobby to catch her hitting, so Evie took a chance and ran out to Court 1, where there was a five-foot-wide, ten-foot-tall bit of exposed concrete at the back of the court. It was no Green Monster—in fact it was a boring old beige—but it would have to do. She took a ball in one hand, tucked a couple of spares in her waist-band, and started nailing the balls as hard as she could—forehands, backhands, swinging volleys—against the wall over and over.

Whack, thud, bounce, whack, thud, bounce.

She was so furious that she was doing some seriously fancy footwork to get in position. Evie was so into it that she didn't notice someone moving stealthily out onto the court. Her pony-tail was going wild as she swung, and that ball was the only thing she saw.

That someone heading for her was the god of tennis him-self. I watched Goran walk out there, and I was annoyed for Evie because clearly he was going to kick her off. I hoped the ten minutes she'd been out there had been enough to get it out of her system, because Goran was about to give her the boot. But Court 1 was Goran's stage, and Lord knew what-ever he did out there would be a crowd-pleaser for every club member who might walk by, so there was no fighting it. The Czech wonder, who should have been exhausted from training all day but was still going strong like the Energizer Bunny, was fixated on my friend as he walked out onto the court.

"Hey, Evie," he said from across the net, his voice bounc-ing off the empty building's gargantuan walls. "I'm waiting for Will to finish work. Wanna hit with me for a minute?"

Evie gulped and looked like she was going to barf. For one thing, the guy had come out of nowhere. If she'd known he was anywhere in the vicinity she would never have set foot out on Court 1. Plus, I think that was quite literally the first time Goran had ever spoken directly to her. I mean, outside of polite hellos in a group of people or asking her nicely to get out of the way. She was too shocked to do anything other than nod, but I knew something was up. I ran inside to find out what the deal was, and went straight to the coaches' office. Evie wasn't stupid, and she'd already been brutalized once today. If they were setting her up to make fun of her, I was going to make them pay. Big-time.

I skidded to a halt outside their office, and on first glance I thought there was no one there, because the chairs were all empty, the desks vacant. But then I noticed Will standing in front of the office window like Thor or Atlas, strong and powerful, arms crossed high over his chest. His mouth was set in a serious line. I observed him watching intently as Goran tossed a ball to Evie. She zeroed in on the ball, skipped up to it, turned to her side, lowered her racket, and whacked it back to Goran. He returned it with a little less power. Evie wasn't exactly light on her feet, but she made it to the ball, set up, and hit it to him. It was weird; she never could've talked to Goran for more than three seconds without cowering in sheer terror, but put her a court's distance away and give her something to focus on and she was like Maria Sharapova on caffeine. Will turned to leave the office, and I moved out of sight and scooted off before he could catch sight of me. He headed out, walking toward the courts. I followed at a distance.

When Will stepped onto the court with me unobtrusively in tow, Goran raised his eyebrows and held up his hand to Evie, who had become red and out of breath. She nodded and let her racket fall by her side.

"I'll be right back! Don't go anywhere," he yelled to her, pointing his racket at her. *Pointing at her.* I suspected Evie didn't care what Goran was up to. His paying attention to her was heaven, I knew. Let it end how it would. For now, she was a princess. Evie stayed put. I casually followed Goran, hanging back far enough so he wouldn't notice (I hoped).

"Did you see that forehand?" he said to Will in a very loud whisper. "I don't think the girl's ever had a lesson and she's already got topspin like that."

Will nodded. He was gazing at Evie under his eyelashes.

"We need to evaluate her properly," Goran went on, putting his hands on his hips, racket pressed against his thigh. "If she really has had no training, this could be . . . But I wonder . . . She must have had lessons at *some* point. I mean, with Lucky as her father, right?"

"I'm not so sure," Will said. "Didn't you say she's here every day? I've never seen her do anything. Set foot on a court. Show an interest."

"That's not really true," Goran pointed out. "She does show an interest—we just never paid attention. She's been watching us all play for the past year or two. Remember when Wimbledon was on? She was always in front of that TV. Right,

Chelsea?" He and Will both turned to me. "Your friend's been practicing, hasn't she?" Goran added. I guess I was caught, and I knew it was a rhetorical question.

Will said nothing.

"If we can get her footwork going," Goran said, shaking his head. "If this is her having never had a lesson, it's—"

"I know," Will said. He couldn't take his eyes off Evie, who was bouncing a ball on the ground, catching it, throwing it down. "I know. I'll take it from here."

"Her feel with the ball reminds me of—"

"I know," Will said one final time, turning to walk toward the net. He whipped around one last time to stop Goran, who was about to disappear under Court 1's back curtain.

"Hey," Will said. "Keep this under your hat, okay? In case we're wrong, we don't want to put any pressure on this kid. Make her feel bad. You know."

Goran nodded and headed inside, but not before throwing a shout and a wave to Evie, who looked as if she were going to pee her pants as she waved back. I stuck by Will, who beckoned to Evie. She scurried over to us. I could only guess she was too tired to be intimidated by the head elite coach standing in front of her.

"Hey, Evie," he said.

"Hey," she said. I realized then she wasn't asking questions about what the heck this was all about, and she was doing as commanded, because she thought she was in trouble for something. I could see it on her face.

"Evie," Will said, "I'm going to throw you a few balls. I want you to aim for the baseline with every shot. Long and deep. Like the elites do. You understand?"

She nodded and returned to the baseline. She got into the ready position, sticking her butt out and swaying her lower body the way she'd seen the elites do on this very court. Will tossed a ball to her forehand and she nailed it down the line, but it sprayed way wide. She got ready for the next ball.

"Shake it off," Will shouted from across the net. "Go again."

He fed her five quick ones in a row, and she nailed them, some deep, some in, some out. "Okay, that's enough," he said after about ten balls, and beckoned her over to the net. Evie stood there dutifully, racket at her side.

He crossed his arms over his chest and looked down at her. "Have you ever had a tennis lesson, Evie?"

She shook her head. "Um . . . no?"

"You must have hit the ball around with your dad. Even if it wasn't a real lesson, you've played with him at the park or something, right?"

She shook her head again.

"Never?"

"No," she said, starting to catch her breath. "Lucky says I'm not an athlete."

Will looked surprised, and then sorry for her. "Do you like tennis, Evie?"

She paused to think about that one. "I guess so," she said

after a few seconds. "I've never really played. I only hit on my own . . . because I get bored. Actually . . . yes." She studied her racket, then looked back at Will. "I do like it."

He nodded, eyeing her and, I think, gauging his gut feeling. This girl had come out of nowhere—and for all three of us standing out there at that moment, this was happening pretty fast. I could see it in his posture, feel it breathing from his skin: Will was going to go big or go home with my friend.

"What would you say," he said, "if I offered to train you? To see if we can turn your raw talent into something?"

I think Evie and I were only somewhat clear on what "something" meant. I could tell she was stuck on the "raw talent" part. No one had ever told Evie she was talented at anything. She looked over at me, and I smiled back. Of course she should go for it.

"Evie, before you say yes, I want you to think about what this means," Will said. "From what I've seen today, you have some real potential, but it's going to take work to see it through. You'll need to get up to train early in the morning, you'll need to work out in addition to your tennis practice, and you'll need to show up when I tell you to. When summer's over, you'll have to get up early and practice before school."

He stood back and examined her. She met his eyes head-on, racket firmly in her hand and pointing toward the ground.

She was taking him seriously and, I suspected, going over in her mind what his offer would mean to her life.

"Not everyone has the commitment it takes to become a champion. Can you stick with this, Evie? Will you do what I tell you, even if it's hard, and you're tired, and you want to stay in bed?"

Evie nodded. "I can do it," she said. And in that moment, I thought, she believed she could. Will seemed to see it, too.

"We're going to need to teach you a few basics, get you in shape before you train with other kids," he said. "Then we'll enroll you in the camp. We'll figure that out with your father and Gene when the time comes."

"Um . . ."

"What?"

"My dad."

Will sighed. I think he was finally seeing what he was up against. He was used to pushy tennis parents. Lucky was the anti–tennis parent.

"We'll cross that bridge with Lucky when we come to it," Will said firmly. "You make sure you show up for me tomorrow and we'll go from there. Deal?"

A giant, genuine grin of joy crossed my friend's face then. "Okay."

"We'll begin tomorrow, before camp starts. Seven thirty."

"I'll be there," she said. I saw something in her eyes I'd never seen before.

Will nodded. "Tomorrow." He directed his chin toward her racket before turning to walk away. "Keep hitting against the wall. Another half hour tonight."

Evie nodded and went straight for the ball hopper. I stayed with her and watched her hit for the next half hour, and I thought Will Temple was definitely on to something.

After

"You two are strange," my mom said to Evie and me, and headed back to her swivel stool behind the reception desk. "But hey. Whatever floats your boat."

She flipped through her out-of-date *People* magazine. *Phew.* Evie's weak explanation as to why we were sitting on the floor leaning on the wall outside the coaches' office—because we wanted a change of scenery—had passed muster. The real reason was that Detective Ashlock was back, and he'd grimly summoned Lucky and Patrick for a private discussion in their office.

Evie and I stayed still. We heard some mumbling from within, and then, clearly: "This is your last chance, Patrick. What happened in the women's locker room the night of the summer kickoff party? Tell me now, or tell me at the police station."

Patrick responded nice and loud. "Oh, for God's sake. It wasn't *me*, Detective. It wasn't me who was weird and violent that night."

Pause.

"It was Annabel."

After Patrick dropped that bomb, we heard only: *Mmmhmm, mumble mumble.*

Then we heard this semi-crisp exchange:

Ashlock: *So you grabbed her arm?*

Patrick: *I had to—she was going to mumble mumble.*

Ashlock: *But you physically touched her.*

Patrick: *To stop her from beating me up!*

Lucky: *Yes, mmmhmm, mumble mumble.*

Patrick: *That's the thing. She flipped out. She seemed so upset— I could hear it, and I was kind of freaked out. She started screaming all this weird stuff, like, "He's not like the rest of them. He's not! I wish mumble mumble leave me alone!"*

For the next few minutes we strained to hear what we could and were able to piece a story together. After Annabel had been spotted peeking out of the locker room, watching the pool party that night when Patrick saw her and went after her, she'd locked herself in a bathroom stall. She was crying, and Patrick heard it and went in. This is where it gets a little foggy for us eavesdroppers, but I gathered he called out to her. She ignored him, but he tried again, and finally he'd slipped under the stall because he was so worried about her.

According to Patrick, Annabel got physical and started screaming about how you can never trust anyone, that people are never what they seem. He'd grabbed her arm to calm her down, he said. Harmony had come in and been utterly confused; then Lucky arrived and told Patrick to let her go. Annabel had run out crying, and no one had seen her the rest of the night. Ashlock, I could tell, was only partly on board with their story. But Lucky's corroboration that Annabel was the flailer and Patrick the flailee didn't hurt.

For a second, there was total silence—we heard not a whisper or a movement. Then Ashlock hit our pal with a whole new bombshell. "Let's say I believe you," he said. "I want to know about the note you left for Annabel. Why did you do it? And how did you get into her locker?"

Evie leaned even closer to the door and almost had her ear to the metal. That's when my mom put down her *People* and shook her head. "Wait a minute. I should've known."

We played innocent and ignored her. "You're not hanging out," Mom said, getting a tone. "You're *eavesdropping.*" She hopped off her stool. We kept our ears to the door. She stood over us and whispered, "Scootch over."

She didn't bother to sit down. She boldly leaned over and put her ear to the door. So Evie and I got up and did the same. Anyone walking by would have thought we were three lunatics leaning on that door. Then we learned a few things about how obsessed Patrick had been with Annabel.

Before

Man, Evie was bad at tennis. I cringed and shut my eyes.
Maybe we'd been wrong about her. Dead wrong. She'd just
thwapped another sinker in the bottom of the net while at-
tempting a forehand during her very first tennis lesson ever.
Will fed her a backhand, which she proceeded to shank into
the wild yonder. The ball ricocheted off her racket frame and
flew clear over two courts.

It was a beautiful morning, steamy but not too hot yet at
seven thirty. There was the slightest chill left over from the
night, but the thick air let you know you wouldn't be spared
the gloopy, hot New England summer soup later on. Evie had
been at the club since six a.m. Harmony was her only chance
of getting here on time in the mornings, and he'd agreed to
pick her up on the way to open the pool bright and early on
those days he worked the morning shift. Lucky, of course,
was out of the question. For starters, he could barely make it
here for nine a.m. on his best day. So Evie had told her father

she was coming here early to get a head start on helping with the camp lunch.

"I can't hit and I can't run," Evie cried after sending another ball shooting into outer space. "I stink at this stupid game. I'm too heavy. This isn't going to work. *I'm. Too. Fat.*"

She stomped to the baseline and faced the netting. I could see her heaving, either crying or trying not to. I couldn't quite tell from the sidelines. I wanted to run to her, but I thought better of it. Maybe I'd give old Will a chance to show if he *got* Evie. Will seemed to pick up on my desire to go comfort her. He crossed his arms on his chest, showing off those big biceps again, and pointed at me with his racket. The tennis dudes love doing that.

"Stay where you are, Chelsea," he said. "This is part of the training. She needs to learn how to take the bad with the good." Lucky for him, I'd already decided to let these two work it out without me.

Then he boomed to Evie, "Come here."

I thought she was going to stay put, but his tone must have jarred her and she slowly turned and walked back to the net with her head down.

"Evie," he said, "you're not fat." This was said so matter-of-factly as to make even *me* believe it. "But you *are* losing your focus. You can't expect instant results. It takes work. Even great champions were beginners once. Serena Williams. Caroline Wozniacki. They're going to be legends, but they had to start out making mistakes just like you will. You're not so special that you get to skip the training part. You're going to have to toughen up. What if Steffi Graf had given up during her first lesson?"

He regarded her for a moment. She was still huffing and puffing a bit and red-faced from the exertion of this gentle lesson. "You need to forget about skinny or fat. We need to turn you into an athlete, and that's the only thing I want you to be thinking about." He paused. "And there can't be any more talk of giving up."

He walked around the net to Evie's side of the court, his own racket tucked under his arm. "Let me see your grip," he said, putting his hand around Evie's on her racket.

He'd been talking about grip all morning, and how it was why she couldn't hit the ball in the right spot, and I could see now that this seemed to be the root of Evie's problems. Will was having her hold her racket a totally different way than she was used to, in a weird upside-down-wrist position that made her look like a circus contortionist with every shot. Nothing natural about it, if you asked me.

"The Western grip is going to feel weird for a while," Will told her.

So *that's* what this weird grip was. It sure was odd looking.

This was Will's life, teaching and studying the game and trying new things to create champions. He was one of the club's top players back when he was a teen, but he was a rare elite who'd avoided the pro circuit. He'd decided early on he wanted to teach, to be around tennis the rest of his life. Will had gone straight from playing for his college team to teaching, and never looked back.

Now he was adjusting Evie's hand, still wrapped tightly around the leather handle, so the racket face was hovering over the ground, not directed at the net, which looked ridiculous. He held the grip with her and brought her through the motion: racket back, wrist twists downward, elbow up, wrist twists the other way so the racket gets under the ball, and then a quick upward motion to whip the ball with both power and extreme topspin.

Evie nodded and said, "I think I've got it."

She was calmer, focused, and determined. I smiled. I'd known it all along, that she had it in her.

"Good," Will said, and went back to his side. He winked at me, then grabbed a handful of balls from his basket. "Get to the baseline. Let's go."

Evie continued to suck for the next thirty minutes, but I figured Will knew what he was doing. Maybe things had to get worse before they could get better when it came to tennis, too.

Before

"What the heck is that?" Will Temple squinted at Evie across the net. It was their third lesson, and this issue was only now coming up. I had no idea what Evie was going to do about it.

"What's what?" she replied with just the slightest tinge of attitude.

I had to chuckle to myself. Talking back! A week ago she wouldn't have said boo to a goose; the girl had been apt to burst into tears at one stern word from someone like Will Temple. He beckoned Evie over, and when she reached him on the other side, he took her racket in his hand like a hammer.

"What is *this*?"

"It's from the bin at the front desk." She brushed her bangs out of her eyes.

"It" was, in fact, a banged-up old Slazenger from the nineties, with an unfashionably small head, that happened to be the best one left in the loaner pile that morning. Evie had had the choice of that or a warped Wilson with a broken string. Will pressed two fingers hard into the racket's sweet spot and the strings succumbed like a tiny trampoline.

"These are way too loose, and the grip is the wrong size for you. How long have you been a six-foot-four man?" He squeezed the handle, getting the feel of the thing, barely wrapping his own hand around the shabby leather. He handed it back to her.

"You need to get your own racket," he said, squinting some more. Will wasn't wearing his glasses today. He looked pretty dashing in his spectacles, but if it was too humid or he was playing a practice match, or maybe if he was in a certain mood, he didn't wear them. I guess his contacts were the wrong prescription because whenever he had to rely on them, frequent squinting ensued. "Tell your father I said so. With his connections, he'll be able to get a decent one for a good price."

Evie nodded. *Right, sure.* She'd get right on that. She was still fighting with Lucky to get some new underwear without holes in it. The tennis racket battle would have to wait. Especially considering Lucky hadn't a clue Evie even knew how to swing a racket, let alone that she'd caught the eye of the elites' top coach and was training with him. Lucky had been easily convinced that his daughter was working early mornings preparing the camp lunch while he snoozed, which was preposterous because it didn't take six hours to put out some cold cuts. I think it made Lucky's life easier to believe her. So I didn't know what Evie was going to do. This was going to be interesting.

After

There was a long pause in the coaches' office, and finally Patrick spilled to Ashlock as Lucky listened quietly. "I was mad, okay? I thought Annabel liked me, but it became clear she had her eye on someone else. It took a while before I realized it was my best friend." He paused. "So when that note fell out of her pocket one day, I picked it up. That's all. I never went through her things or anything."

Ashlock cleared his throat. "So you found this note, and you thought it would be appropriate to write cruel taunts on it for Annabel, who you say you cared about?"

Patrick insisted, "I only added a few things. Look, I'm not proud of it. But someone else loathed her—not me. The original note was much worse. I don't remember exactly what it said, but it was typed out and it said stuff like, 'Everybody hates you,' 'No one wants you here,' stuff like that."

My mother knew nothing about any of this. She said in the loudest stage whisper ever, "What in the world is going on?" and we shushed her.

"Were there any threats in this note?"

"I don't know," Patrick said. "The whole thing was a threat. It was harsh, you know? But did someone threaten to kill her or something? No."

Ashlock said calmly, "How did the note get into her locker?"

That was an easy one. Gene had put in these shiny, smooth, wooden lockers that were mostly about appearance. They weren't exactly bank vaults. "I waited until after hours and slipped it under the locker door," Patrick said, sounding more relaxed now that he'd unburdened himself. "What's going to happen to me?" he asked.

"That depends," Ashlock replied. "There's something you're not telling me. Annabel Harper was not someone who would let a few insults destroy her. *What was in the note?*"

Patrick heard Ashlock's tone and told the whole truth. "The note was anonymous, and typed." He was talking fast now. "There were more, too. Annabel had talked about 'notes,' plural. They were meant to make Annabel think Goran was a creep who was seeing all these girls at his school in Lexington, and even one in Connecticut from the tennis circuit."

Ah, the "rumors"! This was all ringing true for once.

"Do you think it's possible that night at the party was the first time she got one of those notes?" Ashlock asked.

Patrick thought for a second. "Yes," he said. "That would make sense."

"Was anything in those notes actually true?" Long, long pause.

"No," Patrick said quietly.

"But you let Annabel continue to believe that about Goran?"

"Yes," said Patrick. "I mean, the girls love that whole international-man-of-mystery thing he has going on—so there were always rumors about who he was dating. But he'd only had one steady girlfriend at school since he moved here, and they broke up last year. A few months after that, he set his sights on Annabel."

"Okay," Ashlock said. "Okay, Patrick."

We heard nothing for a moment and my mom jerked her thumb toward the desk. We had to get outta there. We scrambled away from the door, then quickly settled down to walk our separate ways, acting normal. I followed Evie toward the lobby, and as I looked back to check on my mom, I saw her watching me oddly. *Uh-oh.* She was seeing something I didn't want her to. I kept moving and acted like everything was hunky-dory. *Nothing to see here. No problem, Mom. Really.*

Evie collapsed on a sofa and I followed suit. She sighed, deflated, and shook her head. *I know, I know.* It was really draining. Even with the drama and overwrought confessing that had gone on around the club lately, we were no closer to finding out who had killed Annabel.

Evie looked up again, past me, out at the courts full of scrambling tennis players.

"Something's been nagging at me," she said. "About this whole thing."

No kidding. It was a terrible burden to have hanging over us.

"Think about this: What's happening with this missing mystery item? I mean, except for the day it was revealed in the *Bee* and everyone freaked out, we've heard nothing."

I had to agree. It was an intriguing facet of the investigation.

"I can't stop thinking about it. I feel like there's something out there I'm not seeing," Evie said, shaking her head and watching those courts like they held all the answers. "Something's just not right. And I'm going to try to find out what it is, because Detective Ashlock doesn't seem to be any closer to finding out who did this."

Before

When tennis lesson number four came along on a cloudy morning out on Court 9, Evie was on edge. She'd desperately hunted around the club for a nice graphite Head or maybe a Prince that was at least from our generation, but the good loaner rackets were gone, and she was left with another dreadful selection. Evie figured she couldn't use the Slazenger again because it had annoyed her coach, so she made a judgment call and chose a ludicrous kids' racket. I'd watched Will for a while now, and while he wasn't a jerk, he had his moods and he took life, and sometimes himself, very seriously.

When he arrived, I could see he was distracted and Evie didn't have a clue how not to take it personally. He greeted her with a quick hello and briskly walked ahead of her, carrying two full ball hoppers like they were pieces of fluff. His eyes were red-rimmed and he was yawning. I would estimate Will appeared exhausted 75 percent of the time. Evie followed, head down, taking his lead. No chitchat, no *how are you*s, no *good to see you*s. Just tennis. When they hit Court 9, Evie went to her side of the net and Will commanded, "Crosscourt fore-hands," then yawned again.

He started feeding her and she nailed a beautiful, hard shot at a perfect angle.

"Where's your topspin? Try again," he yelled.

Evie approached the next ball with fierce concentration, this time sending it flying into the court's back netting. "Check your grip," Will urged. "Come on. Concentrate."

She *tried* to concentrate, but I could see she was panicking. She repositioned her grip, held it tight, but when she came into contact with the next ball she went for the topspin so hard that she barely followed through, which made the ball whip up and land just before the net on her side. Plus, the kids' racket was way too light to give the ball any oomph.

Will beckoned her with three quick flicks of his index finger. Evie ran up and met him at the net. He took her right hand and adjusted it to the correct position on the racket handle.

"Line up your V here," he reminded her.

The V between your thumb and index finger is very important in tennis, no matter what grip you're using. A tennis racket grip is an octagon whose edges provide a guide for how to hold it for various shots, and depending on what edge your V is on, you can hit flat, topspin, or underspin. Will was so tired he hadn't noticed her racket. Yet.

"Yes, you have to get under the ball," he said to her, "but you also have to follow through or it'll slam into the net every time. Let's go again."

Evie turned to walk away. *That* was when Will figured it out: Evie had shown up with another bad racket. Whether he understood why she had to disobey him, I couldn't tell. His eyes flitted to her undersized racket, then back to Evie, then down at his ball hopper. He frowned, took a deep breath, and let it out as if to calm himself. Evie was braced. I was braced. He said only, "Keep that grip firm. Remember to flick your wrist as you get under the ball."

Evie got it and walked back to her position on the other side, taking a deep breath of her own. Will was pretty much irritated for the rest of the session, though when Evie started hitting some killer topspin backhands he was quick to praise her. She was coming along nicely, in my opinion. I couldn't tell what Will was thinking, but I thought he liked my friend and her prospects, today's hiccup aside.

Then again, I'd been wrong about stuff before.

After

In the hours after Patrick confessed his sins to Ashlock, Evie and I suffered from low-energy syndrome. In an effort to cheer ourselves up, we took in some sun outside the club's entrance, warming our buns on the hot concrete steps. We had to head back in when we started to overheat, which didn't take long on another sweltering August day. When we walked back into the club, my mom was giving me a weird look from her perch at the front desk. *Oh, crap.* It was clear then that she totally knew.

"Come here, Chelsea."

Evie tightened her ponytail and waved goodbye to me with a half smile as she headed to her haven to read. I dutifully walked over to Mom. She had *that look* on her face, and I felt a stab of dread. I didn't want things to change. Not now.

"Sit down," she said, sliding off her stool.

Yep. She'd seen me limping. I saw in her eyes she was fighting the inner battle she always did when my injuries acted up. It was a clash of profound sadness and powerful anger I worried might get her into trouble one day. She sat on the scratchy, well-trafficked gray carpet with me and took my right leg gently in her hands.

"Let's see . . ." she said, as she worked my knee. I cried out and she shook her head. "And the ankle?"

She rotated it gently and man, it hurt. *Ouch.* Maybe I'd overdone it this summer. Maybe running around on the court with Evie and the Pee Wees had been too much.

"I'll get you an ice pack from the café." She met my eyes, and then she said in a happier voice, "Well, then. Time to go see Dr. Mac again." I love Dr. Mac. He is known as "the best" in our little part of Massachusetts. We certainly couldn't say he hadn't warned us. Last checkup he'd said, *Chelsea, you're going to have a long and happy life. But you have limitations. Don't overdo it, okay?* My mom had pounded it into me: *No overdoing it.*

The people I lived with before weren't my actual mom and dad. I don't remember my real parents, but I was okay with that because Beth was my mom now. Those people used to tie my legs together with a frayed old rope that smelled of gasoline. Then they'd hang me upside down from a sturdy branch on an ancient oak in their backyard. Sometimes, they said, they were just "fed up" with me and I had to "*learn.*" Of course they used to hit me, too, and they liked to kick, but that didn't leave any long-term scars (on my physical being, anyway) and they got bored of that after a while. The rope left permanent marks behind, stretched tendons in my knees and

204

ankles, wrecked cartilage, and jiggled some things out of joint inside me. Struggling only made it worse, because I'd be bobbing around, off balance, and it hurt everything from my back to my head to my hips. The ropes were so thin. I never thought I'd wish for thicker rope, but the way this rope wrapped around me stretched me all the more and made my legs numb, like, immediately. Whenever they got the rope out I knew what was coming, and I had nowhere to run. We had a tiny house set among a big stretch of open fields, so I didn't even have woods to hide in or anything.

Gene came out of his office and said, "Everything okay out here?" He gazed at me with concern.

"She'll be okay," Beth said. "She just needs some ice and an aspirin. It just makes me so angry, what they did to her. And they're still out there. That makes it even harder . . ."

"I know," Gene said softly. "To this day I can't believe the cops never caught them." To me he said, "I'd like to get my hands on them myself, if I'm honest, Chelsea. But I'm afraid of what I might do."

I knew Gene and all the rest of the crew here would go to battle for me if the time ever came. But I didn't need that, really. I was okay with the way things were. The important thing was that the police found me, and that Mom took me in and made us a family.

Gene shuffled back into his office, shaking his head. I was pretty sure it would make them all even more worked up if they knew the entire story. The grownups in my life think

I don't remember a lot of it. My mom doesn't know exactly what those people did. She knows I'm afraid of rope, and horrified by the smell and sight of bourbon, but she doesn't know why, and I think it would send her off the deep end if she knew. I just can't tell her, and I hope she never learns about how, sometimes, those people would drink bourbon and laugh at my cries. No one seemed to hear me, no matter how loud I cried out. No one came for me, anyway. Then I'd pass out, and as I was coming to, they'd be yelling about how it's not as fun when I'm not struggling and crying, and they'd take me down.

There was always bourbon. Always. Luckily I rarely come across that smell nowadays because my mom doesn't drink it, so it isn't a factor in my life anymore.

Before

It was the dog days of summer, a dead zone in late July when the buzzing of the cicadas signaled another scorcher was coming. It was so hot at seven in the morning that Evie had to wipe her palms on her shirt every few minutes so she could keep hold of her racket. She was practicing her serve out on Court 9, far away from prying eyes.

She stood sideways at the baseline, her feet firmly planted right behind the white painted line. She stared at a spot on the other side of the net like it was her mortal enemy. She bounced her ball slowly, over and over, and then, abruptly, she tossed it up in the air, whipped her arm around, and nailed a serve into the corner of the service box, her ponytail flying.

She did a little hop and turned to me. "What do you think, Chelsea? Does it look like one of Celia's serves, or what?"

I thought it was darn good. That serve had a serious bite to it. I would definitely not count the ten or so serves before that one that had not made it anywhere near the box.

"That hit the spot," she pronounced. "I'm getting pretty good, right?"

Oh, yes. She sure was. She'd kept to Will's nonnegotiable training prescription with the determination of a pit bull. She had to be at the club four days a week by seven thirty a.m. On Tuesday and Thursday mornings she dragged a ball hopper outside and practiced her serve. On Mondays and Wednesdays she'd have private lessons with Will, with another evening or morning session during the week if he could fit her in.

For the rest of the week, Will told her to hit the stationary bike or take a walk. On Friday mornings, nice and early so no one would know what she was up to, she'd ride the Exercycle like a mad girl for forty-five minutes. It was heaven because she could read at the same time. I knew Will was going easy on her, though. If things went well, Evie would be running the lines and doing tortures soon enough. But Will seemed to realize she wasn't only a beginner at tennis—at the age of twelve, she was a beginner at life.

I knew Evie was worried about autumn. She'd have to come clean with Lucky and Will because there were no free courts in the wintertime. She'd have to pay or she couldn't play. Plus, Lucky, like so many other summer tennis camp coaches, would go back to teaching the game only part-time at the club. Lucky made ends meet with his second job as a part-time salesman of those cool stairlifts for senior citizens.

But that was a worry for another time. For now, Evie was blossoming, and I was having a blast observing her. And through it all, not a soul at the club knew what she was up to, and that's the way Evie wanted it.

After

"Look at this adorable pink coat," my mom said to Evie. "I mean, how wicked cute would this be on Chelsea?"

My mom was flipping through L.L.Bean's Christmas catalog. ("Seriously? In August?" Lisa had sneered when she walked by earlier.) Mom folded the catalog over and held the glossy page out for Evie, who was sitting up on a stool next to her.

Evie stretched her T-shirt down over her knees and leaned sideways to take a look at the jacket. "Pretty," she said.

"It would look *so cute* on you," my mom gushed, shoving the page in my face.

Oh, please. Totally not my style.

"For winter!" She would not stop. "It's so pretty and look—it's totally *in* this season. You can't even get it in stores."

I thought it looked uncomfortable. Who thinks about coats in the summer? My mom was always planning ahead for those bleak New England winter days, when the snowdrifts rose so high we couldn't get out our front door in the morning without help, and the windchill hovered around ten below. I preferred to live in the now, when it was boiling.

Evie said, "Let me see that again?"

Beth was thrilled to have validation and handed the catalog to her, crinkling the pages in her excitement. Evie squinted at the page like she was confused or something.

"Pink. Pink. Pink . . . *hmm* . . ."

Evie handed it back to my mom, saying to herself again, "Pink . . ."

I'll be honest, she was worrying me a little bit.

"Pink," Evie said. Again. "Pink! That's *it*."

Evie hopped off the stool and smiled at my mom. "Thanks, Beth."

She raised her eyebrows at me and I was *in*. We took off and I looked back to see my mom watching us go, shaking her head like we were both wacko. "Slow down, Chelsea," she reminded me in her best Mom voice, and I did, but not enough to lose Evie. I knew my friend, and I could see she had something up her sleeve.

Evie sat on her usual crate in the back room and I clambered up next to her. She twisted her torso and reached behind her, whipping out a notebook from behind a tub of wholesale generic ketchup. "This," she said to me as she opened the notebook with a flourish, "is how we're going to help Detective Ashlock solve this mystery."

I raised my eyebrows. *Really?* How were we going to do that?

"Annabel's necklace," Evie said, taking her favorite purple pen from the notebook's spine. "That's the key. I'm sure of it. We've heard nothing about the dog with the pink sapphire eyes since she died, and yet that charm was her most cherished posession. It *has* to be the missing item. I'm sure of it, Chelsea." I guess writing helped Evie think, because she was scribbling away, à la Ted Ashlock. "When your mom was talking about the pink coat, it made me think about the necklace. Annabel was always wearing it. Remember?"

I did remember. Annabel was always fiddling with that dog charm, the one she'd never take off.

"I bet you if we can find that necklace," Evie said, "it will have fingerprints or maybe even DNA on it that leads to the killer. I bet you anything. But where *is* it? And who sent those evil notes?"

I looked over Evie's shoulder and saw she was doodling now. She'd drawn a face in the *P* for Patrick's name, and put hearts over the *i* in "Lisa." "That note to Annabel was so awful," Evie said. "Patrick added to it, but Lisa has to be the prime suspect for the person who actually wrote it in the first place—before Patrick slipped it into Annabel's locker."

Bingo, I thought. Who else was threatened by Annabel, just because she was Annabel? Evie was staring at her names and doodles, brow furrowed, as determined as I'd ever seen her. "Now, we know Patrick never actually broke into Annabel's locker, but other people did—the cops," she continued. "They also searched the garbage, of course, and they tore apart the men's and women's locker rooms. There's no way the necklace was in Annabel's locker. So is it in Lisa's? Patrick's? The killer's?"

I was as stumped as she was.

"Wait a minute," Evie said, her eyes wide now. "Oh my. Now I remember. Annabel's locker was searched, and probably some staff's were, too, but the cops couldn't search other members' lockers, right? How could they? It would be a clear violation of their rights."

Yep. That was her cop shows talking, I knew. Probaby *Law & Order: SVU*, in this case. Annabel's locker remained double locked and taped up, but hers was the only one.

"Which means I bet you a million bucks I know where that necklace is. Remember the night she drove me home? She was using the mirror in her locker to brush her hair, but she was also using Portia's locker to borrow her perfume and stuff. I didn't think much of it at the time, but if the killer really was someone she knew, it follows that they might know her locker combination—and maybe Portia's. Annabel's locker is right above hers, and Portia's been in Europe all summer. Oh. My. God," she said. "That's it. I can *feel* it. If you wanted to hide something in plain sight, put it in the locker of the girl who was a continent away the night Annabel was killed."

I shivered. Her theory had promise. What if we could help

Ashlock? What if we could help Nicholas and the rest of us start healing, finally? This could be huge.

Except one problem. "We need to think about how to get into Portia's locker. It may be impossible," Evie pointed out.

We thought about that. But then, a minute later, it came to me—and to Evie, too, I guess, because we leapt to our feet at the same time.

"*Duh*," Evie yelled. *Duh* was right. It should have been obvious to us from the get-go. The master key to the club's lockers was accessible to anyone with enterprise and necessity. And right now, that was us.

After

We had to wait for the perfect moment, which presented itself the very day Evie concocted the Great Locker Caper. It was a carefully planned operation, with Evie arranging to hang out with me at the front desk during my mom's evening shift.

The club grew quiet around nine. My mom picked her cuticles and yawned. Evie was tapping her foot. I was starting to feel jumpy when, thankfully, it happened. "Hold the fort, girls. I gotta go powder my nose," Mom said, sliding off her stool.

Evie instituted phase one. We ran to Gene's office tucked behind the reception desk. There, nailed to his wall, was an unlocked steel key cabinet. I acted as lookout as Evie found the key we needed, which opened a closet in Gene's office. (I know, I know. It isn't exactly Fort Knox.) Evie unlocked the closet and flipped on the light, revealing a tower of Gene's old rackets, tennis balls, and *Tennis Monthly* magazines. She put the first key back in the steel cabinet. There was yet another steel box, inside the closet, that held the key we needed.

Eavesdropping was one thing, but this was breaking and entering and my heart pounded as Evie rattled around. She must've knocked something loose, because a bunch of files and tennis rackets crashed out of the closet.

As she scrambled to shove the stuff back in, I heard my mom calling us. *Oh, crap.* I gave Evie the red alert, which involved jumping and gesturing. She had to hurry or we were dead meat. I heard footsteps padding along the worn carpeting, then a *clunk*. I turned back to see Evie frantically scooping up a handful of Gene's old rackets. I quickly turned back and there she was. My mom.

"What in the name of everything that is good and holy are you two getting up to this time?" She narrowed her eyes and blocked the doorway to Gene's office.

Evie came out of the closet and slammed the door behind her. "Oh, hey, Beth," she said, sweet as could be. I thought, forget tennis: this girl should get into acting. "I was looking for a racket for Mr. Biederman. He wasn't happy with the ones in the loaner bin."

Good one. Mr. Biederman was always complaining, and the front desk staff had a running mandate from Gene to keep him happy—no matter what.

"All right," Beth said wearily. "But let's come out of the boss's office now, shall we?"

Phase two involved sitting in the lobby facing the women's locker room entrance until after the pool closed to be sure the last woman had wrung out her bathing suit and headed home. When the clock struck ten thirty, phase three kicked in, and we scooted into the changing room; we only had a small window of time because Mom would start making her pre-closing rounds in ten minutes. Evie and I made sure there was no one left in the stalls or the showers, and then we zeroed in on Portia's locker. I sat next to Evie, our shoulders touching. She stuck the key in and it made a jarringly loud grating sound. I flinched as she turned the key and pulled at the door. It opened immediately.

And voilà—we were in.

After

Evie sat on her knees in front of that locker, staring. We were faced with the totally boring contents of Portia's locker: A neatly stacked pile of fashion magazines shoved against the back wall. You had your basic *Glamour*s and a smattering of *Vogue*s. It was so quiet, and the smell of chlorine, smelly feet, and baby powder was pungent.

"I was so sure," she said. "I had that *feeling*, Chelsea. You know?"

I did know, because I had the same feeling. And since this was our only shot, I wasn't going to back off so easily. I stuck my head in to see for myself, and in the process I knocked down the pile of magazines. Those slippery magazines collapsed and spilled onto the floor.

But my clumsy move turned out to be a good thing—I got a close look, and then Evie leaned in and saw something shiny. It was delicate, small, and unmistakable. She squealed with excitement and dropped back to her knees. "I can't believe it, Chels. We *did it*. Now, don't touch anything. We better leave it here. I'll tell Detective Ashlock tomorrow," she said. "He'll know what to do."

I saw it dawn on Evie then that it wasn't just an exciting find. It was a serious, perhaps dangerous piece of evidence we'd found: it was the dog charm with the pink sapphire eyes.

"I guess," she whispered, "no one thought to check Portia's locker because she was a continent away in Europe when Annabel died." Evie gently put the magazines back in and quickly secured the lock, and we plodded to the front desk to face our next hurdle: returning the key.

As closing time approached, only a few of us were left in the club. Joe Marbury and Lisa Denessen were chatting at the far end of the front desk. They both smelled of chlorine, so I assumed they'd been hot-tubbing. Nicholas, who'd been lifeguarding that night, walked by us after closing the pool, head down, lost in thought as always lately, and threw us a smile and a "G'night." Evie and I smiled back, but it was hard because we were riddled with guilt; we'd found a major piece of evidence in his sister's case and we couldn't tell him. My mom took off to do her closing rounds, and I kept watch at the desk while Evie snuck into Gene's office. She came back ten seconds later with good news. The key was safe in its home, and we'd gotten away with it. *Phew.*

Before

Evie and I were hanging in the lobby when the elites came off the court for a break a few days after Will ordered Evie to get her own racket. She stared at Serene, who was chugging grape juice. "How much do you think Serene's Volcano X costs? Or even Celia's Prince?" Evie whispered to me. I didn't have a clue. A hundred million bucks? Ten bucks? It didn't matter—Evie didn't have a cent to her name. Serene got one of the first Xs ever made because she, like Goran, was sponsored by Volcano.

"Will's going to dump me if I don't get a new racket soon," Evie moaned. "What am I going to *do*?" She rose from the couch to get a better look, pausing outside the women's locker room and eyeing Serene's racket. Out of nowhere, the girl caught Evie's eye and said, "It's pretty awesome, right?"

Evie flinched, but then seemed to realize Serene was being genuinely nice to her. "It's so cool," Evie replied.

Serene held out the racket. "Here. See for yourself."

The Volcano X was the prettiest baby pink you'd ever

seen. It was made of a new shiny material that apparently gave you amazing control and power. Evie held the grip and felt the racket's smooth, glossy neck. She handed it to Serene with a smile and came back to sit with me. We had to think of something, or Evie might be in trouble. She told me she'd have more thoughts to share with me the next day, after she went home and slept on it.

After

Detective Ashlock raced over as soon as Evie called. At precisely nine forty-five a.m., he entered the club. He ignored my mom at the front desk (resulting in a glare behind his back) and strode to the lobby where Evie and I were waiting.

"You did the right thing by calling me," he said. "But you have to stop your amateur sleuthing—now. You're going to get hurt. Do you understand?"

We understood. Evie relayed our locker story to him in a whisper, told him how we'd snagged the key that night and again this morning so we could show him Portia's locker. For the first time ever, I saw Detective Ashlock startle. This man did not startle. But now his eyebrows shot up to the top of his forehead.

"I figured you never searched her best friend's locker," Evie explained. "Since she was in Europe. You couldn't have known how much everyone shares around here."

"You're right. But I do now," he said as if fascinated by our way of life. He adjusted his hat and said, "Show me."

Evie and I led him to the women's locker room. She issued the club's standard cry of "man in the house," and hearing nothing, we gave Ashlock the all-clear sign and he entered. When Evie pointed to Portia's locker, he pulled out two latex gloves and snapped them on, and a little powder flew up and made me sneeze.

"Stay back," he said. "And don't touch anything."

When he opened the door, a cascade of magazines poured out onto the floor in front of us. Evie and I exchanged glances. This was odd; we'd left them stacked perfectly last night. Ashlock pawed through the magazines and felt the back of that locker, the sides, the front. There was no sign of any solid-gold necklace or sapphire eyes.

Evie was scouting around frantically, knowing our credibility was on the line.

"Well," Ashlock said, rocking back on his haunches and reaching up to his head to make sure his hat was firmly on. "I'm afraid that whatever was here isn't here anymore."

He pursed his lips and turned to look at Evie.

"Sorry," she whispered. "I swear, Mr. Ashlock. I mean, Detective. I swear it was there last night."

"Don't be sorry," Ashlock said, shoving the magazines back into the locker and slamming the door shut. We got to our feet, and Ashlock motioned for us to leave via the poolside exit, because we heard female voices coming in from the lobby end. "Life is a series of peaks and valleys," he expounded as we entered the pool hallway, that place where we had first laid eyes on him. "This is one more challenge we'll have to over-come."

"I guess you probably don't believe us," Evie said when we exited the locker room.

"Of course I believe you," the detective said. "Every word."

"You do?" She looked up in surprise. Her eyes, greener than ever, were popping more dramatically the healthier she got, and those rosy-apple cheeks were positively adorable.

"You know what I think?" There was a warning in his eyes. "I think you're not the only ones who've been spying where you don't belong. I think someone's been snooping on *you*. I think you've made someone very nervous. Any number of people could be aware of your movements over the past few weeks."

Uh-oh. The eavesdroppers, eavesdropped on? Ouch. Beaten at our own game.

"But if we hadn't left the necklace there, you might've solved the case—" Evie shot me a guilty look, the same one I'm sure I had plastered on my face.

"If you'd moved anything, it would have compromised our investigation," Ashlock assured us. "Our forensics team will examine that locker. Plus," he said conspiratorially, "you rattled someone. And a rattled bad guy is a sloppy bad guy." He corrected himself. "Or girl."

I wondered whose fingerprints would be all over that locker. Who had been spying on us?

Before

Evie was pacing around the lobby at six in the morning before her lesson with Will, her mouth set in a worried frown. The girl was convinced he was going to quit on her. My mom had no idea what Evie was doing, and paid her very little attention. She was lost in her own world, fiddling with the radio, grumbling about the heat and about Lisa leaving the desk a mess last night when she'd closed up, pencils and scrap paper everywhere, *God*.

At precisely seven twenty-nine, Evie came back behind the desk, sighed, and reached for the dinky old Slazenger.

She walked toward the outdoor courts, racket in hand, to wait for Will. She knew she was in for it, but she wasn't going to let her new coach spill the beans to Lucky under any circumstances. For starters, there was the practical consideration that Lucky might not like Will teaching her, because Lucky himself was an excellent teacher and might wonder why his daughter hadn't asked him to train her. But more likely in Evie's mind, I'd gathered, was the prospect of the put-downs Lucky might throw at her while claiming he "didn't mean anything by it." Like the time he "didn't mean" to make her feel bad about not having many friends: *Ha-ha, you must be doing something wrong, kid. Back in my day only losers didn't have friends.* The worst, of course, was how he kept leaving her behind at the club and how he refused to apologize for it.

I walked alongside Evie as she made her way to Court 9, the outdoor court farthest from the club. She preferred to be as far away from people's prying eyes as possible, and Will had honored that, even though the outdoor courts—and their viewing patio—were 100 percent empty at that time of day. It was another hazy morning, the air thick with heat and humidity.

Will came out five minutes later. "Morning," he said. He smiled at me and then at Evie, his bulging racket bag on his shoulder and a ball hopper in his hand. He unzipped his racket bag and laid it on one of the two chairs that were on every court for tired match players to take a load off between games.

"We're going to practice some rallies today," he said.

Ooh. This was exciting. Rallies were for advanced kids only. Evie waited for further instructions and kept the Slazenger behind her back.

Will stood up, his Head graphite in hand, and did some trunk twists. "Whatcha got there?" he inquired, nodding to Evie's right hand.

Her smile faded, and she reluctantly brought the racket out from behind her.

226

Will stopped stretching and reached his hand out. "Give it here."

She did. I stayed quiet, but tense, sitting on the sideline. He examined it as if it were a weird object from outer space and said, "You can't play this game with a piece of junk. It's not a racket for a serious tennis player. Are you a serious tennis player, Evie?"

"Yes, but I—"

Evie had tried everything and there was no way out. She hung her head, so she didn't see what I saw: Will removed two extra rackets from his bag and was holding one in each hand.

"I think you *are* a serious player," he said. Evie looked up. "And you need a serious racket. So." He waved the rackets in her general direction. "Choose."

In his left hand was a rugged silver graphite Prince just like Celia's, and in his right was a Volcano X like the one Serene used, pretty and pink but also powerful and special.

"What?" Evie seemed stunned.

I practically leapt up and started jumping around. *Oh my God oh my God oh my God.*

Will couldn't keep up the stern act. He broke into a smile, his eyes twinkling.

"Come on, Evie. Pick the one you want, and it's yours." Evie was still confused. "Personally, I think this one's a better fit for you."

Will handed her the Volcano X. Evie took it, and never looked twice at the Prince. She felt the grip of her new racket

227

in her hands, tested its weight, hit the strings against her left palm. The face was huge with a juicy sweet spot; this weapon looked like it could slay dragons. I wasn't fooled by the pretty color.

"I can use it the whole summer?" she said. Her eyes were welling up with tears, her expression pure and joyful. I'd been waiting a long time to see this.

Will said with mock exasperation, "Evie. The racket is *yours*. To *keep*."

Evie opened her mouth and again, I thought the girl was going to cry, and I think Will thought so, too, because he got back to business superquick.

"Okay. Let's try that thing out. Back to work."

She stayed there for an extra second, though, and looked him in the eye. "Thank you."

Will smiled and gave her a nod before turning to get to his side of the court. I knew, and I think Will did, too, that she was thanking him for more than that racket. I couldn't stop hopping in place, I was so happy. Evie gave me a wink and I wanted to scream with joy.

She skipped to the other side of the court, staring at the racket as she went. She stood behind the baseline in the ready position, and Will hit her a ball, and Evie brought her new Volcano X back and hit a smooth, deep forehand crosscourt that kicked up right to Will's forehand. I watched her and Will and that racket practice for the next hour, and I think I felt as content then as Evie did. For once in her life.

After

Detective Ashlock pushed open the club's glass front door two days after the charm necklace debacle. Something was different. My mom sat up straighter on her stool at the reception desk. Even she could see it would be a bad idea to mess with Ashlock today. His face was ashen, not its normal shiny bright white. For the first time since we'd known him, his head was bare. He still had his fedora, but it was clutched to his chest like an old-time Southern gentleman bearing bad news.

He was accompanied by a short, portly police officer. As Ashlock began to speak, I was mesmerized by the view of his head unconcealed. There had been more than one bet going around that the hat was hiding a colossal bald spot. In reality, it had been hiding a pate covered in close-cropped brown curls with streaks of gray.

At that moment he was thrusting a crinkly piece of paper in my mom's face. "I have a warrant to search the women's locker room and all its lockers," Ashlock told her.

My mom turned toward the back office. "Gene," she croaked. *"Gene."*

"Please give us the keys and show us the way," Ashlock ordered.

Gene came out of his office, blinking and appearing confused. My mom walked up to him, showed him the paper, and whispered in his ear. Gene got it pretty quickly and went back into his office to retrieve his keys. Everyone headed for the women's locker room. Curious members walking in and out of the club were eyeing the cops, who made a big show of *not* noticing that every single human being in the lobby was focused on them. A bunch of us brazenly stayed in step with them. Mom and Lisa, who had appeared out of nowhere, fell in behind the police, and Evie and I brought up the rear. Patrick and Goran joined us when they saw our group traipsing through the lobby. Lucky sensed something was going on and slipped in with the crowd. Someone must have buzzed Nicholas down at the pool, because suddenly he was there. By then, there were probably a dozen of us.

My mom yelled the requisite, "Man in the house. Everyone decent?" We heard "All clear!" from a woman inside, and Detective Ashlock walked in, followed by the cop, followed by the rest of us. I, for one, could feel Nicky's tension. Lisa, apparently very forgiving, hooked her arm through his, holding it tight. Out of the corner of my eye I saw him wriggle away. I didn't think Lisa was going to date him in the end.

Ashlock took a step toward a block of lockers, and you

could feel everyone's minds working to recall who had lockers in that row. He took another step, and another, until he was standing in front of a row of three lockers, all in the top row: 127, 128, and 129. Lisa Denessen, my mom, and the lunch lady were their owners. The detective snapped on another pair of those dusty latex gloves. The cop shook open a plastic evidence bag, and Ashlock held his hand out to Gene, who gave him the master key. Ashlock slowly reached out toward the lockers—and then someone let out an almighty yell.

"*Hey!*" It was the lunch lady. "Don't! Stop this. These are our private things. You can't do this."

She was panting now, tendrils of her jet-black hair going wild. My mom said, "I'm afraid he can. Let's let him do his job. If we're not guilty, we have nothing to hide. Right?"

The detective reached out until the key was touching one of the three lockers. As he did, some of us gasped and some of us let out an involuntary *Oh!* Ashlock believed one among us was guilty, and we could all see which person's life was about to change.

Ashlock slid the key in, turned it, and unlocked number 127. *Lisa's locker.* Ashlock opened it, and Lisa's mirror, her collection of lipsticks, her poster of Joe Manganiello, and worst of all, a pair of granny underwear, were on show.

The detective was focused on his job, even when Lisa screamed, "*No!*" The cop held her back as Ashlock riffled through her things. "What are you doing? Leave my things alone. *Please* don't . . ."

Lisa squeezed Nicholas again but Nicholas again ripped his arm from hers. Guilty until proven innocent, I guessed. The detective used a pen from his jacket pocket to lift up a gray sweatshirt Lisa wore a lot. Underneath that was something shiny. Ashlock let the sweatshirt drop to the floor, then stuck his pen into the locker and gently pulled out a gold necklace. Those pink sapphire eyes flashed, and for one brief moment I thought I saw Annabel's soul in them.

"It can't be," my mom breathed. "How?"

She turned to Lisa questioningly. Lisa had started crying. "I don't know how that got there. Who's doing this to me?"

Nicholas turned to her with a look of realization, and then of hatred. "You" is all he said, his voice gravelly. *"You."*

I was afraid someone was going to have to restrain him, but Nicholas shook his head and stalked out. Ashlock turned to Lisa. "This," he said, "is the necklace Annabel Harper *never* took off. Yet it wasn't on her when she was found. We couldn't locate it—until now."

He let it fall gently into the plastic evidence bag the cop was holding. To give him credit, Ashlock wasn't crowing or gloating or putting on any airs. He was doing his job.

"Lisa Denessen, you are under arrest for the murder of Annabel Harper."

The cop took out his cuffs and grabbed her arm, rather roughly I thought, and brought her arms behind her back as Ashlock was saying, "You have the right to remain silent . . ."

"But I didn't kill her," Lisa said through her tears.

My mom, choked up, said, "I know you were jealous of her, but why do this? Why kill an innocent girl, Lisa? You've thrown your life away."

Lisa looked around at everyone and found no supporters among us. She opened her mouth, but no sound came out. She closed it, then closed her eyes, and I realized she'd given up. I felt sorry for her, I really did. My mom added, "Someone should call her parents."

Patrick was saying, "No way, no way, no way," over and over and, finally, Evie started crying. She began to sniffle, then cry, then bawl, and then she ran out before Ashlock finished talking about Lisa's rights, and I followed her. She went to that back room and cried and cried and cried until she couldn't cry anymore.

Before

Will and Evie didn't bump into each other much outside of their scheduled lessons, given his crazy schedule and her penchant for hiding. But one day she ran into him in the lunch line, and I watched her hand shaking as she held her plate with turkey on rye, a leaf of romaine poking out of the sandwich.

"What's up, Evie?" Will said. He was distracted, rushed, hungry.

Evie was mortified to be caught eating. "I know I shouldn't really have this ... It's too much ... I was getting it for someone else," Evie lied. "Up at the desk."

She looked down, turning red, embarrassed, *yada yada yada*. Will didn't even notice her preteen angst. He was too interested in feeding his body. He took a loud bite of carrot as he scanned the table, probably wondering if he could get away with spearing an entire pound of roast beef. That man was a walking calorie furnace.

"You need to eat, Evie," he said, reaching out to fork a

rubbery slice of ham. "You need your protein. I don't want to see you starving yourself." He looked at her briefly, politely, and some might say cluelessly, then continued making his sandwich. Evie was so used to Lucky telling her she actually didn't need to eat that she almost fell over. I couldn't wipe the grin off my face. *You go, Will Temple. You go, my friend.*

Evie turned sideways, brought her racket back, and smashed a forehand crosscourt. She hit it so deep it looked like it was going to fly out of bounds, but Evie's fierce topspin pulled it back in and it hit the intersection of the baseline and the sideline with such an angle that, if there had been an opponent on the other side, it would have zinged away from her.

Evie's face lit up. It was a wicked good shot. Will, who was feeding her balls from the service box on the opposite side, looked behind him, then back at Evie.

"Do you know what was wrong with that one?"

"No," she said flatly. "It was exactly what you've told me to do—deep and hard and right on the line."

"Exactly."

Evie sighed loudly. I knew her well; she was frustrated with Will's odd grip. For every killer forehand she hit, she'd hit another one flying off or plopping like a rock into the net.

"I'll tell you what was wrong with it. It hit the line," Will said. "Never aim for the lines."

"Why not?" Evie had her racket out in front of her, ready for more forehands.

"Because if you aim for the lines, you're not giving yourself any room for error. You're going to miss too much of the time. Aim for a foot inside the line. If you do hit the line, it means your aim was off."

He fed her another ball, and Evie whaled on it and hit it past the baseline. Will raised his eyebrows at her. She pretended she didn't see his expression. He fed her a few more, and some shots looked great, but more often than not, the ball would be too topspinny and not hard enough so it landed short, or it would fly into kingdom come. Evie had progressed like the star I knew she was, but I think she felt she was struggling to learn the game, which was to be expected considering she'd never played a sport in her life.

"At some point you'll be taught by someone else during drills or clinics or camp. They'll try to change your grip. Ignore them," he'd ordered her from day one. "They'll tell you your grip is only good for clay court players. Slow, plodding players who can only hit high moonballs until they put their opponent to sleep. They're wrong."

To prove his point, he'd have her feed him a low, hard passing shot to his forehand and he would whip under it and scoop the ball up, aiming it over the net where it kicked up with pace on the other side.

"*See?* Did you see that? Of course you can get under the ball with this grip. And you can hit it much harder when you do."

One of the most fun things about Will was his passion. And also the way he yelled to Evie with just the slightest flavor of a Boston accent when he was teaching her, like when he got really excited: *Come owan, Evie. Try it again. Yoa almost thee-ah.*

At the end of the lesson about aiming for the lines, Evie was frowning as she walked to the center post, and she kept frowning as she slipped her Volcano X into its case.

"Your forehand is coming along nicely," Will said, zipping his own stuff in his bag.

I thought again how lucky Evie was to have him. The guy now had a full eight hours of coaching elites ahead of him.

"I guess," Evie said. "I can't seem to get that grip."

"What are you talking about? You're doing great. It's going to take time. It'll come."

He smiled briefly at her and together they started the walk across four courts to get back inside the club. "Let's focus on what's going well. Like your serve. Not many people your age can hit it as hard as you. Someday you could have one of the most powerful serves in your age group in New England."

"Okay," she said, mostly to herself. "I know I can do it. I *know* I can."

I knew then that she, too, had been reminded of what an amazing thing it was to have Will coaching her. "Thatta girl." He smiled, waving goodbye in the café area as he bounded up to the lobby to start his day.

Even Evie's bad days on the court were better than our previous life. Our story changed when Will Temple came on the scene, our days no longer made up of slinking through the lobby so Evie wasn't noticed, or killing time in the back room she'd turned into a dungeon. Now the day was broken into segments of how Evie could do better at her training. Could she find time to do the stationary bike? Could she and I get Harmony to let us hang out at the pool to catch some rays, if we promised to stay on the lawn? And when could she slip onto the court to practice her serve? She'd found the perfect hiding place for her Volcano X, stashed against the back wall behind boxes of pineapple juice that had cobwebs on them. It was the best time ever.

After

I wanted to jump up and down with excitement at our luck. A major revelation was walking right toward us—you could feel it. Evie, my mom, and I were having lunch and catching some rays out on the lush lawn by the pool, reflecting on how weird it was that Lisa wasn't here today because she was, as far as we knew, still in jail, when Gene circled through the revolving door and approached us.

"We need to talk," he said to my mom, nervously clasping his hands in front of him. She tilted her head toward me and Evie, and Gene said, "They can stay. No more secrets."

A glob of tuna plopped out of Mom's sandwich and fell onto the grass, and as she picked it out, Gene sat down on a corner of her quilted blanket.

"Lisa is innocent," he pronounced. Evie almost choked on her tuna.

"How could you possibly know that?" Mom grew alarmed and laid her sandwich back in its Saran wrap.

"Because I'm her alibi," Gene said. "And it's time I cleared this up."

My mom put both her hands up, as if to stop an assault. "Whoa. *What?*"

Gene took a deep breath. "I was with Lisa the night Annabel died. She came to my house around midnight, desperate to talk. What was I supposed to do? She was crying. I couldn't turn her away. She was upset about school, her future, her life. She was so insecure and was always comparing herself to Annabel. It was so late, I couldn't send her home. She crashed on my living room sofa bed. She has no one else to go to for guidance. You know what her parents are like."

Yes, we all knew. It wasn't like they beat her or anything, but apparently they liked to drink a *lot* even when she was a little kid. Gene had no kids of his own, and he'd always let the teenagers around here know they could trust him if they ever needed help—and they did.

"So how do you know she didn't sneak out?"

"Because," Gene revealed, "we were up talking until three a.m., after Annabel was killed. There was no way. Look, Beth—the girl's lost. She has brains and ambition, but no direction. I wasn't going to turn my back on her."

"Okay," Mom said crisply. "I guess we were wrong about Lisa. But why didn't she say all this when she was arrested? She could've avoided this whole mess entirely."

"Because," Gene replied, "she's more decent than any of you give her credit for. She was worried how it would make me look." He looked down. "I should have spoken up right away."

My mom, who had calmed down some, said, "I have to admit I'm relieved. I heard her screaming at Annabel the night she died and thought . . . Well, it was a pretty awful fight."

Evie and I had kept quiet as Gene confessed everything. "So now you know," he said. "Someone else got there after Lisa left." And off he went to get Lisa off the hook. I just hoped he didn't end up in jail himself for his lies of omission.

Before

The court surface was still cold early in the morning, but the sunshine was warming me up as I sat on the sidelines and watched Evie train. She was doing side-to-sides. Will would feed her a forehand, then a quick backhand, then a forehand, and so on. The ball rolled off her racket as she moved in a smooth rhythm: *Smack, run, shuffle, smack, run, shuffle.*

Evie was getting *good*, and she was moving like a real tennis player, lighter on her feet, more confident. It took me a minute to identify the most important difference of all today, though. She was wearing shorts! Her oversize pink shirt looked cute now that it was paired with her new white stretchy Champion shorts. Her legs were suddenly tanned, and they were smooth and shapely. She looked great.

Will called time on the side-to-sides, and Evie nodded and walked to meet him at the net, wiping her brow with her shirtsleeve, tucking her racket under her arm. She had blond highlights from the sun, clear eyes, and a straighter posture. She was standing taller than ever.

He started to rewrap his sweat-absorbing grip tape, and as he did, he told her, "Your backhand is looking great. You're going to be a real threat, you know."

Evie—I could see her mind working—wanted to shrug it off but fought the instinct to turn his compliment into a negative.

"Thanks," she said. "It feels pretty good."

Will finished wrapping and secured the velvety tape. He checked his watch.

"We've got five more minutes," he said. "Let's finish up with some sprints."

Evie nodded and laid her racket down next to his. I knew this moment was coming, but I didn't know if Evie could handle it. She'd seen the campers do it many times. She and Will ran the lines for five full minutes, each moving at their own pace, with Evie holding her own as she managed to keep going no matter how bad she wanted to quit, even once when I caught her gagging from the exertion. She sucked it up and kept running. So Evie wasn't the skinniest person ever, and she wasn't the fastest kid on the block, but all of a sudden she was fit and healthy and awake, and to me that made things pretty darn perfect.

After

Lisa came back to work the day after Gene confessed everything to Detective Ashlock. One would think being accused of murder would be horrifying. For Lisa, though, it seemed to be a fun way to get more attention. She sashayed into the club at nine in the morning in her workout gear and what looked like professionally blown-out hair. She grinned at us like nothing had ever happened. She stood at the front desk and was approached by one person after another, all of whom fawned over her and proclaimed some form of the phrase *I knew you were innocent the whole time . . .*

Evie and I watched this homecoming from behind the desk with my mom, who I knew felt absolutely terrible about what Lisa had gone through. But I also suspected she'd secretly hoped Lisa might learn something, too, maybe a modicum of humility or subtlety. No such luck. At one point we heard Lisa say, "Detective Ashlock had to practically *grovel* when he let me out. He gave me his phone number and told me to call him *anytime* if I thought of anyone who could have planted the necklace in my locker."

My mom listened to this and said to Lisa, "It's a shame you were caught up in this, Lisa. But let's not celebrate quite yet. If it wasn't you, then the killer is still walking around free." That quieted everyone down real quick.

Later that day, I was alone in the lobby when Evie plopped down next to me on the sofa. She whispered a secret meant only for me: *Ashlock's back.*

I sprang up off the sofa. *What now?* We walked at a normal speed toward the club's entrance; I had to force myself not to run. As we rounded the corner and caught sight of the great granite reception desk that was the heart of our club, I stopped short. Ashlock was here, all right. He was talking to my mom. They were standing facing each other, whispering, at the far end of the desk. Evie frowned at me, like, *When did they become pals?* I had no clue. I tried but couldn't hear a single word they were saying. We saw Ashlock hand my mom a mysterious manila envelope. I had to know more. I inched closer to the desk, one step at a time, to try to hear something. Evie followed, but we couldn't get any closer without being noticed.

I felt the same foreboding chill I'd been feeling for a while now, right down to my toes. My mom put her palm to her forehead as if to self-soothe and kept it there for several moments. Then she reached out to touch Ashlock's shoulder. He nodded as if to say, *You're welcome for this mysterious manila envelope.*

She removed her hand and he backed away, so we could at least hear his parting words. "When you're ready," Ashlock said to my mom, "read it. Then destroy it, because I'm breaking a lot of rules doing this."

"Then why are you?" Mom asked. The envelope shook in her hand.

Ashlock didn't reply. He tipped his hat to my mom and walked away, so Evie and I didn't get the chance to ask him about the case, about our ongoing safety fears, or about the necklace's reappearing act. On top of that, we now had a new conundrum: What had he given to my mom, and why did she look like she'd seen a ghost? I decided to stick close to her for the day. I had to know what was up.

A couple of hours later, Gene emerged from his office and my mom said to me, "Keep an eye on the desk, Chels."

Me? Watch the desk? Did she think I was an idiot? She grabbed Gene for a quiet chat, and I could clearly see her clutching the manila envelope Ashlock had given her.

"Let's talk in my office," he said. I faked like I was gonna stay put, but I waited until Mom and Gene were in his office with the door shut and went to listen.

"I can't do this," my mom was saying. "Please, keep it for me."

I heard low talking from Gene, then sniffling from her and some papers shuffling.

"What? What is it?" my mom asked.

I heard Gene say, "It seems to be a lot of what we already know, Beth. She'd managed to get away and made it to a neighbor's house nearly a mile away, where she collapsed on their porch. The first responders were shocked she was even alive, let alone walked a mile on a fractured ankle and that wrecked knee."

There was another long pause, and now I knew he had to be reading from pages that my mom couldn't bear to read. This was why Ashlock had looked at me oddly a few times. He *did* know about my case. That manila envelope, I knew now, contained the police report they'd never shown my mom, because the fact she'd adopted me "didn't give her the right to confidential police files." That's what she'd been told every time she'd tried to learn my full story. The thing about my case, famous as it was, was there was only so much information the police made public. The rest was confidential.

"Chelsea was in shock when they found her," Gene was saying, his voice cracking. "She was malnourished and de-hydrated. Clumps of her"—another clearing of the throat—"of her hair were observed to have fallen out or been pulled out in patches."

Then it sounded like he was reading straight from the report: "'Upon inspection of the property, authorities found several nooses hanging from trees, bloodied tools including pliers, bloody bandages, and . . . a cage . . .'"

"Pliers? A noose? A cage?" My mom repeated his every

word. "Oh, God. No. No more. I don't want to know any more. As long as she doesn't remember, it'll be okay."

Gene said something quietly that sounded like, "I'll cough on the font," which maybe, on second thought, was actually, "I'll stop if you want."

I guess it should have been a horrible moment for me, but hearing my mom and Gene talking about it made me feel safer, maybe because letting the light shine on the horror of my past life took away some of its power. Seeing or smelling things that reminded me of that time was a different story, but just hearing about it seemed to make the evil more impotent than ever.

"Beth," Gene said. "There's more. It's pretty huge. But I think if you face it head-on, it will help you and Chelsea move on for good."

My mom must have bravely read the part he was referring to because things went deadly quiet, and then she gasped loudly and proclaimed, "That—*that*—oh, there are no words for what that man is. You're wrong, Gene. This isn't over, not by a long shot."

Gene was talking again but I could barely hear him, and anyway I'd had enough. I already knew what had happened to me. Whatever this shocking new revelation was, it would be dealt with in due time. I got to my feet and walked slowly away to find Evie.

After

Evie was looking fit and healthy now, and she was tanned, with glints of sun-infused highlights in her silky hair, and her bangs had grown just long enough that she was forced to clip them back with a barrette so her eyes were finally exposed. Celia had told her she looked a little like Taylor Swift, with those delicate features and great skin, and I had to agree. All in all, Evie, along with the rest of us, had managed to get on with things since Annabel's death. That's not to say we weren't grieving and uneasy about a killer being at large, but we were making do.

Still, Evie could *not* catch a break. Tad Chadwick was tormenting her again in front of everyone in the lobby when she made the mistake of stopping by the TV to see "Summer Cool" sung live on *The Brenda Lampley Show*. Tad, munching on ham on white, was asking her what she had on tap for the afternoon: *Sitting, or more sitting? When will you find time to feed your face? Ha-ha-ha*. In front of the counselors he wouldn't call her his usual list of names, but he could still pick on her. I really wanted to teach him a lesson, but Will saved me the trouble.

"That's enough," Will commanded. "You're here to play tennis." He took a large bite of his turkey sandwich, and an uncooperative piece of lettuce tumbled down his chin.

"But she's always hanging around here and she doesn't *do anything*," Tad sniped, defying Will with the confidence of a kid whose life was already laid out for him on a red carpet. A classmate of Evie's eating lunch with Serene guffawed; Serene shot the classmate a warning look.

Will finished chewing his last bite with great gusto. "Mr. Chadwick," he said. "I'll tell you what. Let's wipe that smirk off your face. Since we can't seem to shut you up, I'm going to make a deal with you."

Now Tad was a bit shaky; having Will's complete attention was intimidating, whether he shone down his approval or shot through you with his laser of disdain. The lobby had fallen silent. Tad was turning red and focusing on his lunch.

Will stood up. "You," he said, jabbing his index finger toward Tad and then toward Court 1, "are going to go one set against Evie Clement."

I think I saw Evie dry heave.

Tad just looked utterly confused. "One set of what?"

"Of *tennis*, you blithering buffoon," Will snapped. "I'm offering you a chance to play a set against her. But if you lose, you will not only apologize to her, you will be her best friend for what's left of the summer. If she wants you to fetch her some juice, you'll say 'Grape or cranberry?' If she tells you to go away, you get outta her face."

Tad's smirk had crept back. "You've got to be kidding."

Will crossed his arms, and he and his bulging biceps got in Tad's space. He jerked his chin toward Court 1. "Do I look like I'm kidding?" He did not.

Tad let out one sharp little cackle: *Ha*. But no one else joined in and he quieted abruptly. They were fascinated by what the heck Will had to do with Evie, and why he was sending this poor lamb out to slaughter. It was bizarre to the point where Celia stood up and quietly made her way to Will's side. She whispered something in his ear and Will patted her on the arm. I saw him mouth something like, *It's okay, it's fine. Trust me.* Celia paused and glanced over at Evie, who was standing frozen. Celia still wasn't convinced, and stayed put next to Will. Serene, on the other hand, had a strangely calm look on her face. Like maybe she wasn't so shocked by this turn of events.

Tad was getting more nervous. "How much do I have to win by? I have to, like, beat her 6–0, or what?"

"You have to *win*, Tad," Will said as if he were talking to a simpleton. "Like with any opponent. That's the rule in tennis."

Tad's little adolescent brain was running at full speed, trying to figure out what the catch was. "What do I get if I win?"

"All the praise and glory you deserve."

251

Tad managed an even snottier expression than he normally mustered. "No problem."

Word spread quickly, and before Evie even had her racket in hand, the lobby had filled up. Everyone knew Tad because he was here all summer, every summer, and most people couldn't stand the little brat.

Speaking of Evie, she'd found her way behind the front desk and was crouched down, her eyes scared like a trapped mouse. I personally thought Will might have gone a bit overboard. Evie's first match ever—against her biggest nemesis? On *Court 1*? I felt a wisp of doom, but then blew it away. She was my friend. I had faith in her.

Will found us behind the desk. "Let's go," he said to her.

Evie slowly rose, her pink Volcano X in hand, and followed him to the door to Court 1. I felt someone behind us, and the person leaned past me and grabbed Evie by the shoulder. We both turned and saw Goran standing there in all his tennis god–like splendor. He broke into a grin and squeezed Evie's shoulder.

"Go get him," Goran said. "You've got ten times the talent of that little dork. Remember that—and keep your eye on the ball." And he was off.

"You've got this, kid," Will said to Evie. "Remember what we've been practicing. Keep that grip firm and snap your wrist on your serve—and *keep your feet moving*. His backhand is his weak spot, so *don't* hit to his forehand. Don't let him

252

rattle you. Don't double fault. And remember—don't aim for the lines. Got it?"

Evie was in shock. Will added quickly, "Oh, um—you know how to score, right? You know the rules?" She nodded. You watch the elites long enough, you figure it out.

I don't know how she found the strength to accept this challenge. But then again, maybe her path to courage started with Will Temple; he'd shown her the way, removed the brambles, and laid the bridges. I hoped Evie remembered while she was quaking in her sneakers that Tad was no elite, and never would be. He played tennis because his rich parents wanted him kept busy. Tad wasn't a *tennis player*. Of course, Evie's measly one month of training with Will would now be pitted against tens of thousands of dollars' worth of coaching. I stayed behind until Evie and I were alone. Her eyes met mine, and I tried to channel my faith and confidence to her. She leaned down and hugged me tight.

Then she rose up, and I watched her walk out into the hall-way toward Court 1, head held high, until she disappeared behind the curtain.

After

Tad walked to the net, put the tip of his racket on the court, spun it, and let it fall. Evie won the spin and opted for him to serve. Tad walked back to the baseline and I saw it in his eyes for a brief second: he almost felt sorry for Evie. He bounced the ball a few times and let loose a pretty good first serve down the middle, which Evie managed to slam into the net. Tad was already waiting to serve again.

This time he hit his first serve long, and Evie called it out. His second serve was pretty lame, and Evie ran around her backhand and whacked a forehand to Tad's backhand. Her shot sprayed a foot wide of the sideline, and Tad didn't even move for it. He stepped quickly to the baseline to serve, which was what tennis coaches called rushing. In 99 percent of cases in amateur tennis, rushing is due to poor mental conditioning.

I closed my eyes and prayed, but Evie lost the first game 40–love without a single rally. They switched sides, and Tad gave a semi-grin to his friends through the window that said something like, *It'll be over soon, but I can't gloat because it's too pathetic*. Meanwhile, there was murmuring in the lobby about how Evie could even hit the ball, let alone serve. She moved to the baseline, evening out her racket strings with her fingernails like the pros did.

Tad took his place near the service line. Evie took time to stare at her racket as if it held the answer to unlocking the win. *Good one, Evie*, I thought. Tad didn't like her setting the pace; he was already jumpy as he waited for her serve. She was controlling things now. She finally served, and snapped her wrist as Will had commanded—so much so that the ball hit the court on her side before it even got to the net.

Even so, Patrick, leaning forward with elbows on his knees and mouth agape, said, "Look at her *move*." He glanced up at Will. "She looks like a tennis player. Who knew?"

So far, Will had been unperturbed by the *oof* noises the crowd was making every time Evie made a humiliating error. He stood twelve inches from the glass, watching without emotion. I was standing next to him with my face pressed against the glass, feeding her my energy. I knew Will's philosophy: it usually took a few games for players to warm up and lose the jitters. He wasn't going to worry. Yet.

Evie's second serve was a cream puff. Tad stepped in and whaled on it—so hard, in fact, that it would've flown halfway to Cleveland if the back curtain hadn't stopped it. Evie looked shocked, then happy. She glanced up at Will, who gave her a curt, almost imperceptible nod. She stepped to the other side of the service line and nailed a first serve deep in the box. Tad took a swing with his backhand, nailing it cross-court to hers; Evie didn't get it back. A few more points later, Evie was down 3–0 and they were changing sides again.

Serene said quietly to Celia, "Holy cow. Look how much weight she's lost. I didn't even notice before now."

I was watching her nail a serve down the line that Tad couldn't touch. The first ace of her life, and Evie looked as startled as anyone. I caught Will making a subtle fist. Then we had some rallies, with Evie scrambling to return Tad's shots, scooping under the ball and whipping it up with killer topspin. Goran threw a glance to Will.

Then stuff really started to happen. The next three points got everyone riled up. There was a cracking crosscourt forehand, three first serves in, a crafty defensive lob hit off an approach shot. They were great points. Unfortunately, Evie lost every one of them.

It was suddenly 4–0. Evie had little chance of beating Tad now, not when she'd never played a set in her life, but she was fighting. Tad, all knobby knees and bored arrogance, wiped his entirely dry brow with his wristband before letting loose on his first serve. It went in, hard, straight to Evie's forehand. She danced over to the ball, brought her racket back, and hit a shot down the line to his backhand. Tad glared at the spot as if wanting to call it out, but everyone knew it was well on the line and Evie ignored him and waited for his next serve. He shook his head and continued glaring.

Tad's pal Marcus said, "What's his problem? That was clearly in."

Tad proceeded to miss his next first serve, after which he looked up to the heavens and mouthed something to the effect of, *Why, God, why?* but he quickly recovered and served up a softball: a big, fluffy cloud of yellow. Evie positioned herself to meet the ball at its crest, and slammed a backhand winner down the line. Will pumped his fist and met Evie's eyes. She was *treeing*, which in tennis means you cannot be stopped.

And what was happening to Tad? He'd gotten overconfident, and Evie had seized the moment, absorbed his momentum. Evie won that game. When it was her serve again she hit another ace. Next up, she slammed one down the middle, and while Tad was busy celebrating over his flat, hard return, Evie was running to the ball and relaying it back even harder so that a startled Tad actually ran *into* the ball and got hit in the ribs.

Evie won that game. I could see she immediately took to the feeling of victory, and won the following game 40–0. This wasn't an entirely uncommon turn of events in tennis. As the momentum shifts, there's a vacuum that can be created, and you can't stop the momentum of a comeback any more than you can stop gravity. I saw Will crack a proud smile. Tad was still winning, but now he was mad. I took stock of the lobby and it was clear Evie was a hero.

With the set tied at 4–4, Lucky turned up. He squinted and said nothing as he watched. No one bothered to fill him in; I guess most people figured he already knew. Patrick sensed his presence and asked, "Where've you been? She's killing it."

Lucky said, "Wow," but it was not a *wow* of excitement.

Evie was nailing every shot and was suddenly up 5–4. Patrick rose from his seat and stood next to Will. He put his hands flat on the glass, and started banging in a slow rhythm. Serene hopped up and fell in next to them, then Celia and Goran. Will unwound his arms and put his hands up. Everyone else, including Harmony, joined them until there was no more room at the window. The pounding created a rumbling thunder that reverberated through us.

Evie tuned us out to focus on winning, and stared Tad down as he stood frozen until the pounding stopped. When it did, she rocked back and let off a serve right into the box. Tad hit a shot that didn't turn out to be too bad, but Evie nailed her return out of his reach. It was clear Tad was getting really upset, so the crowd collectively ceased their thumping on the window for good. The score got to 5–4, 40–0, triple match point for Evie. A rally ensued, and she nailed a forehand crosscourt. Tad hit it back short, drawing her to the net. He hit a lob over her head. Will winced. An overhead smash for a beginner under pressure was a lot to ask.

Evie turned sideways, galloped backward with her head tilted up and her finger pointing at the ball like she was calling it to her, bent her elbow back, and smacked that ball down. She hit the ball so hard that it flew off the court far above

Tad's head, and he heroically jumped for it but he never had a chance; it disappeared behind the curtain. The entire lobby erupted in whoops and screams and more pounding on the window.

Evie's mouth dropped open, and she turned to look at us before breaking into a wide grin and giving a hop of excitement. She waved at me and then she looked to Will, who was shouting at the top of his lungs for her, *"Yes!"* and laughing and grinning and whooping.

On the other side of the court, Tad's face had crumpled. He was red and sweaty, and his swagger was gone, his shoulders slumped. When people noticed this, the cheering quieted significantly. He was just a kid. No one wanted to give him a nervous breakdown. The point had been made, and everyone knew it, and that was enough. Evie would agree with that, I knew. She was not mean-spirited. But she *was* scarred, and I could see she was bracing for abuse as she approached the net with a shy smile and held out her hand for the customary shake. Tad was still in the middle of the court, racket on the ground, head in his hands as if he'd lost in the finals of the US Open. He couldn't bring himself to look up at us, so when he finally took his hands away from his face, we saw something we'd never expected to see there: humility. I couldn't believe it, but Tad picked himself up and walked purposefully to Evie, held out his hand, and met her gaze as they shook.

We could read his lips easily: *Good game.*

They walked off the court, Evie first, Tad lagging behind. As we waited for them to make it back to the lobby, Lucky said, "Guess she has her old man's genes." He caught Will's eye. "She's good, isn't she?"

Everyone was out of their seats now, some moving on, some still talking about Evie and what the heck had happened to that girl, and our little group—Celia, Will, Patrick, Goran, Lucky, Serene, and my mom—ran down to the café area to meet Evie coming off the court.

Will nodded, watching for Evie to come out, and Lucky said, "How did this happen?"

Patrick looked sideways at Will. "I think Will's been secretly teaching her."

Lucky looked incredulous. "No way."

"Yes way." Patrick stretched and looked around at the campers in the lobby, ready to get the camp day back on track.

Will turned to face Lucky. "Evie said she wanted to be the one to tell you," he said flatly. "I'm sorry, but I thought you knew. I'm happy to answer any questions after you speak to her, but this is between you and your daughter."

Will walked off to greet his protégée, but turned back briefly. "Look," he said. Lucky raised his eyebrows. "You should know that your daughter's got it. She's a real talent."

Lucky, lost in thought, said nothing. Will clearly was not impressed with Evie's dad, but he kept his counsel and went to meet her. Evie never made it to the lobby because a bunch of campers had surrounded her and Tad in the café area. I

260

was down there like a shot, and I weaved my way through the crowd.

Celia was hugging her, asking with wonder, "Where'd you get that forehand?"

Goran raised his fist in triumph and shook it toward Evie, who I thought was going to explode with happiness. Will made his way to her, and she looked up at her coach with a proud smile. He clamped his hand on her right shoulder and squeezed. "You did good," he said. "Where in the world did you learn an overhead smash?" Will wasn't a hugger, so he slapped her awkwardly on the back, as if she were choking on a piece of steak, and then left to go back to work.

Evie saw me then. "I couldn't have done it without you, Chels," she cried, hugging me so tight it hurt. I didn't mind. As we jumped up and down together, we heard a sudden sharp, "Hey!" shouted from the top of the lobby steps. *"You!"*

What?

It was Serene. She was pointing at Evie and glaring. She had her hands on her hips, and was staring straight at us. "I never doubted you for a second, girl." She broke into a twinkly Serene grin and walked down the four steps toward us.

Evie, utterly confused, said, "You knew?"

Serene threw her head back and laughed, eyes shining. She leaned in and said in a stage whisper, "Where do you think your Volcano came from?" Then she winked. So *that's* where Will got such an expensive racket. *Wow.* It wouldn't have been easy for Serene to secure an extra free racket from the company that sponsored her, but she had done it. For Evie.

"Happy to help," Serene said. "I look forward to meeting you on the tennis court someday." She winked at us again and jogged off, tennis skirt swishing away.

As Evie absorbed everything, I could see my mom right behind her, and she didn't look thrilled. She clearly saw what I did: Evie's glow was fading. She was glancing around, swiveling and searching. But she couldn't find him. She couldn't find her father anywhere, couldn't find the spot where he was waiting to congratulate her.

When things died down, we skipped up to the front desk. We were riding a high knowing Tad would never bully her again, and even if he did, Evie had a new legion of supporters who would jump to her defense. She had Goran's attention, Serene's approval, Celia's affection, Will's respect.

"Hey, Beth," Evie said. "Have you seen Lucky?"

Mom gave her a grin and a thumbs-up for the game, then said, "No idea." *No idea.* He was MIA, and therefore not enveloping his daughter in the proudest hug a dad could ever give. Evie shrugged, but not like she didn't care. Like she was done with Lucky. It was an angry shrug. My mom looked bored flipping through the new *People*, which had a big picture of Prince Harry smiling out from the cover.

"Chels, stay with me awhile. I need some company," Mom said.

I couldn't really argue. I got my run of the place enough of the time, so I waved goodbye to Evie and stayed with my mom. Evie said she was going to go read. I should've known something was wrong, but after what had just happened I assumed she was okay. Even considering Lucky's latest offense. The tip-off should have been that she'd just had the most triumphant moment of her life, and she'd snapped back into a mood darker than I'd seen her in in a long time.

After

Evening came with a fresh wave of humidity and a hazy pink sky. Camp had let out at five o'clock as usual, and a few of the coaches braved the stifling heat to play some doubles on the outdoor courts. I was still stuck at the desk. I batted my eyelashes at my mom.

"Oh, go ahead," she said.

Off I went to find Evie. I checked the obvious places first, including the storage rooms, but no dice. I headed to the outdoor courts and saw Lucky swatting at a volley from Patrick, but no Evie. I was starting to get nervous. My instincts were going berserk, but it was a nonspecific kind of dread and I didn't know what to make of it. I ran to the front desk, where my mom was chatting with a member about the elliptical versus rowing machines.

"Nope. Evie's not here," my mom said when I approached. "I haven't seen her in a while, come to think of it."

I went to check behind the Dumpster, but I already knew in my gut what I would find: no Evie. I wanted to avoid alarming anyone, but something was off. Evie was missing, and while I had to consider that she had run away, I couldn't help thinking about this killer on the loose. The police seemed to be no closer to identifying Annabel's murderer, and if Evie had isolated herself as usual, she'd be an easy target for someone who wanted to attack young girls. I sprinted back out to the courts and ran right onto Court 6, where Celia was getting ready to serve. The four counselors looked at me like I was nuts as I stood in the middle of the court. Celia giggled and said, "Watch out—my serve's a killer!"

I walked up to Lucky, who glanced behind me, as if to look for his daughter. He stood up straight.

"What is it, Chels?"

The thing about Lucky was, he'd always counted on everyone else at the club to watch out for Evie. So even *he* knew that when the rest of us couldn't find her, something was wrong. He acted quickly when he saw me. He waved to Celia, Will, and Patrick with his racket and yelled to them, "I gotta go."

"What is it?" Patrick was jogging over to our side.

"Have you guys seen Evie recently?"

Patrick shrugged. "Not since after she wiped the floor with Tad."

"I'm going to go have a look around for her," Lucky said. "Carry on without me."

Will shook his head, and Celia's eyes were wide with worry. With Annabel's death still unsolved, no one was messing around. "We'll help. I'll take the back of the club," Will said. "Celia, why don't you hit the pool, and Patrick—check *everywhere*."

Patrick nodded, put his head down, and bounded away. We went our separate ways.

Ten minutes later, everyone met back at the front desk. My mom was concerned.

"You checked the convenience store down the street?" she asked, her voice a little shaky.

"I talked to the staff, Beth," Patrick said, shaking his head. "They haven't seen her."

Lucky cleared his throat. "Okay. We'd better call the police."

I actually had one more area to try. I had a feeling that maybe this was the one place Evie would go if she hit rock bottom; she'd observed once that it was a location *everyone saw but no one ever visited, a place where you could disappear.* Lucky saw me heading for the front door and said, "Beth, hold off for now. I think there might be one more special place Chelsea and Evie have that we haven't checked yet."

My mom took one look at me and nodded. "Okay, Chelsea, but if you guys don't find her this time, I'm calling the cops."

Lucky agreed and followed me out. We jogged across the parking lot. I kept going past the Dumpster, and Lucky stopped and looked ahead at the landfill in the distance.

"Really?" he said.

Yep. Really. It was a last-ditch idea, but no one seemed to have a better one. Together we ran across the weedy, dusty vacant lot between the landfill and the club, and easily hopped the halfhearted three-foot wire fence marking the boundary.

"Now what?" Lucky wiped sweat off his brow, smearing dust on his face as he did.

A mountain of garbage loomed in front of us. It looked surprisingly un-rubbish-like from here, more like a big dirt hill with a layer of junk sprinkled on it. Lucky looked up at the monolith and said, "I don't see her up there. Let's walk around it."

The landfill was closed, so it was Lucky and me alone in the dusk, walking around this place that, oddly, didn't smell very bad up close, scanning for Evie. Lucky froze on the dirt path at the base and pointed. He raced to a colorful patch of junk. I saw then what it was: four dirty fingers sticking out of the pile. He knelt down and frantically pulled everything away, and I joined him, desperate to see what was underneath.

After

Lucky let out a long breath and buried his head in his hands. "Thank you, God," he said, pulling out a latex glove that, because it was covered in grime and buried under all that junk, had looked like it could've been a twelve-year-old girl's fingers.

A gust of wind blew by then, and I looked toward the top of the dump, and then I knew where Evie was. Lucky stood up and followed me, and we picked our way up. Finally, on another, higher crest, we saw her. Evie was sitting on a filthy yellow couch cushion she'd found, surveying the town of St. Claire and the club below, hugging her knees.

Lucky said, "Hey, kid."

"Hello," Evie said coldly.

She wasn't surprised to see us; I guess she'd heard us scrabbling around in a panic. Lucky made his way to her and sat on some garbage. I stayed where I was, watching and listening. He stared off into the distance with her for a moment. It was pretty cool up here, actually, if you didn't mind the germs and gunk everywhere.

"I saw part of your match. You were incredible."

Evie hugged her knees harder and glared into the yonder. "Yeah? So where were you afterward? Even *Tad* congratulated me, but not you."

"Hey," he said, still trying to meet her eyes. "I looked for you, but you were surrounded by fans and I didn't want to interrupt that. Then I couldn't find you—"

"I was at the front desk, *Dad*."

Lucky took a loud breath in through his teeth. "Okay. I should have found you. It's not that I didn't want to, but . . . it was kind of a shock. I was surprised you hadn't told me about it."

She *tsked* in that way teenagers do when they are disgusted. "That shouldn't matter," she countered. "A normal father would be happy for me."

Lucky shook his head. "Hey, kiddo. I'm not sure I *want* you playing tennis. You should be focusing on school—"

"Please do *not* be a hypocrite," she said, finally meeting his eyes.

"It's not that," he insisted. "I've been there, kid. I *know* better. Putting everything you have into the game is a path to disappointment. They tell you how great you are, but when you're on tour fighting your guts out, and living in crappy motels trying to qualify for some lame tournament in Bangalore, you realize how hard it is. You're totally on your own."

Evie sighed and gesticulated dramatically. "But that's just *it*. Who cares about going pro? I want to play the game. Why can't you be happy for me?" She stuck her head back between her knees, so her next words were muffled. "Why can't you just be a normal father?"

Lucky rubbed his eyes with his palms and said nothing. Evie popped up for air and added for good measure, "My friend was murdered this summer. Killed. Annabel—she was really nice, Dad. She was my friend. Do you even care?"

Lucky, ill equipped for fatherhood at even the most basic level, appeared bewildered as she continued. "And don't even get me started on you constantly leaving me here! I'm always making excuses for you, and it's *so* humiliating. I don't want to hang around here anymore. I've had it."

"Look, honey," he said, tilting his head down to try to meet her eyes. "I know I've done a lot of things wrong. I'm not the best parent. But I'm doing the best I can. When your mother left—"

"Whoa. Don't blame *her*." Evie lifted her head and sniffed. "At least she's honest. She didn't want to be a mother in the first place. Dads are supposed to *protect* their daughters. A dad is supposed to tell the world that if anyone messes with his daughter, he'll step in. But you just forget me and ignore me. I bet you wouldn't even save me if I was drowning."

Lucky looked like he'd been slapped. "You really believe that?"

I'm not sure she did, but she had a point. Still, right now he looked genuinely pained.

"I was trying to give you some freedom," he said, his brow furrowed. "When I was a teenager, my parents didn't let me do *anything*. They never trusted me, gave me a crazy curfew, didn't want me dating girls or going to parties. And you know what happened?"

"What?" Evie asked.

"I rebelled—I only wanted to sneak out and go to parties. My parents didn't trust me, so I said, *Whatever. I have no reason to try to please them because they already think so little of me.* I wanted you to know that I trusted you to be a good person and to behave yourself. How could you find out who you really are with me bearing down on you?"

Evie tried to process that, and despite its heartfelt intention, I knew it wasn't quite good enough. "But—"

"I know," Lucky interrupted, putting his arm around her shoulders with a rueful smile. "There's such a thing as going too far the other way. I get it now. You've been neglected, sweet Evie, and I haven't meant to do it. I really haven't."

Silent tears rolled down my friend's face.

Lucky cleared his throat. "Your mom popped up here from New York, told me I had a child, and it was like—it was a shock. I was so happy."

Evie looked up at him in genuine surprise. "You *were*?"

The tanned, leathery creases around Lucky's eyes crinkled

up as he said, "Of course, Evie! I loved you the minute I saw you."

I don't think Evie or I or anyone around here really thought that was the case. Good old Lucky. He was so flawed, but he officially had a heart and that was a start, at least. He took a good look at his daughter and said, "What do you say we both try to do better, and see if we can have the best year ever?"

Evie smiled and sent me a sidelong glance. "What about the tennis?" she asked.

"What about it? I don't need Will Temple to tell me my daughter's a star. It's in the genes." He winked and smiled. "Look, kid. I'll help you any way I can, and you and I can play some in the winter, too. We'll work something out. I promise. Now, I've got a rat nibbling on my butt, so can we please go back inside?"

Evie giggled, and together we made our way down, the three of us helping one another as we went so none of us fell.

After

Evie was staring into space. She'd gone through all the stages: fury, impatience, sadness, boredom, and back to anger. Why? Because Lucky had really done it this time and we were stuck with the world's most annoying front desk staffer. Things had started to get better between him and Evie, and he'd taken her with the gang a couple of nights ago to see *Take Me Out*, the white-hot movie everyone would be talking about when school started. Their new deal was to alternate R-rated movies with PG flicks that she could go to, and he'd vowed to never leave her stranded again when they had plans together.

Tonight the gang had gone to see the R-rated *Iron Fisted*, so Evie had gamely agreed to stay at the club and hang out with me. Harmony was lifeguarding, and we had fun sitting with him at the pool when the sun set and the club got quieter. Lucky was supposed to be back by nine thirty to pick up Evie, but when Harmony closed the pool at ten they still hadn't returned. "I can't leave you guys," he said to us, "obviously. But, hmm . . . I do have a date."

Because the front desk staffer wouldn't close the club until eleven, we assured Harmony we'd be fine with her. We called Lucky's cell over and over. Evie grumbled, "He always forgets to pay his phone bill. It's not surprising we can't get through."

The movie had ended long ago. The court lights had been turned off and the members were long gone. It got later, and still Lucky hadn't come. At precisely ten fifty-nine, Margee, the desk staffer, glanced at the clock on the back wall and shrugged. "I've gotta close up," she said. "I need my beauty sleep." Evie appeared alarmed and Margee, who had spent a lot of time hiding in the women's locker room (we suspected she was chattering on social media), added, "You know, I can't be responsible for your parents being late. That's not on me. You both practically live here anyway. You'll be fine!"

Really? Being left alone in a sprawling, dark, empty building with no grownup in sight and a killer on the loose was kind of a big deal. And now that the police were back to square one with Annabel's murder, we were edgier than ever. It suddenly occurred to me that in our current situation we were equally vulnerable whether this psycho was a club regular or a random maniac roaming the St. Claire area. We sat at the desk, frozen. The eerie yellow parking lot lights shone through the club's glass front door with a muted glow. It was disconcerting to see more outside than we could inside; the lobby behind us was an endless pit of black tar we couldn't see through for the life of us. You can't simply flip on a light in a place like this. There's a massive panel of switches. Every light is connected to another, and some of them take fifteen minutes to come to life. So we made do with the little desk lamp and waited.

"Do you believe in ghosts, Chelsea?" Evie asked, her voice struggling to be nonchalant, tinged with bravado.

As it happened, I did believe in ghosts because I saw them sometimes and I couldn't always tell if they were good ghosts or bad ghosts. But that is another story. For tonight, as I stared into the darkness of the lobby and the tennis courts, everything just felt wrong. As I was thinking this, from out of nowhere came an alarming bright light through the glass doors. We heard a *thud* in the distance, but I couldn't tell what it was. Somehow, it felt more frightening being a sitting duck inside that club than being outside in the semi-lit, wide-open world. Evie hopped off her stool and grabbed the heaviest racket she could find in the loaner bin under the reception desk. She took a practice swing and nodded to herself.

"Stay close, Chels. I'm sure it's nothing, but we should check it out."

We headed outside, where it was immediately apparent where the light was coming from. We moved stealthily toward the pool area, which jutted off the main building to the right, tiptoeing along. The pool lights were on full blast. We stood at the gate, pausing to listen for any movement. Evie put her finger to her lips and we waited. After a few seconds, we heard a voice behind the fence.

"Why, Annabel? Why did you leave me? *Whyyyyyyy?*"

It was a male voice, visceral and hysterical. I couldn't for the life of me recognize it. Evie mouthed, "I'm going to see who it is."

The latch had already been undone by whomever was in there, so Evie took hold of the handle and gently swung the wooden gate open a few inches. She peeked inside and I scrunched down for a look, so both our faces were poking through, one on top of the other.

Oh, God. Nicholas Harper was kneeling on the lawn by the back fence, facedown on the grass right where Annabel's body was found, crying, "Come back, Annabel. I didn't mean it . . . Please . . . I'd give anything to see you one last time . . . We're forever young . . ."

Hearing Nicholas's masculine voice morphed into this shrill falsetto curdled my blood. Evie looked stricken. This uncomfortable emotional scene was about as appetizing to us as a haunted tennis club, so we froze and looked at each other: *Do we back off or let him know we're here and try to comfort him?*

"Oh, Annabel," he was saying over and over. *Annabel . . . Annabel . . . Annabel.*

Poor Nicholas. It didn't look like he'd be recovering from his sister's death anytime soon. We heard a few sobs, and then he was babbling again. Evie and I exchanged horrified glances. Inevitably, it was at that moment that something went wrong. The wooden gate got caught in a gust of wind and the door, like a great wooden sail, blew out of Evie's grasp and banged against the fence. Nicholas looked up, startled at first, still in that strange position, his head turned sideways toward us, cheek pressed into the grass. And then—well, then I saw it in his eyes. His face changed from sobbing and surprised to a bitter glare. He narrowed his eyes and scrunched up his face in one great realization, like he'd just identified the cause of all his problems.

He sprang to his feet and gestured to us awkwardly. "Come in," he said, his voice oddly syrupy. His eyes were puffy and bloodshot. I felt Evie shiver next to me.

"What are you girls doing here so late, huh? Come on in. Don't be afraid."

He saw we still weren't moving and he cocked his head. He looked at Evie; Evie looked at him. Then Nicholas dropped the pretense. The three of us knew we weren't here for a pool party, that nothing about this scene was normal. He walked across the deck to the lifeguard bench, opened it, and removed something we couldn't see from thirty feet away.

While he was doing this, Evie had begun to back away slowly like she'd encountered a wild animal in its natural habitat. But I didn't. I moved laterally until I was standing between her and Nicholas. Evie backed away a little more. We watched Nicholas come toward us. He was wearing jeans and a white T-shirt, his biceps like little hills rising up from the joints of his arms and back down before his shoulders, his abs rippling through the white tee under the bright lights. At the end of summer, his tan was a part of him now, every bit

277

of visible skin a deep brown, with a tinge of pink at the tip of his nose. His hair was too long. His blond curls, usually tamed by a short cut, were wild and out of control, like he was.

That much I could see now. Because he was pointing a gun at us.

After

Evie gasped and reached out to squeeze my shoulder. My adrenaline was pumping, and I held my ground as Nicholas approached us. I could see his fly was half-open, and it looked to me like his trendy jeans were missing a button. I knew, I just knew, that Nicholas's missing button had to be the same one Ashlock had found at the pool that day. Suddenly, it all made sense. I could hear Evie's breathing above the frenzied crickets. We were in the parking lot now, out of the pool area, standing under the glow of the streetlights.

"You have to understand," Nicholas said slowly, gesturing with the gun as he spoke, "that I never meant to do it. You have to understand that it was an accident."

Evie croaked, "But how?"

"How?" He smiled maniacally. "How? Because of that greasy Russian, that's how. If it hadn't been for him trying to hurt my sister, none of this would've happened."

Goran. I think we both gauged it was best not to ask questions, so we let him talk. He started pacing. Evie still had the racket in her hand, but now it didn't seem like much of a weapon. "I—I won't tell anyone, I promise, Nicholas. It's none of my business. No one will believe me, anyway."

Nicholas ignored her. "I was only trying to keep her from getting hurt. She didn't know what that—that—*person* was really like. Who he really is. I told her she was too good for him but she was like, 'You don't know him. He's not like that.'" He growled that last part. "She didn't *listen*. She was stubborn, and she kept talking about how they were in love and if I got to know him we could be friends. *Please*." He was pacing frantically.

He stopped again and faced us squarely. "I was supposed to protect her. That was my job. But I failed . . . because she wouldn't let me." He looked at us pleadingly. In that brief moment, I think he wanted us to believe him. To forgive him. To absolve him.

"Oh, yes, I think you're totally right," Evie said softly. "It wasn't your fault . . ."

Her words, meant to comfort him, only got him more worked up. Nicholas bent forward at the hips and covered his head with one hand, that gun flailing about unchecked again in his other. He let out an animalistic cry. "Ohhh God, Annabel. I didn't mean it . . . but there's no going back, is there? Why did you fight me on this? *Whyyyy?*"

I'm sure Evie was thinking what I was: *If he's saying Annabel fought him, did something terrible happen by accident?* He was sobbing now. He stood up and faced Evie, who smiled nervously. But just when I'd thought he might calm down and believe we were on board with his story about an accident, he seemed to lose his grip entirely. Something was happening to him—something sinister. Something that was not our Nicky.

"I understand, Nicholas. It's going to be okay. Clearly it wasn't your fault . . ."

I think Evie believed we were starting to get to him, bond with him, make him realize no one would pay any attention to a wild tale born in the imagination of a kid. That we could walk away from this and everything would be fine.

I knew better, and I saw it long before Evie did. The change in his eyes. The almost imperceptible twitch of the hand that held the gun, and the pheromones blowing off his skin, all signaling to me he was going to attack. I could smell it.

I lifted my face to the wind and wiggled my nostrils, and I knew.

Before Nicholas could shoot my best friend, I crouched so low my stomach brushed the ground, and then I rose up with all my might and leapt at him with everything I had, aiming my jaws for his neck and my paws for his eyes.

But he'd sensed my intentions, too.

While I was in the air flying at him, Nicholas shot me in the chest. I went down, and everything went black.

After

Next thing I knew, Evie was hovering over me, glowing with a heavenly aura. My first instinct was to smile at her. I was so confused I can't even explain it. I didn't know where I was, what I was waking up from, and why Evie looked so terrified.

I felt a sort of numb pressure on my tummy area, and I was panting hard. "You're going to be okay, sweetie," Evie promised. She whipped off her new sweatshirt and I felt her press on my chest. "You're such a good girl. We're going to take care of you, don't you worry."

But her voice was thick and shaky as she fought tears. That's when the pain broke through the numbness—it was a slow, throbbing alarm that something was terribly wrong. I could breathe okay, which gave me hope. Everything came back to me in one great rush when I heard a man scream, *"Oh, God,"* and then I saw it was Nicholas, still holding a gun— and pointing it straight at Evie's head from less than ten feet away. Right—he'd shot me. *Nicky?* Why? My focus was going in and out, but I was alert enough to see now that the aura lighting up Nicky and Evie was from the yellow parking lot lights, that we weren't in heaven, and that we were still all alone with this angry person we'd thought we knew.

"Look what you made me do," Nicholas shrieked. He sounded so crazed he gave me the shivers. "I'm sorry, Chelsea! I'm so sorry, girl. I had no choice . . ."

I had to move. I had to get up. To stop him. I wouldn't let him hurt Evie, and he of all people should know I'd fight to the death. I tried to wriggle on the rough pavement, still warm from the sun beating on it during the day, but Evie held me down gently so I stayed on my side. *Don't move. Don't move, Chelsea.*

"Drop it, Nicholas," a smooth, sure voice broke into the night.

I knew that molasses-like sound so well. Detective Ashlock was here.

"Don't move or I'll shoot the girl," Nicholas yelled back. He took a step closer to us. I tried again to get up, but Evie held me down, her sweatshirt helping to stem the blood.

I heard the *click* of metal on metal, and Ashlock—who had materialized out of nowhere and was standing on a patch of grass to Nicholas's right—yelled back, "Another step and I'm going to have to shoot you, Nicky."

"Detective, he shot Chelsea. We have to get her to a vet,

like, *now*," Evie cried. I could feel blood trickling through the sweatshirt, a wet stickiness that had begun to mat my fur. "It's going to be okay, girl. Stay with me."

"I know, Evie," Ashlock said calmly. "Backup is on the way. We'll sort this out, right, Nicholas? And then we'll get Chelsea straight to the vet."

"Oh, *please*," I heard Nicholas say. "I'm a dead man walking and you know it."

"Not if you stop this right now," Ashlock said. I almost believed him. "Not if we find out this was a terrible accident. But you have to help me, Nicholas. You have to come in peacefully and help us sort this whole thing out."

I could feel Evie shaking, and I couldn't blame her; the scene was surreal. Nicholas, our golden boy, the hero, was suddenly possessed by the soul of an evil demon. We had to somehow process two dimensions colliding—the one where Nicholas was a heroic Boy Scout and the one where he was a scary murderer. It appeared he had either lost it completely, or he was finally showing his true colors.

"It *was* an accident," Nicholas said defiantly. "And no one feels worse about it than I do. But it was also self-defense. *Annabel* attacked *me*."

I started to fade, and I heard a distant, muted cry from Evie. *Chelsea, Chelsea* . . . It was such a sweet sound, but I didn't know if it was enough to keep me there.

Ashlock, his voice more urgent now, shouted, "Nicholas, I believe you. You were trying to talk sense into your sister, right? But she wouldn't listen. So you had to—you had to grab her so she'd hear you. Then what? Maybe she hit her head and fell into the pool?"

I couldn't keep my eyes open anymore, but I heard Nicholas say, "She was at the club that night to meet that—that *ape*, and I found her dressed . . . *provocatively*. She told me she'd started to believe the stories about him, but they'd talked it out and were meeting to profess their undying love for each other. I told her he was wrong for her, but she wouldn't listen, so I grabbed her. But I let go—I let go. And then she lunged at me, started punching me . . ."

Nicholas's confession trailed off, so Ashlock picked it up. "You had to stop her from hitting you, right? So you grabbed her, maybe around the neck. And maybe before you knew it, she was in the pool, passed out. By then maybe you thought it was too late. It wasn't your fault, Nicky. We know that now."

Nicholas was silent for a moment, and when he spoke he was bawling again. "I would *never* have hurt her. Never. I only wanted her to know the truth about him. About that girl over at Long Hills Country Club. He says he was there to train her, but everyone knew—he used her and dumped her, and then he did the same to another girl in Connecticut."

Ashlock sounded totally on board with his story. "You didn't mean for any of this to happen, and when you realized what you'd done you got sick, didn't you? You were so sorry that you vomited on the pool deck."

Nicky kept that gun leveled at Evie and said softly, "That's right."

Ashlock continued. "Okay, Nicholas. That's good—you getting so sick means you have a conscience. Now drop the gun before someone else gets hurt."

Nicholas hung his head, but then snapped it right back up, perhaps realizing he had to pay attention or Ashlock could wrest control from him.

"Annabel died in the pool, Nicholas," Ashlock said. "Tell me, how did her hair get dried and styled?"

"She—" Nicholas couldn't seem to get the words out. He cleared his throat. "I *loved* her. I wanted her to look beautiful. She was always so beautiful. I carried her back into the bathroom and fixed her hair, dried it, brushed it. Like she would've wanted."

I was so tired, and getting so cold. I shut my eyes and started to drift away.

"She was found in her bikini top. Why leave her exposed like that?"

"Because," Nicholas said, "her shirt got dirty when I got so sick. I wanted her to be clean, and she was. She was all clean."

Ashlock said, "I get it, Nicholas. But why frame Lisa? It was brilliant the way you got into her locker to plant the necklace. You had us all fooled."

Nicholas snorted, angry again. "It wasn't hard. We share everything at this club, remember? After the way she treated my sister, I didn't care if she was wrongly accused."

As I listened to these bombshells, I wondered: Is Nicholas good, or is he bad? Is he a great kid who's gone off the deep end, or is he secretly rotten to the core? Have we missed the little signs along the way that he isn't quite the golden boy we like to think? Like I always say, people are strange.

Ashlock also confirmed we'd been stalked. "Well, the police department was impressed that you stayed one step ahead of us. How'd you manage it?"

Nicky laughed again, an eerie, unnatural sound. "I saw Evie spying on you. I heard everything. And yes—I was there when she was telling Chelsea all about her necklace theory. So, yeah, I followed Evie to her hideaway behind Court 5 and from there, it was easy to check in on her to see how close she was getting."

I was getting woozier, and I didn't know how Ashlock could stop Nicky on his own. If he tried to shoot Nicholas, Nicholas could shoot Evie first.

"Let's talk about this at the station," Ashlock pleaded. "Let this be over." My eyes were closed, but in the silence that followed I imagined the boy fighting with himself, wanting to do the right thing, not sure how. I felt a blissful sleepiness come over me, and I took one sharp breath.

"Detective, I'm losing her. Please." Evie's voice was a cry. I let that breath out, and again everything went black.

After

Was I dreaming? I was in a bizarre world where my mom was suddenly with me, crying, begging me to stay with her, and I really wanted to. I was just so drowsy. I could hear everything crystal clear, but I didn't have the energy to open my eyes.

Lucky was there, too, pleading with Evie. "Thank God you're okay! I'm *so* sorry, honey. We got a flat tire on the way back from the movie and my phone was dead, so I called the club a million times from Beth's phone but it went straight to voice mail. We were stuck, and when I couldn't reach you I called Detective Ashlock. He rushed over to check on you."

I, for one, believed him. It sounded like Evie did, too. *"Margee,"* she said sharply, realizing what had gone wrong. "She must've put Call Forward on before she even closed the club. It's okay, Dad," she said. Her theory made sense. Desk staff always put the phones on Forward at closing time, which meant calls went straight to voice mail without ringing. Margee clearly hadn't wanted the phones to interrupt her secret tweeting in the locker room and had shut them down hours early. I had a feeling she'd be fired ASAP.

Lucky, voice rising in a panic, asked, "Where's the animal hospital ambulance?"

I heard Evie again, soothing me, saying, "You're such a good girl," and "We love you, Chelsea." I felt her gentle touch on my head, and someone else's firm pressure on my belly. I tasted blood in my mouth.

I heard a cacophony of tennis people's voices and I weirdly remembered they'd gone to see *Iron Fisted*. Someone was yelling, *"What happened? What happened?"* The same thing Nicky had screamed on the day Annabel's body was found. We'd come full circle, I thought. Lots of stuff was running through my mind, let me tell you.

Now I heard a deep, accented voice above me. "You're my good luck charm. You hang on, girl. You hear me?" It was Goran.

I heard the distant wail of sirens, but they got louder mighty quick, until they were so close it was like they were in my ears. "There's only one," Lucky yelled. "*No.* Where's the second ambulance? For the dog?"

I heard doors slam and urgent footsteps.

"Let's have you sit down, sir," one of the paramedics said.

"It's only a graze," Ashlock's fierce radio-announcer voice replied. "I'll take myself to the hospital later. I'm waiting here for backup."

"I understand, Detective," one of the guys said. "But you've been shot, and we really need to take you over and make sure you don't go into shock. It's procedure."

What the heck had happened? Evie seemed to be okay, Ashlock was still talking away, but he'd been shot? How? And where was Nicholas?

"The boy is over there, cuffed to the fence," Ashlock told the paramedics. "No ambulance needed. Take this dog straight to Margot Animal Hospital. Now."

"But, sir—"

"It's a scratch. *Take the dog,*" Ashlock ordered in a voice you'd have to be an utter moron to disobey.

The guy must've gotten the message, because within seconds I felt new hands touching me. "What have we got?" the medic asked someone.

Lucky explained crisply, "Female golden retriever–pit bull mix, about six years old. Gunshot to the abdomen. One bullet. We've been applying pressure now for several minutes . . . since it happened." He lowered his voice. "She's lost a lot of blood and it sounds like her lungs are filling up."

That sounded scary, and I started to get nervous again. My mom seemed panicky and said, "Just take her. *Please.* I'll follow behind."

The paramedic asked sheepishly, "Who's assuming the vet bills? Sorry, but they're going to need to know this is covered. You know, what kind of measures to take."

"This dog's bills are guaranteed for any amount," Gene boomed. "They are to take *all measures,* do you understand?

Tell them to do whatever they can to save her." I think I smiled then, but I'm not sure if I did, or if I dreamed it.

I felt four hands sneak underneath me, and the two life-savers lifted me deftly onto a stretcher and strapped me in. That was the most scared I'd been this entire time. The straps. The strangers. I admit it, I began to whimper, and I cried a little. Evie gasped, "I'm going with her."

The paramedic guy balked again. "I'm afraid—"

I wanted to laugh because it was hilarious hearing Ashlock at his wits' end with these clowns. He said, "The girl is going with her dog. That's the end of the discussion. *Now move it.*"

"You heard the man. Move it!" That was my mom. Good old Mom. I hoped I'd see her again.

This time, when I faded out, I felt like whatever happened was going to be okay, because even if I had to leave this world for good now, my people were okay, and that's what mattered. If it was my time, then so be it. I felt a peace wash over me, and I let it take me.

After

Well, surprise—I made it. I was unconscious for days after the shooting, stuck in a coma that scared everyone. My mom told me Evie had stayed by my side at the hospital every day. I kind of knew she was there; she read to me and a part of me could hear it, because I had so many new images running through my head when I woke up. She got through *Matilda*, and then shared the gossip about the tennis camp, and how Justine was going to be back on the court when school started and was as healthy as anything, and how Patrick and Goran were back to their old antics, like nothing had ever happened.

Only Celia and Patrick were treading on eggshells for now: that secret confrontation behind Court 5 had been about the things he'd written to Annabel, and Celia was still wary of him, but I knew they'd reconcile. They'd been close for too long to let this destroy them.

I'd lost a couple of pints of blood and my liver had been grazed by the bullet, but both parts of my body could regenerate, and so one day, out of nowhere, I came out of my coma. I'm wicked lucky, too—I only had a 50-50 prognosis of survival, according to my mom. Evie, of course, was there when I came to. As my blurry eyes began to focus, I saw her smiling at me and, even with a giant bandage wrapped around my midsection and dripping with tubes and IVs, I managed a few gentle half wags in greeting: *thwap, thwap, thwap* against the blanket.

Evie gently stroked my head and told me she loved me, and I wagged my tail some more. "What took you so long?" she asked, and if I could've shrugged, I would've. It takes as long as it takes, as my mom likes to say.

Vis-à-vis the whole murder mystery, it wasn't until later that I got the full story as my mom relayed it to Evie. It was pretty crazy stuff. For starters, Ashlock was a total hero. It turned out that during Nicky's gun-waving semi-confession, Ashlock had begun to suspect the boy might be ready to die—and take us with him. After I'd passed out, he'd baited Nicky with taunts about Annabel in order to trick him into aiming at the detective instead of Evie. Nicholas *had* shot at Ashlock—but the bullet only grazed his shoulder and then hit the fence, and that turned out to be Nicky's last bullet. Ashlock jumped him, saving pretty much everyone's life, including Evie's.

Evie also informed me the dog charm necklace had Nicky's fingerprints and DNA on it, along with blood they think got

there when he cut himself ripping it from Annabel's neck.
Ashlock had already started suspecting Nicholas, but had
had to dig deeper. He found an old police report about the
Harpers calling the cops ten years ago, when Nicholas had
gone crazy and was holding his sister hostage in her room
with his dad's shotgun. He was only seven at the time. The
siege had gone on for hours, with their dad, Herbert, assuring
police he could talk Nicky down, that nothing would happen
to Annabel. In the end, their mom had coaxed Nicholas out.
The cops had been persuaded to hush up the whole affair
because they were only kids. *But why would Nicky do that?*
Evie had wondered. *Those two were so close.*

Exactly, Ashlock had told her. We spent so much time
wondering who hated Annabel when all along we should've
looked at who loved her most. What he couldn't legally tell
Evie and my mom about Nicky's mental health, they found
out on their own through the St. Claire grapevine: Nicholas
had gone straight into therapy and was diagnosed with an
anger-related explosive disorder after that childhood siege.
Basically, he'd get extremely mad sometimes, and when he did,
he couldn't stop himself from losing it. I guess the therapy
hadn't worked. Ashlock said Nicholas, at seventeen, was con-
sidered an adult in Massachusetts, and that he'd almost certainly sit in prison for many years for killing his sister, even if
he ended up making a deal to avoid a trial. He was currently
locked up while the lawyers sorted through the tragic case.

When Evie told me how everything had ended, I thought about Annabel and Nicholas, so beautiful and kind and happy, splashing around at the pool like they didn't have a care in the world, their whole lives ahead of them. Now I hoped Annabel, at least, was sunning herself in heaven.

After

With the mystery solved, there was only one more chapter to close. My favorite people came to see how it ended, and sat with my mom and me in front of the TV in the club's lobby on a crisp fall day.

My mom shushed everyone when we saw the big *5 Live* logo splash across the screen. She and Evie were sitting on the floor on either side of me, and Detective Ashlock was sitting to my right on the blue foam love seat Evie and I often occupied in the summers, a fittingly somber look on his face. The news guy introduced my story, which they'd told my mom would be a feature tied to today's big news. Beth hadn't given *5 Live* an interview, but she'd chimed in with some helpful facts and had given them a couple of photos of me. I thought the guy had a nice enough voice. And thank God for it, because it wasn't the easiest news in the world to deliver. I'll try to relay it exactly as it happened:

Meet Chelsea. (A picture of me. Not my favorite photo, because you can see some food stuck in my whiskers if you look really close, but I'm smiling and lying on the pool lawn, so at least it's not the worst angle.)

Will there be justice for this heroic local rescue dog? We're live as a judge prepares to render his decision any minute in a Nashville court, where a Massachusetts man is due to be sentenced today in the horrific abuse of more than a dozen dogs (footage of an old Southern courthouse with lots of random people milling about).

Who could forget the case that rocked the Boston area and the upscale suburb of St. Claire (footage of the fanciest street in St. Claire, lined with mansions and majestic red elms) *three years ago, where this tragic canine was found emaciated, dehydrated, and stumbling as she picked through the garbage at the home of a local family?*

Chelsea miraculously managed to escape her abusers and limped for miles through woods and streams (cheesy reenactment of a hazy beige blob that was supposed to be an injured golden retriever–pit bull mix, I guess) *and found the neighbors' house.*

Yep, that was pretty accurate. I'd waited day after day after day, week after week, month after month, for my owners to be so drunk they would forget each of the following steps: chain me up, lock the cage door, *and* secure the padlock to the musty, ramshackle shed where I was kept. Finally, one day, they were so drunk on bourbon that they forgot the first two steps, and sloppily screwed up the third. I'd nosed the cage door open, and then the shed door, and inhaled the fresh air. But freedom, too, was scary; I didn't know where I was or where I could go, and I didn't know at the time that their land backed up against one of St. Claire's largest expanses of conservation land. I could see the dark shapes of endless hills lit up only by the moon. So I'd hobbled along, rocks and twigs digging into my paws like a million little daggers. I caught the scent of barbecued chicken, and I followed the smoky aroma, only to find, after what seemed like hours of walking, that the barbecue had been the night before. There was no food and no people, just a cold grill coated with remnants of charred meat.

News guy: *Joan and Ralph Lee couldn't believe their eyes when they saw the desperate animal nosing through their garbage.*

(Cue footage of Ralph and Joan's interview.) *The sound woke me up. I thought it was raccoons in the trash, so I had Ralph get the broom out to shoo them away. Then I saw this poor creature. It was horrific* (said Joan). *I gave her some cold cuts and water and called 911 right away.*

Ralph: *I'm not even a dog person, and seeing her licking an old yogurt container, with her bloody ears and the fur under her eyes stained with tears, well, let me tell you—I cried a few tears myself. I'm not ashamed to admit it. She cowered so low when I came out with that broom, it broke my heart.*

It's true, Ralph and Joan had both cried for me, but they couldn't cuddle me because it hurt too much and I yelped when they tried. But let me tell you, that bowl of chopped-up bologna, turkey, and rice they gave me was the best meal I'd ever had—to this day. I got a little sick after, but compared to what I'd been eating, it was a small price to pay. Then again, maybe it wasn't the cold cuts after all that made me so sick.

News guy: *Chelsea* (that photo of me again) *had broken teeth from gnawing at her restraints over two years, a flea infestation so brutal she'd lost her hair in large patches, and infections in both eyes. Worse still, vets had to pump her stomach after animal control realized she had an obstruction. They found paint chips, bits of carpeting, and splinters of wood, the only items she could find to stave off hunger during her captivity.*

(News guy is back, in front of some woods.) *But where did Chelsea come from? When she was first found, she was officially labeled a stray. Publicly, police said the investigation remained open and that they had no solid leads—and no one would admit to owning her. This peaceful suburb is one of the safest in the state, and residents were horrified something like this could happen in their town. St. Claire detective Ted Ashlock began looking at the case again this summer* (everyone looked over at him, and I smiled and wagged, and he patted me on the head) *after hearing about the Nashville case and doing some digging based on what he calls "a gut feeling."*

Detective Ashlock, who joined the St. Claire force several months after Chelsea was found and wasn't involved in her initial investigation, recently spoke to 5 Live.

(Cue Ashlock's voice over a scratchy telephone.)

The hairs on the back of my neck stood up when I saw the Nashville case. I went back to our archive and found the records—and learned police had searched a property in St. Claire when it happened, and were 99 percent sure they had their man. But they couldn't definitively tie Chelsea to the property or the abusers.

News guy: *Authorities now say she was held in a tiny cage too small for her to stand up in on a twenty-acre spread, where she was strung up, beaten, starved, and caged for two years by this man, former St. Claire resident Max Marbury* (footage of stocky, ruddy-faced Max Marbury walking toward the courthouse with a smirk on his face).

See, that was the kicker: Max Marbury, Joe Marbury's thirty-year-old son, did this. When my mom gathered the courage to read the report Ashlock had slipped her, we finally knew who did it—and I knew then why hot tub lover Joe Marbury had always provoked a feeling of doom in me that I could never entirely explain. I could smell Max on him; I could catch the scent of the son's DNA coming off the father.

News guy: *Marbury lived with his wife, Miranda, on a twenty-acre parcel of land owned by his father in St. Claire, before moving to Nashville two years ago. Sources tell 5 Live that his powerful father, home-building mogul Joe Marbury, allegedly used his influence to quash the case, leaving Max Marbury to go unpunished—and to strike again. He won't be tried for anything he allegedly did to Chelsea, who was quickly adopted by St. Claire resident Beth Jestin* (photo of my mom, looking stunning).

Instead, Max Marbury will be sentenced today for his role in a dog-fighting ring in suburban Nashville. Marbury, thirty, pleaded guilty to twelve counts of animal cruelty, among other

*charges, to spare the state the cost of a trial and in return receive a
reduced sentence.*

(News guy is now live in front of the courthouse.) *So we
await the final sentence, which could be as many as twenty years
behind bars or as little as six months. Whatever the punishment is,
it will have to be enough for this dog, who, as 5 Live viewers will
well remember, saved the life of twelve-year-old Evie Clement
last month but will never get justice for her own trauma.* (Ah,
finally, a beautiful photo. This one was taken after the Boston
paper did a story on me and Evie, for which they sent a professional photographer. Evie is kneeling on the lawn in the
pool area, hugging me as I sit on my haunches next to her,
those spectacular summer flowers in the background. My
eyes are closed as I shower Evie with kisses, my ears relaxed
and flopping back on my head. Evie is grinning and hugging
me, and the moment that photographer captured was as close
to bliss as I can imagine.)

"Oh my God, shush," my mom yelled to the already quiet
crowd, taking a massive breath so as not to cry. Evie was already crying, but she was smiling, too, as she looked at me and
stroked my fur. "The sentence is in."

We now bring you breaking news. Max Marbury, the announcer said, genuinely choking up, *will go to jail. And* (crin-
kles some paper, then his nose), *wow. I can reveal that Max
and Miranda Marbury will each go to prison for fifteen years!*

That was much more than we'd been expecting, and it was

great news, because now they couldn't hurt anyone else for a long time. No one whooped, but somehow I thought we could all feel one another's inner whooping. Evie said to me, "No one will ever hurt you again, Chelsea. I promise."

All I felt was love.

So there you have it—my whole story. As we say in my pack, *Dogspeed, my friend.*

Epilogue

I wouldn't have survived that summer without Chelsea. She was like a furry angel who wouldn't let me give up on myself. Those days when Chelsea *had* left my side, I was too dumb to see what she was trying to tell me.

Every morning that summer she would hang outside the club's front door to wait for me. She'd sit on her haunches, alert, eyebrows scrunched together as she looked out for me. Everyone who walked in or out would speak to her or touch her; there wasn't a single person who didn't at least smile at the regal, seventy-five-pound ball of love. She'd give them a wag or a cuddle, but beyond that she couldn't be moved. She'd stay there until she caught sight of me walking from the back parking lot with Lucky. As soon as she saw me, she'd start jumping up and down and grinning, eyes shining and wide, her tongue flapping away, tail going ballistic. Some days near-hyperventilation would ensue.

She'd stay with me most of the day, and the times she did go off on her own she'd always come back to me. I'd be sitting behind Court 5 reading, listening to music, thinking everything was hopeless, and in she'd trot, her nails making a *click-clack* sound on the concrete, smiling and wagging. She'd look at me expectantly. *What now, Evie? What now? Let's play!* And we'd find some adventure, maybe go out back for a walk around the grounds and I'd laugh as she scurried after lizards or chased a bit of scrub brush blowing in the hot wind. Or sometimes we'd find somewhere to sit and watch the world go by.

Chelsea had a beautiful face, with a wide jaw and a sweet wet nose, and the shiniest golden coat the color of spun gold. When I spoke of serious things she'd lie flat, her head resting between two paws with dog-calendar cuteness. Her whiskers would twitch sometimes when I cried, and sometimes she'd cry with me, little high-pitched whines. That would make me stop immediately. I never wanted to upset her. I'd cheer up for her, and she for me.

The unconditional love in her eyes was always enough to soothe me. When I spoke to her, her eyes told me she knew me; her eyebrows would rise and furrow and react just like a human's. Her giant, chocolate-brown eyes would change, too, and when I looked into them I felt like I was looking into a special soul who understood everything I was saying. It didn't matter if it was true or not, because I believed it.

When that humiliating encounter with Tad Chadwick and his friends happened, Chelsea was there, growling and barking at them with a ferocity I'd never seen from her, and I thought Tad was going to pee his pants. For effect, she'd even shown some teeth. When it was over and she came back to the storage room with me and put her head on my knee and wagged furiously, I almost felt human again. When Annabel died and I was terrified and my father wasn't able to make me feel safe, Chelsea did. The love and joy in her eyes brought me so much comfort that sometimes I almost cried from relief; maybe that day wouldn't be so dire, after all. I wouldn't have to walk through that packed lobby alone. I'd have one of the club's most beloved members by my side, and there was nothing I could do to make her love me any less.

Every day I see the beauty of her understanding and the purity of her loyalty. There is a perfection about dogs we humans will never achieve, even the best of us. The dogs who drag their owners out of burning houses, who sniff out skin cancers on their leg, who guide their blind masters across deadly streets and through hazards they cannot see. Dogs understand more than we realize, sense things we'll never see, give more than they take.

They're here for a purpose, and Chelsea's was to be my guardian angel. Because when I saw her face every day as I lumbered toward the building that held all the people who thought I was a useless speck of nothing, it confirmed what I believed about myself.

And every time I rounded that corner and saw Chelsea waiting for me, I knew I was somebody who mattered.

I can see Chelsea right now. She's far away from where I'm

standing, but I smile at the sight of her golden curls. This is my moment, maybe the only chance I'll get. Seeing Chelsea clears my mind. I'm hopping on my toes and focusing on my breathing as the warm-up begins.

It's my first tournament ever. I'm steeling my mind, the way Will taught me, to be tough and treat this like any other match. But it's hard when you're playing a girl who was born with a racket in her hand and is rumored to be quitting school next year to hit the pro circuit. She's number one in New England in the fourteen-and-unders.

It's the last tournament of the summer and it feels only slightly less steamy than the August Annabel died. Beyond the stadium are woods and grasslands and even in here we can hear the buzz of the cicadas, which will be gone soon. I am thirteen, about to go into my last year of junior high. I have become an athlete in one year, strong and fit and happy. I'm still not as skinny as they seem to want—the popular girls at school, the boys in my class, the fashion magazines I try to avoid. I've sprouted up to five feet eight inches already, so I can handle a little extra weight, and personally I think I carry it well.

Luckily, I have tennis, and Will, and we only care about how fast I can move and how hard I can hit my serve and still get it in. Serene helps, too. She is a friend now, and we even sit together at lunch at school sometimes. *We just deal with whatever comes our way,* she often tells me, eyes twinkling, *and kick butt on the tennis court.*

My players' box is full. Oh, wait—did I mention I'm in the *finals* of my first-ever tournament? The championship matches of each age group at this massive event are held at the Yale Bowl, a modest stadium in Connecticut that nonetheless reminds me of a big-deal Grand Slam–type tournament so I am trying not to freak out. Will is sitting next to Lucky, and Goran is there with his new girlfriend. He easily won the boys' eighteen-and-unders yesterday—launching him firmly from number two to number one in New England, so he's riding a major high—but he stayed in New Haven to cheer me on. My mom sent flowers from Portland, where she's still finding herself.

My dad, Will, Beth, and Chelsea are sitting in the front row. There are no dogs allowed inside the Yale Bowl, but Beth pulled off a miracle with her renowned bull-in-a-china-shop fearlessness. I hear she really laid it on thick about me and Chelsea. When the usher heard the story, he voluntarily pronounced Chelsea a service dog, winked, and let her in. *I can't take the underdog's dog away from her,* he'd said with a smile. *No way.*

My friend is slower on her feet now. I mean, she really didn't need a bullet to the chest after all she'd been through, but I know she's happy. She still bounds about, still loves me, still sits courtside when I train, still helps me gather up balls when lessons are over, still watches out for Beth and me.

I get the signal and I walk to the net for the racket spin for serve. Starting in ninety seconds, I will either pull off one of the biggest upsets in New England junior tennis history, or I will do exactly what is expected of me and lose, maybe humiliatingly badly. I inhale the smell of summer's end, and I wonder if I will beat this girl, and I wonder how long we'll have Chelsea with us given her health challenges, but I'm not going to worry about either of those things. What will happen will happen, and I'm not going to waste precious time carrying a sadness about things I have no say over, things that might never happen. If and when life takes a new turn, we'll deal with it then. Chelsea taught me that.

After a brisk warm-up, I take my position halfway between the baseline and the service line, the crowd goes silent, my opponent serves, and from that moment on I never take my eye off the ball.

ACKNOWLEDGMENTS
(major spoiler alert!)

I got to tell this story because my indomitable agent, Steven Chudney, took hold of my book and wouldn't let go; because the brilliant Janine O'Malley championed it and made it readable and beautiful with help from Angie Chen, Andrew Arnold, and their team; and because I was lucky enough to have family and friends who helped along the way and always believed I would someday be in print even after five hundred million rejections: Chris, Vicki (Mom), Jed, Liza, Jason, Samm, Christi, Rob, Linda, George, JIB, Angie, Ed, Bob and Anne, Laurie Anne Tarkington, Cheryl Holmes, Eileen Makoff, Peggy Davis, Tania Schnapp, and Rebecca Tauber (you are missed). THANK YOU, ALL.

Huge thanks to the people who first paid me to write, or then helped me do it better, to name but a few: Bryan Alexander, Simon Perry, Monique Jessen, Sally Bray, Nicky Briger, Bill Holstein, Judith Chilcote, Kristin Lindstrom, and the gang back at the paper—Rus Lodi, Mike Sereda, Gene Cassidy, Dwight Blint, Scott Matson, Meredyth Inman, Andrea Haynes, and many more.

And here's to the eighties tennis/pool/frozen yogurt crowd who helped inspire Evie's story: Peter Blacklow, Kathy

Bradford, Maura Bannon, Ross "Just One Pepsi" Ginsberg, Megan Kelly, Katherine Parker, Shane Sibley, Cori Sibley, David Stolle, and to David Brown for saying nice things when I was young (keep saying them to your tennis kids; we remember even if you don't).

To my friends in the rescue community who I've watched risk their sanity and their relationships to save animals like Chelsea, I salute you. I hope this book will help educate those who aren't aware about the extent of pet overpopulation in this country, and about how thousands of sweet, perfect dogs and cats are euthanized each year because of a lack of spaying and neutering and a culture of overbreeding. There is almost no breed or age of dog or cat you cannot find in a shelter or with a rescue organization. Visit your local shelter to find your own Chelsea. Our fosters and rescues have been the biggest gifts, and we thank Los Angeles–based Molly's Mutts and Meows and Connecticut's CT Animal House, who allowed us to foster and save abandoned dogs Brody, Billy, and Maggie; and Friends of the New Haven Animal Shelter for giving us Guinness. (All are local, grassroots organizations that survive on donations.) When people abandon their pets, it's saviors like Molly Wootton, Chris Lamb, Mary Beth Stark, and their dedicated teams who rescue them, often from death row. Save a life—adopt, don't shop. Let's clear the shelters.

To all the underdogs, human and otherwise—this is for you.